15

THE BOOK OF DISQUIET

'Unceasingly I feel that I was an other, that I felt other, that I thought other. I am a spectator of a play produced with different scenery. And I am a spectator of myself ... I created myself, crevasse and echo, by thinking. I multiplied myself, by introspection ... I am other even in my way of being.'

Fernando Pessoa writes under a variety of guises, or 'heteronyms': aspects of himself who exist in their own right – autonomous fictions; thus Bernardo Soares, a clerk in a Lisbon office, is the nominal author of *The Book of Disquiet*. Comprised of internal reveries and everyday impressions, the narrative is in turn an intimate diary and a prose poem. Reminiscent of Rilke's *The Notebooks of Malte Laurids Brigge*, anticipating the works of Beckett, Nabokov, Borges and Pynchon, *The Book of Disquiet* is a masterly demonstration of the workings of the exquisite machinery of a solitary intelligence and of the literary imagination, and evokes the city of Lisbon – the heart of Portuguese language and culture.

Published posthumously in Portugal and Spain to great critical acclaim and never before published in Great Britain, this selection (c. 1910–30) from *The Book of Disquiet*, Pessoa's unique work in prose, reveals a highly original vision of the meaning of both writing and of human existence, akin to that of Pirandello and Cavafy. Unquestionably Portugal's greatest twentieth-century poet and one of the founders of the Portuguese *modernista* movement, Pessoa is foremost among those who have shaped contemporary European thought.

FERNANDO PESSOA

Fernando Pessoa was born in Lisbon in 1888. He was brought up in Durban, South Africa, and returned to Lisbon in 1905 where he lived precariously as a commercial translator, publishing the occasional poem in magazines and admired by a small group of followers. He died in 1935. Much of his work was published posthumously.

FERNANDO PESSOA

The Book of Disquiet
A Selection

Translated from the Portuguese and with an Introduction by
IAIN WATSON

QUARTET ENCOUNTERS

Quartet Books

Published in Great Britain
by Quartet Books Limited 1991
A member of the Namara Group
27/29 Goodge Street, London WIP lFD

Originally published in Portuguese under
the title *Livro do Desassossego por
Bernardo Soares*

British Library Cataloguing in Publication Data

Pessoa, Fernando, *1888–1935*
    The book of disquiet.
    I. Title   II. Livro do desassossego . *English*
    869.141 [F]

ISBN 0 7043 0153 9

Typeset by AKM Associates (UK) Ltd, Southall, London
Printed and bound in Great Britain by
BPCC Hazell Books
Aylesbury, Bucks, England
Member of BPCC Ltd

*For Charete and Amalia
Gobartt del Castillo*

INTRODUCTION

The I as a Ventriloquist

The bare facts of Fernando Pessoa's life can be summarized very briefly.

He was born in Lisbon on the 13 June 1888. His father, Joaquin de Seabra Pessoa, came from the provincial nobility and worked during the day in the Ministry of Justice. At night, he indulged his true passion for the opera and was the music critic for one of the leading newspapers of the time. Well educated, with fluent English and French, he married late, at the age of thirty-seven, only to die soon afterwards in 1893 from tuberculosis. Pessoa's mother, Maria Madalena Pinteiro Nogueira, was born in the Azores and was also a fine linguist who shared her husband's passion for music. (Two further facts are not without interest: his maternal grandmother, Dionisia, had frequent bouts of insanity, and a Marrano ancestor had appeared before the Inquisition in 1706.)

Two years after her first husband's death, his mother married Commander Joao Miguel Rosa, the Portuguese consul at Durban. So, Pessoa spent his childhood and adolescence in South Africa. First educated at a school run by Irish nuns, he then graduated to the Durban High School, where a little later his future translator, Roy Campbell, was also educated. Shunning all forms of sporting activity, he was a brilliant academic pupil who had no friends. At the age of fifteen, he won the prestigious Queen Victoria Memorial Prize, choosing as his reward works by Keats, Tennyson, Ben Jonson and Edgar Allen Poe.

At the age of seventeen, without any regrets, he left Durban and returned to Lisbon, where he remained until his early death. Quickly abandoning his philosophical studies at the university, he attempted to set up a printing press. But the enterprise immediately failed and for the rest of his life he worked as a commercial translator for different business friends, a clerk like his near contemporaries Kafka and Kavafy.

Between 1905 and 1920, he led a bohemian life in rented rooms before going to live with his mother on her return to Portugal after the death of his stepfather.

The main friends of his youth died young, mostly by suicide, and Pessoa lived an increasingly solitary existence, meeting acquaintances in cafés and restaurants.

Extant photographs (which he hated having taken) show him dressed formally in the English fashion, with white shirt, bow tie and Homburg hat. Being myopic, he wore spectacles. He was reserved in speech and gesture, had a cutting sense of humour, smoked eighty cigarettes a day and drank quite heavily. He was never on time for an appointment, always arriving silently either too early or too late.

Fernando Pessoa died on 30 November 1935 from kidney problems, leaving behind a gigantic trunk which contained 27,543 documents and texts, few of which had been published in his lifetime.

Already at fourteen, Pessoa had made the following observation: 'If a mystic can claim to have a personal knowledge and a clear vision of Christ, a human being can claim to have a personal knowledge and clear vision of Mr Pickwick.' And this reserved, misanthropic man created in his head three other personae who wrote three distinct types of verse, establishing him as one of the major poets of our century. Whether entirely true or not, his account of this genesis, in a now famous letter to the critic Adolfo Casais Monteiro, explains how these alter-egos, or heteronyms, came about.

One day – it was the 8 March 1914 – I went over towards a tall chest-of-drawers and, taking some sheets of paper, I began to write standing up, as I always do whenever I can. And, one after the other, I wrote about thirty poems in a sort of ecstasy whose nature I cannot define. It was a day of triumph in my life and I could never have another one like it. I began with a title: 'The Keeper of the Flocks', and there followed the appearance in me of someone to whom I have since given the name of Alberto Caeiro. Please excuse the absurdity of the phrase: my master appeared in me. Such was the immediate sensation . . . The moment Alberto Caeiro appeared, I made haste to discover – instinctively and subconsciously – his disciples.

The disciples were called Ricardo Reis and Alvaro de Campos. Pessoa 'makes' Caeiro die quietly in 1915. Reis, the neo-classic, dies in 1919. Alvaro de Campos, the violent experimentalist, lives on until Pessoa, the hermetic and metaphysical poet, himself dies.

The 'author' of the *Book of Disquiet* was finally called Bernando

Soares, whom Pessoa described as a 'demi-heteronym, a literary personage . . . or rather a simple mutilation of my own personality'.

Portugal between the years 1920 and 1935 was in a state of considerable political, intellectual and artistic ferment. Turning away from Symbolism, Pessoa's generation took up Futurism and Modernism with great enthusiasm. Art and literary magazines were created quickly and died equally rapidly, but often had an importance far beyond their brief existences. For example, the unique issue of *Portugal Futurista* (1917) published texts by Apollinaire and Cendrars, brought by Sonia and Robert Delaunay who spent the war in the north of Portugal, as well as translations of the Manifestos of Marinetti, Boccioni, Carra, Balla and Severini.

Later, Pessoa was to say that although he was no doubt influenced by these ideas, as well as by the accounts sent to him from Paris by his friend, the poet Sá-Carneiro, about a new movement, called Cubism, in fact the influence was linked to the ideas provoked by these various theories rather than by their actual content.

In short, during this period, the established order was being assaulted from every direction by painters and writers promoting an eclectic range of ideas which covered everything from the defence of homosexuality, and apologies for fascist-anarchist monarchies, to messianic and Rosicrucian speculations.

As for Pessoa, perhaps the strongest consistent tendency in his work is a personal *sandosismo*, a nostalgia for his country based on its heroic past, 'when it gave worlds to the world', and a retreat from 'reality', perhaps disgusted by the bigotry of a Salazar for whom he had nothing but contempt.

What sort of creature is the *Book of Disquiet*? It is not a well-polished creation like the *Confessions* of Jean-Jacques Rousseau. We have absolutely no idea how Pessoa would have organized his texts for publication: the majority were written in two distinct periods. The first half was composed between 1913 and 1919: the second between 1929 and 1934. It is not a so-called intimate journal like those of Gide or of Julien Green, purporting to disclose the private side of the author's life. It has little in common with the *Journal* of the Swiss, Amiel, except perhaps that they both have a fragmentary form.

As has been pointed out with reason, however, the crisis of the I is related to the romantic notion of the double and, in this sense, Pessoa is closer to the *Monsieur Teste* of Paul Valéry or the *Oeuvres*

Complètes de A.O. Barnabooth of Valéry Larbaud or *Niebla* by Miguel de Unamuno.

Perhaps the closest comparison is that made by Antonio Tabucchi when he relates the *Book of Disquiet* to *The Notebooks of Malte Laurids Brigge* by Rilke; both books insist on the importance of learning how *to see*, of defining the relationship of the *Ego* to the outside world.

English readers will, no doubt, remark that from time to time Pessoa's ruminations on aesthetics are not unrelated to those of Oscar Wilde. He defined himself as a playwright, capable, like Shakespeare, of shedding his own personality and of distancing himself from his own creations: 'My heart is a gigantic stage.' One should never forget that he was totally bilingual, equally conversant with Pope as with an obscure seventeenth-century Portuguese Jesuit theologian.

In short, *The Book of Disquiet* is the product of an exquisite and exacerbated sensibility. Pessoa's responses to the outside world are as fluid as quicksilver. In this selection, I hope that the reader will have a reasonably clear vision of the two major strands in his prose: the first is an extraordinary capacity to paint lyrical word-pictures; the second is the research made by a highly acute intelligence, probing with Talmudic precision and persistence the philosophical problems surrounding true boredom. Because of these two qualities, we have a text which is as germane today as it was at the time of its writing, over fifty years ago. No other writer explored so thoroughly the consequences and the responsibilities of creating 'mythologies'.

Like so much in the author's life, the history of the publication of the *Book of Disquiet – Livro do Desassossego* – requires a short explanation.

In his lifetime, Pessoa had published a few extracts from it, in 1912 and 1929. At the outset, the 'author' was called Vincente Guedes, before he became Bernardo Soares.

In 1960, Jorge de Sera began a long effort to publish the manuscript, before finally abandoning the task. It was only in 1982 that a full edition was published in Lisbon, the text having been transcribed and assembled by Maria Aliete Galhoz and Teresa Sobral Cunha, and the preface and organization having been under the supervision of Jacinto do Prado Coelho.

The selection published here comprises roughly half the contents of the full edition. Prado Coelho decided to group the texts more or less by themes rather than to follow a strict chronological order whenever that could be established. This edition follows closely the selection made jointly by Prado Coelho and Robert Bréchon, published by Christian Bourgois in 1988, which, for the present moment, seems the most elegant solution if the full text is not to be printed. Works by Fernando Pessoa have already been translated into more than fourteen languages.

I should like to thank Pauline Hall whose secretarial skills and profound grasp of the Portuguese language have been invaluable to me.

Iain Watson

14 March 1916*

I am writing to you today, urged on by a sentimental need – a sharp and painful desire to talk to you. As can be deduced very easily, I have nothing to say to you. Simply this – that today I am in a bottomless depression. The absurdity of the phrase tells all.

I am in one of those days where I have never had any future. There is nothing but a fixed now, fenced in by a wall of anguish. The opposite river bank, since it is on the other side, is never the near one; that is the entire reason for my pains. There are ships which succeed in mooring in poets, but not one will tie up at that quay where life gives up creating suffering, and there is no dockside where one can forget that. All that happened a long time ago, but my sadness is even older.

During these days of the soul like the one I live today, I feel, with the entire consciousness of my body, to what an extent I am the wretched child maltreated by life. I have been put in a

---

* On the 14 March 1916, Pessoa wrote to Mário de Sá-Carneiro, one of the best Portuguese Modernist poets, who committed suicide in Paris the same year at the age of twenty-six.

corner from which I can hear the others playing, I feel in my hands the broken toy I was given with a pathetic irony. Today – 14 March, at ten past nine in the evening – that is all the flavour, that is all the value of my life.

In the garden I half-see through the silent windows of my imprisonment swings tossed up over the branches; they are twisted high up there; so the idea of an imaginary flight cannot even avail itself of the swings in order for me to pass the time.

That is more or less, but stylelessly, the state of my soul at this moment. I am like the *Vigil Nun of Marin*, my eyes burn me for thinking about weeping. Life hurts softly, with sips, in a book whose binding already comes unstuck.

If it wasn't to you, my friend, that I wrote at this moment, I would be obliged to swear to the sincerity of this letter, and that all these things, hysterically linked to each other, sprang spontaneously out of what I feel I live (am). But you well sense that this unplayable tragedy is of a shredded reality – all full of here and now, and that it comes into my soul like greenness into leaves.

It is highly probable, if I do not post this letter tomorrow, that I re-read it. I tarry by typing it in order to include certain of its elements and phrases in my *Book of Disquiet*. But that will not take away any of the sincerity with which I write it, nor the aching inevitability with which I feel it.

That is my latest news. There is also the war with Germany, but, well prior to that, pain provoked suffering. On the other side of life, that should be the text under a cheap cartoon.

That is not truly madness, but madness must produce a surrender to that from which one suffers, a pleasure, cleverly relished, in the joltings of the soul – little different from what I feel now.

I feel – what colour can that be?

I clasp you to me a thousand, thousand times, yours, always yours,

Fernando Pessoa

P.S. I wrote this letter without stopping. Re-reading it, I see that, in effect, I shall copy it out tomorrow before sending it to you. Truly, I have very rarely described in such detail my psyche, with all its emotional and intellectual facets, with all its fundamental hysterico-neurasthenia, with all those crossings and intersections in the consciousness of one's self which are its major characteristics . . .

You agree I am right, don't you?

❦

There are in Lisbon, a certain number of smallish restaurants or bistrots which possess, over a well-proportioned room, an *entresol* which has the sort of heavy family comfort of restaurants in small towns with no railway. In these mezzanines, scarcely used except on Sundays, quite frequently there are odd fellows, physiognomically totally without interest, a band of aliens.

The desire for peace and the reasonableness of the prices led me, at a certain moment in my life, to frequent one of these *entresols*. Whenever I dined there, about seven o'clock, almost every day I ran across a man who I first thought to be without interest but who, little by little, aroused my curiosity.

He was a man about thirty, very round-shouldered when sitting, a little less when upright, and dressed somewhat negligently but not entirely so. On his pale face with no features you could catch a look of suffering which added nothing to them, and it was truly difficult to define what type of suffering was translated by that look – it appeared to reveal several types of hardship, anguish, and, in addition, that of a suffering born of indifference, which is itself born of an excess of suffering.

Every time, he ate a light dinner and smoked cigarettes he rolled himself. He was extraordinarily observant of those around him, not suspiciously, but he watched them intently; not scrutinizing them, but giving the appearance that they interested him, without going to the length of staring at their faces or analysing their characters. That was the curious fact which first aroused my interest in him.

3

I began to perceive him more clearly. I observed that a look of intelligence enlivened his features, albeit in an undefinable way. But a desolation, a glacial stagnation so frequently hid his expression that it was hard to see beyond it.

One day, by chance, I learned from one of the waiters that he was a clerk who worked in an office next to the restaurant.

One day, there was a street incident, just under our windows – a fight between two men. All those who happened to be in the *entresol* rushed over to the window. I did likewise, as did the man I am speaking about. I made a brief banal remark to him; he replied in an identical tone. His voice was lack-lustre, full of hesitations, the voice of those who have lost all hope, since it is totally futile in their case to hope for anything at all. But perhaps it was absurd to pay so much attention to my evening fellow-diner.

I don't really know why, but from that day on we began to greet one another. Then, one evening, brought into proximity by chance, a ridiculous coincidence that we were both dining at half-past nine, we struck up a desultory conversation. At one moment, he asked me if I wrote. I replied yes. I talked to him about the magazine *Orpheu** which had just begun to appear. He started to praise it, even highly, a fact which completely took me aback. I allowed myself to show my amazement, for the sort of writing which appears in *Orpheu* is aimed, in fact, at very few readers. He replied that perhaps he was one of them. Moreover, he added that sort of writing provided him with nothing that was new; and timidly he continued that, having nothing better to do, no place to go, no friends to see, and no urge to read, he spent his evenings, in a room in his *pension*, he too in writing.

I envy – without really knowing if I truly envy – those men whose biography can be written or who are capable of writing

---

* A short-lived but highly important magazine started by Pessoa in 1915. It had two issues.

their own. In these chaotic impressions, without any link between them and purposely so, I recount with indifference my autobiography devoid of facts, my life-story without a life. All this in confidence. And if I tell nothing, it is because I have nothing to tell.

What can one recount that is interesting or useful? All that has happened to us, either has happened to everybody else, or to us alone; in the former case, it is not new, and, in the latter, it is incomprehensible. If I write about what I feel, it is because in doing so I diminish the fever of feeling. What I admit to is without interest as nothing holds any interest. I perfectly understand those women who do needlework because of sorrow, and those who crochet because life exists. An old aunt of mine played patience during the infinity of evening after evening. These admissions of my feelings are my sort of patience. I do not interpret them as one who needs cards to know the future. I do not listen to them since, as in the game of patience, the cards, if one is accurate, have no value. I unroll myself, like a polychrome caterpillar, or rather I create for myself those cat's cradles, made of string by children, in complicated form, on their taut fingers, and which they pass from hand to hand. I only take care that the thumb does not let slip the strand which belongs to it. Then I reverse my hands and a new form appears. And I start all over again.

Living is crocheting with the wishes of others. Nevertheless, as the crochet needle advances, one's thoughts remain free, and all the Prince Charmings can stroll about in their enchanted gardens, between the clickings and clackings of the ivory needle with its crooked end. Crochet of things . . . Intermezzi . . . The Void . . .

Now that the last rains have quit the sky to remain on earth – limpid sky, humid and mirror-like earth – the most intense brilliance of life, following the blue, has gone off again up into the heavens, has elated itself with the freshness of these

5

showers fallen down here, and has left behind a little of its sky in our souls, a little of the freshness in our hearts.

We are, despite ourselves, slaves of time, of its shapes and colours, meek subjects of the heaven and earth. He who drills down into himself, disdaining all around him, that same person does not drill the same shafts depending on whether it rains or it shines. Obscure transmutations, which perhaps we do not perceive except in the most intimate part of abstract feelings, can take place simply because it rains or stops raining, can be experienced without our truly feeling them, since, without sensing time well, we have felt them nevertheless.

Each one of us is multiple in our unique selves, is myriad, is a proliferation of ourselves. That explains why the being who disdains the air around him is not the same as he who savours it or who suffers from it. There are beings of many sorts in the vast colony of one being, who think and feel differently. At this very moment I write down (a well-deserved moment of relaxation in a day little burdened by work) these scanty words – or impressions – I am at one and the same time he who writes them down, with an unflagging concentration, and he who is elated at not having to work at this moment, and also he who looks at and sees the sky outside (a sky invisible from where I sit), he who thinks all that, and further he who senses his healthy body and his slightly cold hands. And all this universe of mine, of people strangers to each other, casts, like a motley but dense crowd, a single shadow – this tranquil body of someone who is writing and which I press, standing up, against the tall desk of Borges, where I went to look for the blotting pad which I lent him a little while ago.

Everything escapes me and evaporates. My entire life, my memories, my imagination and its contents – all escape me, all evaporate. Unceasingly I feel that I was an other, that I felt other, that I thought other. I am a spectator of a play produced with different scenery. And I am a spectator of myself . .

Often it happens that I find again pages I once wrote, when still very young – short pieces when I was seventeen or twenty years old. And some of them have an expressive power which I don't remember having had at that time. Some sentences, some passages, written just as I was ceasing to be an adolescent, appear to me to be the product of the being I am today, shaped by years and things. I am obliged to recognize that I am well and truly the same as that which I then was. And, despite all, feeling that today I have greatly progressed from what I was, I ask myself where is the progress, and if I already was the same as I am today.

There is in all that a mystery which diminishes and oppresses me . . .

On whom, then, my God, am I the onlooker? How many am I? Who is me? What then is this gap between myself and me?

I well know it is facile to elaborate a theory about the fluidity of things and souls, to apprehend that we are an interiorized stream of life, to imagine that what we are stands in for a great number, that we pass through ourselves, and that we have been a multitude . . . But there is something more here than a mere discharge of our personality between its own banks: there is the other the absolute other, an alien being which belonged to me. That I may have lost, with age, the imagination, the emotion, a certain sort of intelligence, a certain way of feeling – that, even though it distresses me, would hardly surprise me. But in what am I participating when, re-reading myself, I believe I am reading an unknown person, who comes from afar? On the banks of what river am I then, if I see myself in its depths?

It also happens that I come across passages I have no memory of having written – which is not surprising – but which I cannot even remember being capable of having written – which horrifies me. Some sentences belong to another mentality. It is as if I found an old photo, of me beyond doubt, with a different height and other features – but indiscutably of me.

❧

My vital habit of believing in nothing, and particularly in nothing which is instinctive, and my spontaneous attitude of insincerity, are the negation of the obstacles which I avoid by constantly making use of these sides of my character.

In fact, what happens is that I make of others my own dream, agreeing with their opinions in order to saturate my mind and intuition with them, to make them mine (since I have none of my own, I can just as well have those as any others), and in order to mould them in my taste and so to make, out of their personality, things linked to my dreams.

I emphasize to such an extent my dreams in comparison with my life that I am capable, in my verbal contacts (I have no others), to go on dreaming, and to continue via the opinions and feelings of the other, in the fluid path of a living and amorphous individualism.

Each one of the others is a canal, or a channel, where only sea water flows as they will it, stretching, under the sparkling sun, its sinuous path, in a way infinitely more real than their own aridity could do.

Hence, often enough, after a rapid analysis, even though it seems to me that I parasite others, that which truly occurs is that I oblige them, the others, to become the parasites of my ulterior emotion. So I live, inside the shells of their individualities. I print their footsteps in the clay of my mind, integrating them in the depths of my consciousness so well that finally it is I, much more than they, who have slipped out and walked over their paths.

In general, owing to my habit of pursuing, by doubling myself, two mental operations simultaneously, or even more, I am able – by adapting myself with lucidity and exaggeration to their way of feeling – to analyse at the same time, in myself, that unknown attitude which is theirs, thus leading to a purely objective analysis of what they are and think. I go ahead, in my dreams, without letting go for a second of the train of an uninterrupted reverie, and I live not only the refined essence of their emotions – from time to time already dead – but even more I go on reasoning and classifying according to their internal logic the diversified forces of their mind, which sometimes lie hidden in the depths of a simple mood.

And in the middle of all that, nothing escapes me – neither their appearance, nor their clothes, nor their movements. At one and the same time, I live their dreams, their instinctual life, and their bodies as well as their attitudes. In a gigantic movement of unified dispersion, I ubiquitize myself in them, and I create and am, at every second during our conversations, a plethora of beings, conscious and unconscious, analysed and analytical, which reunite together in a wide-open fan.

My soul is a hidden orchestra; I do not know with which instruments it plays and resonates in me, strings and harps, cymbals and drums. I only know myself as a symphony.

❦

Suddenly, today, I had an insight which was both absurd and accurate. I realized, in a flash, that I am no one, absolutely no one. When that flash lit up, there where I believed was a town, instead was an empty plain; and that sinister illumination which had shown me myself did not uncover any sky stretching out above it. Even before the world was, my capacity to be had been stolen. If ever I have been obliged to reincarnate, it was without myself, without me, myself, being reincarnated.

I am the suburb of a non-existent town, the prolix commentary on a book never written. I am nobody, nobody. I am a character in a novel which remains to be written, and I float, aerial, scattered without ever having been, among the dreams of a creature who did not know how to finish me off.

I think, I think endlessly; but my thoughts contain no reason, my emotions contain no emotions. I fall without cease, out of the bottom of the trap-door up there, through infinite space, tumbling down in a fall without any direction, infinite, multiple and void. My soul is a black maelstrom, a vast vertigo spinning around the void, a movement in an infinite ocean, around a hole in nothingness; and in all those waters, which form a turbulence more hectic than water, swim all the images of what I have seen and heard in the world – houses, faces, books, packing cases, shreds of music and scattered syllables flash by in a sinister, endless whirlwind.

And me, what is really me, I am the eye of all that, a centre which has no existence, except that postulated by the geometry of the abyss; I am that nothing around which that movement rotates, without any justification except to rotate, and without any independent existence, except that every circle has a centre. Me, what is really me, I am the well with no walls, but with the viscosity of walls, the centre of all with nothing encircling it . . .

To know how to think! To know how to feel!

My mother died very young, and I did not even know her . . .*

❦

I created myself crevasse and echo, by thinking. I multiplied myself, by introspection. The slightest event – a change produced by light, the spiralling fall of a leaf, a yellowing petal falling, a voice on the other side of the wall, or the footsteps of someone who is speaking next to another who is probably listening to him, the half-open gate of an ancient garden, a patio opening its arcades among the houses huddled together in the moonlight – all those things, which do not belong to me, enclose my sensitive meditation within the bonds of resonance and nostalgia. In every single one of those sensations I am other, I painfully renew myself inside each undefined impression.

I live off impressions which do not belong to me, I dilapidate myself in renunciations, I am other even in my way of being.

I have created these separate personalities in myself. I create these characters endlessly. Every one of my dreams is without fail, as soon as it is dreamt, incarnated by somebody else, who begins to dream it, he, and no longer me.

To create me, I destroyed myself; I have so exteriorized inside myself that in my interior I only exist on the exterior. I

---

* In fact, it was his father, not his mother, who died.

am the living stage where different actors enter, playing different plays.

❧

Amiel said that a landscape is a mood, but that phrase is the pathetic discovery of a mediocre dreamer. The minute the landscape is a landscape, it ceases to be a mood. To be objective is to create, and nobody would ever say that a poem, already made, is the mood of someone who is thinking about making one. To see is perhaps to dream, but if we call that seeing instead of dreaming, it is because we distinguish the act of seeing from that of dreaming.

When all is said and done, what use have these speculations of verbal psychology? Independently of my person, grass grows, it rains on the growing grass, and the sun gilds the expanse of grass which has grown or is about to do so; mountains have risen up for a very long time, and the wind whistles in the same way as when Homer (even if he never existed) could hear it. It would have been more accurate to say that a mood is a landscape; the phrase would have had the advantage of not implying a theoretical lie, but much more the truth of a metaphor.

These few words, written by chance, were dictated by the vast expanse of the city, perceived in the universal rays of the sun from the terrace of São Pedro de Alcántara.* Every time I gaze over a large expanse and I slough off the one metre seventy of height and the seventy-one kilos of weight which make me up physically, then I have a vastly metaphysical smile for those who dream that the dream is dream, and I love the truth of the absolute outside with a noble virtuous spirit.

Down in the depths of the Tagus is a blue lake, and the hills on the south bank seem those of a flattened Switzerland. A small ship (a black steam cargo boat) leaves the port, over by Poço do Bispo, and makes its way towards the estuary, which I cannot see from here. May all the gods preserve, until the hour

---

* One of the finest views in Lisbon, opposite the Castle of St George.

11

when my actual aspect shall disappear, the clear notion, the solar notion of exterior reality, the instinct of my unimportance, the comforting idea of being so small and of being able to conceive of happiness.

A SHRUG OF THE SHOULDERS

In general, we give our ideas of the unknown the colour of our concepts of the known: if we call death sleep, it is because, from the outside, it looks like sleep; if we call death a new life, it is because it appears to be something different from life. It is via the play of these minor misunderstandings with reality that we build our beliefs, our hopes – and we live off bread crusts which have been baptized cakes, just like poor children who play at being happy.

But it is like that for the whole of life: at least as far as concerns that particular system of life which is normally called civilization. Civilization consists in giving something a name which is unsuitable, and then dreaming about the result. And the name, which is false, and the dream, which is true, really create a new reality. The object becomes really different, because we, ourselves, have caused it to be different. We manufacture realities. Primary matter always stays the same, but form, provided by art, prevents it in reality from staying the same. A pine table is truly made out of pine, but it is equally a table. It is at the table we sit, and not at a pine tree. Life is a sexual instinct: after all, we do not love with our sexual instinct, but begin with the hypothesis of another feeling. And that hypothesis is already, in fact, another feeling in itself.

I have no idea if it is because of a subtle light effect, an indistinct noise, the memory of a smell, or a music echoing beneath the fingers of some outside influence or other that, abruptly, as I was walking along the streets, I produced these divagations which I write down without haste, as I nonchalantly sit down in a café. I have no real idea where I was about to guide these thoughts, nor in which direction I would have liked to push them. The day is composed of a light mist, humid and lukewarm, sad without being threatening, monotonous without reason. I feel painfully a certain sensation whose name I ignore. I sense a certain proof is lacking of something or other. I have no nervous willpower. I feel sad over and above consciousness. If I write down these lines, in truth hardly structured, it is not to say all that, nor even to say anything at all, but uniquely to occupy my distraction. Little by little, I fill up with the slow and soft strokes of a blunt pencil (which I have no desire to sharpen) the white paper which is used to wrap sandwiches and which they gave me in the café since I needed no better and any old paper would do so long as it was white. And I consider myself satisfied. I lean back comfortably. It is nightfall, monotonous without rain, with a light tinged by a morose and vague tonality . . . And I stop writing because I stop writing.

❧

And down from the majestic heights of my dreams – here I am assistant accountant in the city of Lisbon.

But the contrast does not squash me – it liberates me; its very irony is my own blood. That which should demean me is precisely the flag I unfurl; and the laughter I should turn against myself is the bugle with which I greet and create the dawn where I engender myself.

What nocturnal glory it is to be mighty without being anything! What dark majesty is that of an unknown splendour . . . And abruptly I experience the sublimity of being a monk in his desert, a hermit divorced from the world, conscious of Christ's substance in the stones and caves of his complete isolation.

And writing at my table, in this room, I am less of a wretched, pathetic anonymous employee, and I write these words which are as it were the salvation of my soul, the ring of

13

renunciation on my evangelical finger, the static jewel of an ecstatic disdain.

I feel sorrier for those who dream of the probable, the near-at-hand and the legitimate than for those who lose themselves in dreaming about the far off and the bizarre. If one dreams of it grandiosely, either one is mad, one believes in one's dreams and one is happy about it, or else one is a simple dreamer for whom dreaming is the music of the soul which cradles him without saying anything. But if one dreams of the possible, then one knows the real possibility of true deception. I can deeply regret not having been a Roman emperor, but I can bitterly regret never having spoken to the seamstress who, about nine o'clock, always turns right at the end of the street. Dreams which promise us the impossible, because of that very fact already deprive us of it, but dreams which hold out the possible to us intervene in life itself and delegate their solution there. The one exists in total independence by excluding all the rest; the other is subject to the contingencies of exterior events.

That is why I possess impossible landscapes, and huge expanses of deserted plateaux where I shall never go. I cannot imagine for a second they will materialize for me. I sleep when I dream of what does not exist. I am about to wake up when I dream of what can exist.

I lean over one of the office balconies, empty at midday, over the street where my distraction perceives, in my eyes, people milling around, but without ever really seeing them from the bottom of its reflection. I sleep, leaning on my elbow which the rail tortures, and I am conscious of nothing, with the impression of wonderful things to come. Details from the motionless street, where numerous silhouettes flit about, become more distinct in a mental distancing: the crates piled up on the cart, the sacks at the shop door a little further down, and, in the last shop window of the corner grocery shop, the vague shape of those bottles of port which nobody, it seems, will ever buy. My mind isolates itself from half of matter. I explore with my imagination. The crowd going by in the street is always the same as a little while ago, it still has the fugitive appearance of someone, stains of movement, trembling voices, unsure things which pass by without ever being capable of consistency.

To take everything in with the consciousness of the senses, rather than with the senses themselves . . . The possibility of different things . . . And suddenly there echoes in the office behind me the arrival, suddenly metaphysical, of the messenger. I feel capable of killing him for so having interrupted the train of thought I did not have. Turning, I look at him in a silence gravid with hatred, I listen in advance, with a tension of latent homicide, to the tone of voice he will adopt to tell me something or other. He smiles at me from the end of the room and loudly wishes me good-day. I hate him like the entire universe. My eyes are heavy with the force of conjecture.

❦

In default of any other virtue, I have at least that of the eternal novelty of freed feeling.

I was going today down Nova do Almada Street and suddenly noticed the back of the man walking in front of me. It was the banal back of an ordinary man, a clumsily cut jacket on the shoulders of a passer-by met by chance. He carried a battered briefcase under his left arm, a rolled umbrella held, by its curved handle, in his right hand.

Suddenly, I felt something approaching tenderness for that man. I had towards him that tenderness one feels for the vulgar banality of humanity, for the daily banality of the *pater familias* going off to his work, for his modest and happy household, for the pleasures both happy and sad out of which his existence is forcibly made up, for his innocence in living without second thoughts – in short, for the totally animal insouciance of that clothed back, there, in front of me.

I stared hard at the back of that fellow, the window through which I captured his thoughts.

My impression was exactly similar to that one feels in front of a sleeping man. All that sleeps turns into a child again. Perhaps, because asleep, one can do no harm, one is not conscious of life – in any case the greatest criminal, the most self-centred egoist is holy, thanks to a natural magic, for as long as he sleeps. Killing a man asleep or killing a child – I cannot see any appreciable difference.

Now, the back of that man sleeps. That creature walking in front of me with the same step is totally asleep. He walks in a state of unconsciousness. He lives in a state of unconsciousness. No one knows what he does, no one knows what he wants, no one knows what he knows. We sleep out our lives, perpetual children of Fate. That is why I experience, if I think in diapason with that feeling, a gigantic, shapeless tenderness for that infantile humanity, for that sleeping social life, for us all and for everything.

It is a direct humanitarianism, without end or aim, which takes me by storm at this moment. I feel a painful tenderness like that of some god looking down on us. I see them all via the compassion of the unique spectator, all those poor human wretches, those poor wretches of humanity. What is all that doing here?

All the movements, all the aims of life, starting from the simple life of the lungs up until the construction of cities and the fortification of empires, I take them to be a somnolence or things close to a dream or resting, which unfurl without wishing to in the gap between one reality and another, between one day and another of the Absolute. And, like a creature abstractedly maternal, at night I lean over my children, good as well as bad, reunited in that sleep where they are mine. I become tender and all-embracing like something of the infinite.

Turning my gaze away from the back in front of me, and letting it wander over those of all the passers-by in this street, I unambiguously enfold them in that same frigid and absurd tenderness evoked in me by the shoulders of that unconscious creature I followed. All that is the same thing; all those young girls twittering about the *atelier*, those young people mocking their office work, those heavy-breasted maids who come back, laden with shopping, those young messengers still adolescent – all that is one same unconsciousness spread out over different faces and bodies, like so many ghosts manipulated by strings all of whose ends finish up in the hands of a being who remains invisible. They pass by encompassing all those attitudes which define consciousness, and they are conscious of nothing, since they are not conscious of being conscious. Some are intelligent, others stupid – and they are all equally stupid. Some are older, others younger – and they all have the same age. Some are men, others women – and they all possess the same sex, which doesn't exist.

There are days when each person I meet – and even more so those who form an inescapable part of my daily routine – takes on the value of a symbol and, either in isolation or together, composes an occult or prophetic script, shadowy image of my life.

In the street, I sometimes hear snatches of intimate conversations, and nearly always they are about the other woman, or the other man, the lover of a third woman or the desires of a fourth man.

I carry off with me – simply from having overheard those shadows of the human discourse by which most conscious lives are preoccupied – a nauseating boredom, an anguish of the exile among the spiders, and the abrupt realization of my squashed state among real people; that fatality of being thought of, by my landlord and all the neighbours, as like the other tenants in the building; and I gaze with disgust, through the bars which protect the windows of the back rooms, at the trash of all and sundry which piles up in the rain in this sordid courtyard which is my life.

❦

Whenever I have lots of dreams, I go out into the street, eyes wide open, but cresting along still in their wake and their certainty. And I am flabbergasted by my automatism which causes the others not to see me. For I go through daily life never letting go of the hand of my astral nanny, while my

17

footsteps in the streets are in time and harmonize with the obscure aims of my semi-sleeping imagination. And yet I walk in the street with a decided step; I do not stumble, I reply correctly; I exist.

But the instant I relax, the moment I no longer need to watch my progress, in order to avoid the traffic or not to bump into other pedestrians, the second I am no longer obliged to speak to anybody, nor have the distasteful necessity to go into a doorway nearby – then I give myself up once again to the waves of dream, like a paper boat with pointed ends, and I go back once again to the languorous illusion which had rocked my vague consciousness of the dawning day, to the clatter of vegetable carts.

It is at that moment, right in the middle of life, that dreams display their vast cinemas. I go down an irreal street of the Lower City, and the reality of non-existent lives tenderly wraps my forehead with a white turban of false memories. I am a pilot, sailing on an unknown sea, in my depths I have triumphed over all, there where I have never been. And it is a fresh breeze that somnolence on which I can sail, keeling over for that voyage on the impossible.

Each of us has his own poison. I find sufficient in the fact of existing. Drunk with auto-sensations, I wander and walk in a straight line. If it's time, I go back to the office, like everybody else. If it's not yet time, I go as far as the river to look at the river, like everybody else. I am like them. And behind all that, there is my heaven where I secretly constellate myself and where I possess my infinity.

During sultry summer evenings, I adore the calm of the Lower City, and even more so the calm emphasized, in contrast, to those parts which the day plunges in agitation. Arsenal Street, Alfândega Street, those long dreary streets which run parallel to the river and stretch off towards the east, the length of deserted quays – all that consoles me with its sadness whenever I plunge into, during these long evenings, its deserted network. Then I am living in an era prior to mine; I feel deliciously that I am the contemporary of Cesare Verde, and I carry in me, not other poems like his, but the very substance which brought about their birth.

I drag along in these streets, up until nightfall, a sensation of a life which resembles them. All day long, they are filled with a pullulation which has no meaning; at night, they are full with an absence of pullulation, which has no meaning either. In the day, I am nothing; at night, I am me. No distinction between the streets of the port and me except they are streets and I am mind, and perhaps the distinction is minimal faced with what constitutes the essence of things. There is an identical destiny, as it is abstract, for mankind and for things – a nomenclature equally interchangeable in the algebra of mystery.

But there is still more . . . During those long empty hours, there arises in me, from the depths of my soul towards thought, a sadness of my entire being, the bitterness that all is simultaneously not a feeling entirely my own but also a totally exterior thing which it is not in my power to modify. Oh, how often my own dreams surge up in front of me, almost real, not in order to substitute themselves for reality, but to tell me how like it they are, owing to the fact that I deny them as well, and that abruptly they seem to me to be on the outside, just like that tram down there which appears, right at the end of the street, or like the voice of the towncrier who broadcasts something or other in the night, but whose call, in a Arab melopy, is just like a fountain suddenly spouting up in the monotony of the dying day.

You see future couples passing by, young dressmakers, two by two, young people passing by, in the pursuit of pleasure; on their eternal pavement, you see smoking those who have retired from everything, and, cogitating about nothing, on the doorstep, those static vagabonds of shopowners. Slow, sturdy or weak, army conscripts somnambulate, sometimes in noisy groups, sometimes in groups which are more than noisy. From time to time, a normal person appears. In this area, at this time, there are not many of them. In my heart rules an anguished peace, and all my quietness is only made of resignation.

All passes . . .

Lassitude of all illusions and of all they entail – the loss of those same illusions, the futility of having them, the pre-lassitude of having to have them in order to lose them later, the wound one keeps from having had them, the intellectual shame of having had them knowing full well that their end would be like that.

The consciousness of the unconsciousness of life is the oldest tax the world has ever known. Unconscious intelligences exist, fugitive sparks of spirit, currents of thought, voices and philosophies which possess as much understanding as our physical reflexes, or as much as the liver and kidneys when they manage their excretions.

❦

I experience huge stagnations. Not at all (like a lot of people's behaviour) that I wait for days to reply with a postcard to an urgent letter. Not at all (like nobody else ever does) that I put off indefinitely the easy gesture which would be useful for me, or the useful gesture which would be pleasant. There is more subtlety in my non-intelligence of myself. It is in my very soul that I stagnate. There occurs in me a suspension of will, of emotion, of thought, and this suspension lasts for interminable days; only the vegetable life of the soul – words, movements, appearance – can still express me in relation to others and, via them, in relation to myself.

In those periods impregnated with shadow, I am incapable of thinking, feeling, wanting. I only know how to write numbers, or doodle. I feel nothing, and the death of a loved one would give me the impression that it took place in a foreign language. I cannot; I have the impression of sleeping, and my movements, my words, my most judicious actions seem nothing else to me but a peripheral breathing, the rhythmic instinct of any old organism.

Thus days and days go by, and I would be incapable of saying what percentage of my life has gone by like that. I imagine sometimes that whenever I cast off that stagnation of myself I do not re-find myself entirely naked, as I believe, but there are still impalpable veils which hide the perpetual absence of my true soul; I imagine sometimes that to think, to feel, to want, can stand in for an equal number of stagnations, faced with a more intimate thought, a way of feeling more entirely mine, a will lost somewhere in the labyrinth of what I really am.

Be that as it may: I allow it. And to God, or to the gods who perhaps exist somewhere, I give over what I am according to what fate ordains and chance accomplishes – true to some forgotten oath.

❦

I am in one of those days when I am overwhelmed, just as much as if I entered prison, by the monotony of each and every thing. This monotony is nothing however, all things taken into consideration, but the monotony of myself. Every face, even that of someone met the previous day, is different today, since today is not yesterday. Each day is the present one and there has never been one like it in the world. It is only in our soul that identity exists – an identity which the soul feels, albeit in a false way, with itself, and through which all is similar, and all is simplified. The world is made of separate things and different angles; but, if we are short-sighted, it is a skimpy, unrelenting fog.

I want to flee. Flee what I know, flee what belongs to me, flee what I love. I want to leave – not for an impossible kingdom of the Indies, or some huge Islands to the south of all the rest, but for some place or other – a lost village or far-off hermitage – which, above all, is not this place, here. I do not want to see any longer these faces, these habits and these days. I want to nest, emptied of this organic mania of mine to pretend. I want to feel sleep wash over me like life, and not like rest. A hut on the seashore, even a cave, at the jagged bottom of some mountain or other, can give it to me. Unhappily, my will all alone cannot do it.

Slavery is the rule in this life, and there is no other, since it is that rule one has to obey, without any revolt or escape. Some are born slaves, others become slaves, and others have slavery imposed on them. That cowardly love we all have for liberty (if we suddenly had it, it would astonish us by its novelty, and we would immediately push it away) is the unequivocal sigh at the weight of one's enslavement. I, myself, who have just said that I want to live in a hut or a cave, where I would be freed from all monotony, that is the monotony of myself, would I be courageous enough to go off to that hut, knowing, without any conceivable doubt, that I would carry everywhere with me that monotony, fundamental to my being? I, myself, who suffocate there where I am and because I am, where then could I breathe more easily, since that sickness is based in my lungs and not in my environment? I, still further, who longs so ardently for pure sun and untrammelled spaces, the sea visible and the horizon in its entirety – what tells me that I would not feel put out by the unaccustomed bed or novel food, or the simple fact of no longer being obliged to go down eight flights of stairs, of no longer going into the corner tobacco-shop, of no longer saying good-morning, as I pass by, to the idle hairdresser?

All that surrounds us becomes part of ourselves, infiltrates the very sensations of the flesh and of life, and the spittle of the Great Spider links us subtly to what is nearby, rocking us in the slender bed of a slow death which casts us to the winds. All is us and we are all; but what use is that, since all is nothing? A ray of sunlight, a cloud – apparent only because of its fleeting shadow – a breeze which gets up, the silence which follows it when it drops, such or such and such a face, voices in the distance, a laugh which sometimes bubbles up among those voices talking to each other, then night where there emerges, stripped of meaning, the fragmented hieroglyphs of the stars.

❧

Today, during one of those reveries without purpose or dignity which make up the major part of the spiritual substance of my life, I imagined myself rid for ever of Douradores Street, my employer Vasquès, the accountant Moreira and the whole lot at the office, the messenger, the groom and the cat.* I experienced in dream that liberation, as if all the Southern Seas had offered me the discovery of the Blessed Islands. Then mine was the rest, the flowering in art, the intellectual fulfilment of my entire being.

But abruptly, during the course of that dreaming – which took place in a café during the short lunch-break – along came a feeling of oppression which attacked me even in that imaginary world: I felt I would suffer. Yes indeed, whether I use one word or many. I would suffer. My employer Vasquès, the accountant Moreira, the clerk Borges, all the fine fellows around me, the young groom who sails off happily to the post, the messenger-of-all-trades and the so-affectionate cat – all that has become part of my life; I could never abandon it without tears, without realizing that this tiny world, no matter how appalling it seemed to me, was part of me and would remain with them; that to leave them would represent the bisected image of death.

Moreover, if I left them all tomorrow, if I divested myself of this uniform of Douradores Street – to what else could I cling (for it is certain that I would cling to something), what other uniform would I put on (for it is certain I would put one on)?

We all have our employer Vasquès, visible for some, invisible for others. As far as I am concerned, he is really called Vasquès, he is a good chap, pleasant, sometimes rude without ulterior motives, interested in money but correct, in the end, and doted with a sense of justice lacking in the majority of great geniuses and other wonders of human civilization, whether on the right or on the left.

Considering that I was not making enough money, one of my friends, a partner in a prosperous business thanks to its relationship with the government, said to me the other day: 'You are being exploited, old boy.' That phrase reminded me that indeed I was; but since we all are obliged to be exploited in life, I wonder if it is not better to be exploited by that man

---

* Gilders Street, a small street, full of shops, is the 'Douradores Street' where Bernardo Soares' office is supposed to be.

Vasquès, cloth-merchant, than by vanity, glory, disdain, envy ... or the unattainable.

There are those whom God himself exploits, who are the prophets and saints in the gigantic void of this world.

And I take refuge, as others do in their homes, in this alien building, this gigantic office in Douradores Street. I barricade myself behind my table as if behind a rampart against life. I feel tenderness – even tears – for these accounts books, at one and the same time mine and belonging to someone else, where I inscribe my things, for the ancient inkpot I use and for Sergio's hunched back, who dockets the slips a little further down. I feel love for all those things – perhaps because I have nothing else to love – perhaps also because there is nothing in the human soul which deserves love; and that love, if we want to give it at any price, out of an emotional compulsion – then why not give it to the wretched state of my inkpot rather than to the vast indifference of the stars.

❧

I feel a physical distaste for ordinary mankind; it is moreover the only sort which exists. And sometimes the whim takes me to dig down into that distaste, in the same way as one makes oneself vomit in order to appease one's desire to vomit.

One of my favourite walks – on those mornings when I fear the banality of the approaching day as much as one can fear being in prison – consists in slowly meandering through the streets, before the shops and stores open, listening to the scraps of conversation which young men or young girls (or both) let drop, exactly like ironic alms in that invisible college of free-wheeling meditation.

And it is always the same group of the same phrases: 'Then she said to me ...' and the tone alone shows what intrigues she is capable of. 'If it's not him, then it's you ...' and the voice which replies protests and I no longer listen. 'You've said it, exactly, you've said it ...' while the dressmaker's assistant insists in a strident voice: 'My mother says that she does not want ...' 'Who, me?' and the astonishment of the young fellow who carries, under his arm, his lunch wrapped up in grease-proof paper does not convince me any more than it convinces, without doubt, that old thing with the dyed hair. 'If it was like that, it was . . .' and the laughter of four youths who cross in front of me covers some obscenity or other. 'So I stood directly in front of the guy and spat in his face – right in his face, José!' and the pathetic creature lies, for his section chief (from the tone of voice, his enemy could only be his section chief) certainly never allowed him, in the middle of the arena formed by desks, to shake his cheap gladiator's fist. 'So I went to smoke in the lavatory . . .' and the boy doubles up with laughter in his shorts mended with multi-coloured patches.

Other people go by in silence, alone or in groups, or else speak among themselves without me being able to overhear, but for me their words are totally obvious, have a worn intuitive transparency. I do not dare to say – I do not even dare to say it to myself, in sentences I would write down only to scratch them out immediately – what I have seen in these distracted looks, in the direction they took in order to cast themselves, involuntarily, filthily, after the pursuit of some object of cheap desire. I do not dare for, whenever one wishes to provoke vomiting, one must do it only once.

'The guy was so drunk that he didn't even see the steps of the staircase!' I raise my head. That small young chap, at least, describes something, and those people are more worthwhile when they describe than when they feel, since they forget themselves in the description. My distaste goes away, I see the fellow in question. I see him photographically. Even innocent slang comforts me. Blessed breeze I feel on my brow – the fellow is so drunk that he did not even see it was a staircase with steps – the staircase perhaps by which humanity goes up chaotically, groping and pushing on the steps deceptively sign-posted up the slope which leads to the back courtyard.

The intrigues, the bitchery, the improved tale of what one has never dared to do, the satisfaction which all those pathetic dressed-up animals get from the unconscious consciousness of their soul, sexuality without soap, jokes which are monkeys' ticklings, the horrific ignorance that they have of their

25

consummate unimportance . . . All that creates in me the vision of a monstrous, abject animal, made out of, in the haphazardness of dreams, damp crusts of desires, masticated left-overs of feelings.

❧

Apart from those banal dreams, which are the ordinary shame of the scrapings of the soul, that nobody would dare to admit and which haunt our waking hours like scruffy ghosts, fatty and viscous abscesses of our repressed sensitivity – what derisory material, undecipherable and horrific, can the soul still dredge up, with what effort, and recognize from its hidden recesses!

The human soul is a lunatic asylum, filled with caricatures. If a soul could show itself entirely, and if there did not exist a deeper modesty than all known and labelled feelings of shame – it would be, just as one says of truth, a well, but a lugubrious well haunted by vague noises, peopled with base lives, by slime without life, larvae stripped of existence, droolings of our subjectivity.

❧

In the light mist of this pre-spring morning, the Lower City awakes, still groggy, and the sun rises with a sort of torpor. A gentle gay quality floats in this air when one still feels half the cold, and life, on the soft breath of the non-existent breeze, an indistinct quivering of the cold already evaporated – in the memory of the cold rather than in the coldness itself, and in comparison with the approaching summer rather than because of the present climate.

The shops are not yet open, except the small cafés and bistros, but this tranquillity is not torpor, like that on Sundays; it is merely tranquillity. A trace of gold floats as an advanced patrol in the air becomes apparent little by little, and the blue turns pink through the mist which dissipates. A beginning of movement is sketched in the streets, the isolation of every walker is defined, and in the few open windows, right up there, a few early risers loom into sight like phantoms. Halfway up, the trams leave their moving, yellow, numbered wake. And minute after minute, very evidently, the streets become less deserted.

I roam, all my attention focused on my feelings, without thoughts or emotions. I woke up early; I went down into the streets without any prejudice. I scrutinize as one who dreams. I see as one who thinks. And a gentle fog of emotion rises up absurdly in me; the mist which dissipates from outside seems to penetrate me slowly.

I realize that, without meaning to, I have begun to think about my life. I did not notice but it happened. I thought I only saw and listened, that I was nothing else, during this lazy stroll, but a mirror of received images, a blank screen on which reality projected colours and lights in the place of shadows. But I was much more, without knowing it. I was also the soul which scuttles away in refusal, and even that act of observing abstractedly was still a refusal.

The sky darkens through a lack of mist, it darkens with an ashen light which one would say was mixed with mist. I realize suddenly that the noise is much louder, that many more people exist. The pedestrians' footsteps, more numerous, are less in a hurry. Abruptly, breaking up that absence, that slow gait of the others, come the fast and deft steps of the *Varinas*,* the swaying of bakers' boys with their gigantic baskets, and the divergent likeness of other tradeswomen only distinguishes itself by the content of their baskets, where the colours are more striking than the objects. Milk-sellers collide, like absurd hollow keys, with the unbalanced churns of their ambulant trade. Policemen stagnate at crossroads, a static rebuttal of civilization at the invisible rise of day.

How much would I like – I feel it at this instant – to see those things without having any other contact with them but that of simply seeing them – to contemplate all that as if I were a grown-up traveller who had arrived today on the surface of life!

---

* Women selling fish in baskets on their heads.

27

Never to have learnt, since the very day of my birth, how to give an acquired meaning to all those things, to be able to see them expressed in the way they see themselves, separate from that which has been imposed on them. To be able to know the *Varina* in her human reality, independently of the fact that one knows she exists and sells fish. To see the policeman as God sees him. To be conscious of everything for the first time, not apocalyptically, like the revelation of a Mystery, but directly like a flowering of Reality.

I hear the hour strike – eight strokes doubtless, but I did not count – in a belltower or public clock. I wake out of myself because of that banality: the time, monks' cloister imposed by social life in the continuity of time, frontier in the abstract, limit in the unknown. I wake up from myself and, looking at the world around me, now full of life and routine humanity, I only see that the mist, which had left all the sky (except that which, in all this blueness, still floats of an indistinct blue), has truly entered my soul, and at the same time has entered into the most intimate part of things, there where they come into contact with my soul. I have lost sight of the vision of what I saw. By seeing, I have become blind. Already I feel things with the boredom of the known. And that is no longer Reality: it is Life.

. . . Oh yes, life where I belong as well and which, in turn, belongs to me; no longer Reality which only belongs to God or to itself, which contains neither mystery nor truth and which, since it is real or pretends to be so, has an existence somewhere, fixed, free to be temporal or eternal, absolute image, idea of a spirit which would exist on the outside.

I slowly wend my way, more quickly than I think, towards the door of my apartment. But I do not go in; I hesitate, I continue on my way. Figtree Square, its motley goods spread out, hides from me, with its plethora of customers, my pedestrian horizon. I walk on slowly, dead, and my vision is no longer mine, it does not exist any more: it is merely that of a human animal who has unwittingly inherited Greek culture, Roman discipline, Christian morality and all the other illusions which make up the civilization in which I have my feelings.

28

Where then are the living?

❧

I sometimes say to myself that I will never leave Douradores Street. That, once written down, it seems an eternity.

My employer Vasquès. I am quite often, inexplicably, hypnotized by my employer Vasquès. That man, what is he to me, apart from being an occasional nuisance, owing to the fact he is master of my time during the daytime part of my life? He deals with me politely, speaks to me in an agreeable way except for those moments of brusqueness due to some unknown worry, when he is agreeable with no one. You agree, but why does he obsess me so much? Is he a symbol? A cause? What is he finally?

Employer Vasquès. I already remember him in the future, with the regrets which in advance I know I shall experience then. I shall live quietly in a small house on the outskirts of some town or other, and enjoy the free time during which I shall never advance further the work which I do not realize today and I shall go on looking, in order not to complete it, for excuses different from those I get away with today. Or else I will be interned in a vagrants' hostel, happy with that total defeat, mingled with the dregs of those who imagined they were geniuses and were nothing more than beggars burdened with dreams, lost in the anonymous mass of all those who were neither capable of succeeding in life, nor able to achieve a sufficiently big renunciation to succeed in reverse. Wherever I may be, full of regrets I shall recall employer Vasquès and Douradores Street, and the monotony of daily life shall be for me, as it were, the memory of never-occurring passions, or of victories I was never fated to win.

Employer Vasquès. I see him today from the standpoint of the future, just as I see him today from this very spot – medium sized, stocky, vulgar but, within certain limits, capable of affection, open and sly, brusque and affable – an employer, apart from his money, because of his hairy slow-moving hands, with prominent veins like tiny coloured muscles, his thick

29

but not fat neck, his cheeks ruddy but firm at the same time, under the shadow of a beard always freshly shaved. I see him, I see his movements bursting with energy, even when relaxed, his eyes ruminating inside themselves exterior things, I feel the shock of the time I annoyed him, and my soul rejoices to see him smiling like the acclamation of a crowd.

It is perhaps because I have never had anyone near me who was higher in colour than employer Vasquès, that, often enough, this boring even vulgar person insinuates himself in my mind and distracts me. I believe there is a symbol there. I believe – or almost so – that somewhere, in a far off existence, that man has been something more important in my life than what he is today.

❧

The essential tragedy of my life is, like all tragedies, an irony of fate. I reject real life as if it were a condemnation; I reject dreams as if they were an infamous liberation. But I live what there is which is the most sordid, the most banal in real life; and I live what is the most intense and constant in dreams. I am like a slave who gets drunk during the siesta – a double downfall in only one body.

I clearly see – with that very clarity with which our reason illuminates in flashes, in the darkness of our life, those proximate objects which constitute it in our eyes – what there is that is vile, soft, flabby and factice in this Douradores Street, which represents my entire life for me – that sordid office, filled with even more sordid employees, that room rented by the month where nothing happens, except that a corpse lives there, that corner grocery and its owner whom I know without knowing, those young things in the door of the café, that laborious futility of each day like the others, that perpetual return of the same people, as in a play reduced to one set, and the set itself back to front . . .

But I also see well that to run from all that would imply either dominating it, or rejecting it; now I do not dominate it since I do not go beyond it in real life, no more do I reject it since, despite my dreams, I always remain there where I am . . .

When you think that I can only make a noble gesture deep inside me, nor have a futile desire which is really futile! ...

That fluid but firm sensitivity, that prolonged but conscious dream which creates in its unity my privilege of penumbra ...

The grandfather-clock down there at the end of a deserted house – for everyone is asleep – gently exudes that quadruple clear chime which rings four o'clock when night comes. I am not yet asleep and no longer hope to be. Without anything holding my attention, preventing me so from sleeping, or any pain in my body precluding thus any rest – I lie prostrate in the darkness, rendered even more solitary by the vague lunar light of the street lamps; I lie prostrate under the weighty silence of my body become alien. I no longer can think, I am so tired; I no longer can feel, sleep evades me so much.

Everything around me is naked, an abstract universe made up of nocturnal dealings. I divide myself between exhaustion and anxiety, and I succeed in grasping, thanks to the sensation of my body, a metaphysical knowledge of the mystery of things. Sometimes my spirit flags, then formless details of my daily life skim the surface of my consciousness, and there I am filling up columns with figures according to the waves of insomnia. Or else I wake from that semi-sleep where I stagnated, and ill-defined images in my empty mind cause to parade noiselessly their spectacle with its haphazard and poetical hues. My eyes are not entirely shut. My fuzzy vision is bordered by a gleam from afar; it is that of the street lamps lit down there on the deserted frontiers of the street.

To cease, to sleep, to replace that interpolated consciousness by better things, melancholic, whispered in secret to someone who does not know me! ... To cease, to flow agile and fluid, flux and reflux of a mighty sea, along shores visible in the night where one really slept! ... To cease, to exist incognito, on the outside, to be the rustling of branches in spaced-out alleys, a falling of light leaves, more guessed at than seen, high sea of the distance and thin jets of water, and everything that is undefined in parks at night time, lost in endless criss-crossings, natural labyrinths of the shadows! ... To end, to cease to be finally, but with a metaphysical existence, to be the page in a book, a lock of hair in the wind, the wavering of a plant climbing in the frame of a half-open window, unimportant footsteps on the path's fine gravel, the final smoke rising from a sleeping village, the carter's whip forgotten on the edge of a morning track . . . Anything at all which is absurd, chaotic, even smothered – anything at all, except life . . .

And I sleep out after my fashion, without sleep or rest, this vegetable life of suppositions, while, under my eyelids free from rest, there floats like the peaceful foam of a polluted sea a distant reflection of silent street lamps.

To sleep and to un-sleep.

On my other side, well behind the play where I lie prostrate, the silence of the building arrives at infinity. I listen to time dripping, drop by drop, and not one of those drops which falls can be heard as it goes down. I feel my physical heart, physically weighed down by memory, reduced to nothing, of all that was or of all that I have been. I feel my head materially lying on the pillow which it dents. The material of the pillow-case establishes with my skin the touch of a body in the penumbra. Even my ear, on which I lie, etches itself mathe-matically on my brain. My eyelids flutter with exhaustion and make the faintest, inaudible sound on the sensitive whiteness of the raised pillow. I breathe, as I sigh, and my breathing is something projected, it is not me. I suffer without thinking or feeling. The clock in the house, established point in the heart of the matter, chimes the half-hour, arid and nothing. All is so vast, all is so deep, all is so black and so cold!

I pass by the lapse of time, I pass by silence, shapeless worlds pass by next to me. Sudden, like a child of Mystery, a cock begins to crow, ignoring the night. I can sleep for ever in my depths, it is morning. And I feel my mouth smiling, gently shifting the creases in the pillow-case stuck to my face. I can abandon myself to life, I can sleep, I can ignore myself . . . And through the recent sleep which obscures me, either I remember the cock which began to crow, or else it is he who, in reality, crows for a second time.

❧

To live is to be an other. And to feel is not possible, unless one feels today as one felt yesterday: to feel today the same thing as yesterday, it is to be today the living corpse of what was yesterday's life, already lost.

To wipe everything off the blackboard, from one day to the next, to find oneself new every dawn in a perpetual revirgini-fication of emotion – that and that alone makes life worth living, or having, in order to be or to have what we imperfectly are.

This dawn is the world's first. Never before has this rose colour, delicately shading into yellow, then a warm white, so tinged the face which the houses on the west slope, their windows like a thousand eyes, offer up to the silence which arrives in the nascent light. Never yet has such a time existed, nor this light, nor this being which is me. What will be tomorrow shall be other, and what I shall see will be seen by reconstituted eyes, full of a new vision.

Sloping hills of the city! Gigantic architecture which the jagged flanks hold back and amplify, floors of buildings separately piled high which the light interweaves with shadows and scorched stairs – you are only today, you are only me because I see you, and I love you, the traveller leaning on the rails, just like a ship at sea meeting another, leaving behind unknown regrets.

❦

Knowing to what extent and how easily the smallest things know how to torture me, I deliberately avoid their contact, no matter how small they are. When one suffers, as I do, because a cloud veils the sun, how could one not suffer from this ob-scurity, from this perpetually overcast day of one's existence?

My isolation is not a search for happiness which I have no courage to look for; nor for tranquillity which no man can obtain, except at the moment he can no longer lose it – but for sleep, effacement, reasonable renunciation.

The four walls of this wretched room are for me, at one and the same time, a cell and distance, bed and coffin. I am happiest when I think about nothing, want nothing, dream about nothing, lost in a vegetal torpor, a line of foam floating up on to the surface of life. I savour without bitterness the absurd consciousness of being nothing, a foretaste of death and vanishing.

I have never been able to call anybody 'master'. No Christ came down to die for me. No Buddha has shown me the way. In the heights of my dreams no Apollo, no Athene has ever appeared to light up my soul.

❦

The ray of sun came in catching me by surprise as I suddenly saw it . . . And yet it was a ray of hyper-intense light, almost colourless, which sliced the black floor of the parquet and reanimated, as it went, the old nails hammered into the floor, the cracks between the boards, black projections on all this off-white score.

Minute by minute, I followed the insensitive effect of the sun's penetration into the tranquil office . . . An occupation worthy of prison! Only prisoners watch the sun move in such a way like one watches the movements of ants.

A quick glance over the countryside, over a wall on the outskirts of the city, frees me more completely than a long journey might somebody else. Every viewpoint is a topsy-turvy pyramid whose base cannot be defined.

❦

Banality is a home. Routine is maternal. After a long incursion in the lofty realms of poetry, up towards the sublime aspiration, the peaks of the transcendent and the occult, nothing is more delicious (all the charm and warmth of life is there) than the return to the inn where happy idiots burst out laughing, where one drinks with them, idiotic in one's turn and, just as God made us, satisfied with the universe we have been given and leaving the rest to those who climb mountains capable of nothing once they have reached the summit.

I am barely moved when I hear that a man, whom I hold to be mad or stupid, is superior to an ordinary man on most occasions or in the business of existence. Epileptics, at the height of their attack, are incredibly powerful; paranoiacs reason as few normal people can; religious maniacs draw crowds of believers as few public speakers (if there are any at all still) succeed in doing, and with an interior conviction that the latter never arrive at communicating to their supporters. And all that only proves that madness is madness ... I prefer the defeat which recognizes the beauty of flowers to the victory in the middle of the desert, reduced to blindness of the soul, alone with its separate nothingness.

How often my own reverie, so futile, leaves me with a horror of the interior life, the physical disgust for mysticisms and contemplations. With what haste I rush out from my house (that place chosen for dreaming therein) until I reach my office; then I see Moreira's face as if I were entering port. All things taken into consideration, I prefer Moreira to the astral world; I prefer reality to truth; yes, I prefer life even to God who created it. That is how he has given it to me, that is how I shall live it. I dream because I dream, but would not tolerate that insult to myself of giving dreams another value but that of making up my intimate theatre, just as I do not give wine, not that I don't drink it, the label of nourishment or vital necessity.

I have always avoided, with horror, being understood. To be understood is to prostitute oneself. I would rather be taken seriously for that which I am not, and to be ignored humanly, decently, naturally.

Nothing would more stir my indignation than to see my fellow office workers finding me 'different'. I want to enjoy alone that irony of not being different in their eyes. I want to endure that hairshirt of seeing them judging me to be similar to them, and to undergo that crucifixion of not being different. There are more subtle martyrdoms than those of saints and hermits. There are tortures for the intellectual just as there are those of the body and of desire. And there is in those agonies, as in the others, a certain pleasure.

❦

. . . Bits of nothing, totally normal, insignificant things of everyday, trivial life – dust which underlines with a taut grotesque line all there is which is base and sordid in my human life.

So it is with the accounts book, wide open under my eyes where life dreams of all the Orients; or the harmless joke of the section chief which offends the entire universe; and then to tell one's employer to telephone, it's his girlfriend – all that right in the middle of meditating on the most asexual part of an aesthetic and intellectual theory . . .

Everybody has a section chief with a gift for uncalled-for jokes, everybody keeps his mind outside the universe in its totality. Everybody has an employer, and the employer's girlfriend, and the telephone bell which rings at the worst moment, just as there is an admirable nightfall – and those ladies who daringly speak ill of their lover, go off to pee, as we others know full well.

But all those who dream, even if they do not dream in an office of the Lower City or in front of accounts books in a draper's shop – yet all have an accounts book, there in front of them, whether it is the woman they married or the threat of a future which falls on them through inheritance – anything at all, from the moment that it exists, positively.

And then friends – really decent chaps, of course, it is so pleasant to talk to them, to lunch with them, to dine with them, and all that, I don't know why, is so sordid, so trivial, so pathetic; you are always in your draper's shop even when you are out in the street, you are always in front of your accounts book even when you are abroad, you are always with your employer even when you are already in the infinite.

All of us who dream and think, we are all employees and clerks in some draper's shop, or in some other shop in some

36

other Lower City. We do the accounts and we lose; we add up and we miss out; we draw up the bill – and the invisible number is always not in our favour.

I write these words with a smile, but it seems to me that my heart could break, break like an object which smashes into pieces, into rubbish, into trash thrown into a box which the dustbin man, in one movement, tosses up on to his shoulder and carries away to the perpetual dustcart belonging to all the townhalls of the world.

❧

In order to feel the delight and terror of speed – there is no need for fast cars nor express trains. All I need is a tram and the astounding capacity of abstraction which I have and cultivate.

Once in a tram, I know, thanks to a constant and immediate power of analysis, how to isolate the idea of a tram from the idea of speed, to separate them completely, including making them real-distinct-things. Then, I am able to feel myself rattling along not in a tram but in its very speed, and if, bored, I want to give myself the delirium of unlimited speed, I can further transpose that idea in the pure imitation of speed and, at will, increase it, diminish it or amplify it beyond all possible speeds of all vehicles and trains in the world.

To run real risks frightens me, that is true; but it is not so much the fear (which has nothing excessive about it) which bothers me, but rather the unflagging concentration on my feelings which irks and depersonalizes me . . .

I never go there where there is risk. I am afraid of becoming blasé of dangers themselves.

❧

It sometimes happens – without my expecting it or anything preparing me for it – that the asphyxia of everyday life grabs me by the throat, and I feel physical nausea for the voices and gestures of those we call our fellow men. A direct physical nausea, directly felt in the stomach and head, ridiculous marvel of awakening sensitivity . . . Each individual who speaks to me, each face whose eyes stare at me, affects me like a vile insult. I sweat from all my pores a universal horror. I faint as I feel myself feeling them.

And nearly always it happens, during those moments of intestinal distress, that a man, a woman, even a child surges before me as the true representation of that banality which sickens me. Not its representative by virtue of a partial emotion, subjective and rational, but truly of an objective truth, really conforming, from the outside, to what I feel inside, and which leaps up by a sort of analogical magic by bringing me to the epitome of the law I have invented.

❧

That black sky, down there to the south of the Tagus, was of a sinister blackness against which, contrastingly, the white flashes of the gulls' wings in their agitated flight were silhouetted. However, the day was not yet stormy. All the menacing mass of rain had piled itself up over the other bank of the Lower City, still humid from previous light showers, which smiled up from the earth to a sky whose north remained bluish with scattered whiteness. The freshness of spring was shot through with a slight chill.

At such times, empty, imponderable, I delight in steering my train of thought towards a vague meditation which leads nowhere, but which retains, in the limpidity of absence, something of the chill solitude of that so clear sky, with its dark backdrop in the distance, and certain intuitions which, like the gulls, evoke contrastingly the mystery of all things against a profound obscurity.

But, abruptly, in opposition to my intimate and entirely literary premises, the dark backdrop of the sky to the south of the city conjures up for me – a true or false memory – another sky, perhaps seen in another life, in a north with a smaller river, with sad rushes, and without the smallest town. Without knowing how, it is a landscape for wild ducks which sprawls across my imagination and, with the clarity of a strange dream, I feel myself close to the vista I imagine.

38

Land of rushes on river banks, a place for hunting and anguish: its irregular banks, like dirty capes, jut into waters of yellow lead, and are hollowed out into muddy creaks, designed for miniature boats, where here and there it opens up into canals whose waters glisten on the surface of the mud, hidden among the green-black stems of the rushes, impossible to walk through.

The desolation is that of an ashen-dead sky, wrinkled here and there with clouds blacker than the prevailing tonality of the sky. I do not feel the wind, but it is there, and the bank opposite finally is a long island behind which can be divined – vast abandoned river – the other real bank, laid out in the flat distance.

No one ever gets there, will ever get there. Even if, by means of a contradictory fleeing in time and space, I could escape from the world into that landscape, no one could ever join me there. Vainly would I wait for something, without knowing what I was waiting for, and, in the end, there would be nothing more but the slow coming of the night, and the whole area would slowly assume the colour of the blackest nights which, little by little, would merge into the abolished sky.

And, suddenly, I feel here the cold from down there. It penetrates my body, coming out of my very bones. I breathe deeply and awake. The individual who goes past me under the Arch, next to the Stock Exchange, looks at me suspiciously like a man intrigued by something he does not know how to interpret. The black sky, coiled up, has dropped even lower over the south bank.

One of my constant preoccupations is to understand how other people can exist, how there can be other souls than mine, consciousnesses alien to my consciousness which, since it is consciousness, must by definition be unique. I fully understand that the man in front of me who speaks to me with words similar to mine, and makes gestures equivalent to the ones I make myself or could possibly make, might well have something in common with me. Exactly the same thing happens, however, with the images I extrude from magazine illustrations, with the heroes I visualize from novels, with the dramatic characters I see on the stage, via the actors who play their roles.

It seems to me that nobody truly admits the real existence of someone else. It may be conceivable that the other is alive, that he feels and thinks like us; but there will always remain an anonymous factor which separates us, a materialized disadvantage. There are figures from days of yore, mind-images contained in books, which constitute for us more important realities than those incarnated indifferences who speak to us over a counter, or casually glance at us in the tram, or brush by us as they pass in the dead haphazardness of a street. For us others are no more than a landscape and, nearly always, an invisible landscape in a familiar street.

I consider more mine, closer in intimate ties of blood, certain characters described in books, certain images I know from engravings than most so-called real people who share in that metaphysical futility called flesh and bones. And 'flesh and bones' is a perfect description: they seem to be chopped-up things displayed on the marble slab of some butcher's shop, dead things bleeding like liver, pigs' trotters and chops of Fate.

I have no shame in feeling like that since I realized that everybody feels like that. What might appear to be a man's contempt for mankind, an indifference which permits us to kill people without really feeling one is killing, as in the case of murderers, or without thinking one kills, as in the case of soldiers, is a result of the fact that nobody pays sufficient attention to the reality – doubtless too abstruse – that others too are souls as well.

On specific days, at specific times brought to me by some breeze or other, when some door or other is opened in me, I suddenly feel that the grocer on the corner is a spiritual being, that the boy at the door bending at the moment over a sack of potatoes has well and truly a soul capable of suffering.

When they told me yesterday that the cashier in the tobacco shop had committed suicide, I had the impression they were lying. Poor thing, he too had had an existence! We had forgotten him, all of us who knew him just as those who had never known him. Tomorrow, we shall forget him even more. But he had a soul too – there can be no doubt about it, since he killed himself. Passion? Worry? Surely . . . but there only remains, for me as for the whole of humanity, the memory of a vapid smile floating above a jacket, cheap, dirty and badly cut on the shoulders. That is all that subsists for me of a man who felt so strongly that he killed himself because he felt too much, since, in the final analysis, nobody kills themselves for any other reason . . . One day, as I was buying my cigarettes, I said to myself that soon he would go bald. Finally, he did not have the time to do so. That is one of the memories of him I keep. What other could I possibly retain since that one, after all is said and done, has no contact with him, but simply with the way I thought about him?

I have a sudden brutal vision of the corpse, of the coffin they put him in, of the totally anonymous grave in which they probably buried him. And, abruptly I see that the cashier in the tobacco shop in a certain way was, with his ill-fitting jacket and balding head, the whole of humanity.

It only lasted a second. Today, now, it is clear that, in so far as he was a man, he is dead. Nothing more.

No. Others do not exist. That is why for me this setting sun with its ponderous wings, its cloudy hard colours, remains fixed. For me, under the sunset, quivers, without me seeing it flowing by, the mighty river. It is for me that this wide square was made, open on to the river which is just at high tide. Did they bury the cashier from the tobacco shop in a communal grave? Today's sunset is not for him. But, with that thought and truly despite myself, he also has ceased to exist for me . . .

❧

I can only envisage as a lack of physical cleanliness this permanent inertia where I lie with an existence always equal to and always similar to itself, resting like dust or refuse on the surface of non-change.

Just as we wash our bodies, so we ought to wash our destiny, to change lives as we change clothes – not to preserve life as we do by eating and sleeping, but in virtue of that detached respect towards ourselves which is precisely what we call cleanliness.

There are many people for whom a lack of cleanliness is not a wilful characteristic, but rather a shrug of the shoulders made by intelligence, and there are many for whom a placid and retiring life is not a consequence of what they willed, nor of a natural resignation faced by a life they have not desired, but of a waning of their understanding of themselves, an automatic irony of knowledge.

There are pigs which repudiate their own filth, but which do not distance themselves from it, held back by the same feeling, pushed to the extreme, which prevents a terrified man from fleeing danger. There are pigs of destiny, like me, who do not distance themselves from the banality of their daily lives owing to that very same power of attraction produced from their own impotence. They are birds fascinated by the absence of a snake; flies which remain stuck to a tree trunk, not having seen anything until the moment they came into the viscous range of the chameleon's tongue.

So I walk my conscious unconsciousness, over my tree trunk of everyday life. So I go, walking my destiny which advances, since I do not; my time which follows, since I do not. Nothing saves me from monotony except these short remarks I make about it. I satisfy myself with the fact that my cell has windows inside its bars – and I write on the windows inside the bars – and I write on to the windows – in the dust of the necessary – my name in capital letters, a daily signature of my compatibility with death.

With death? No, not even with death. When you live as I do, you do not die: you end, you go away, you devegetalize yourself. The place you were at remains without your being there, the street you used to take remains without your being seen in it, the house you lived in is inhabited by a non-you. That is that, and we call that nothingness, but we cannot even act out to applause that tragedy of negation since we do not even certainly know if truly it is nothing, vegetables as we are both of truth as of life, dust equally thick on the interior and on the exterior of the windows, grandchildren of Destiny and adopted sons of God, who married Eternal Night when she was widowed by Chaos which engendered us all.

❧

In the rectilinear perfection of the day, the air still stagnates, replete with sun. It is not the present tension of the approaching storm, malaise of amorphous bodies, ill-defined flattening of the truly blue sky; it is the tangible torpor of insinuating idleness, a feather skimming across the skin of a dozing face. A sultry serene summer. The countryside beckons even those who dislike it.

If I were an other, I say to myself, it would be a happy day for me, since I would experience it without further thought. I would finish my work with anticipatory delight: my work made up out of daily normal monotony. I would catch the tram for Benfica together with a few friends. We would dine outside in a garden under the last rays of the setting sun. Our shared happiness would form part of the landscape, and would be recognized as such by all who saw us there.

However, since I am me, I extract a certain pleasure from imagining myself to be that other. Then, later that other me, sitting under a barrel or a tree, would eat twice the amount I am capable of eating, would drink double the quantity I normally drink, would laugh twice as much as I can possibly imagine laughing. Later him, now me. Yes, for a second I was that other; I saw, I lived in that other the humble, pleasant pleasure of existing like an animal in rolled-up shirt sleeves. What a marvellous day which evokes such dreams! All is blue and sublime up in the sky as in my ephemeral dream of being a commercial traveller, bursting with health, having an agreeable evening somewhere or other.

❧

When the dog-days arrive, I become morose. Even the acrid luminosity of summertime ought to be sweet for someone who does not know who he is. But no, it is not sweet for me. The contrast is too extravagant between the exuberant life outside and what I feel, without knowing how to feel or to think: the everlasting unburied corpse of my sensations. I have the impression I am alive, in this shapeless land called the universe, during a period of political tyranny which, though not directly oppressing me, nevertheless gives offence to some occult principle in my soul. And then heavily there descends over me the anticipated nostalgia of possible exile.

Above all, I feel sleepy. Not with that sleep which encompasses latently, like all sleeps, even morbid ones, the physical privilege of repose. Not with that sleep which, at the point of forgetting life and perhaps distracting us with dreams, brings on a tray, sliding towards our soul, the peaceful offerings of a profound abdication. No: this is a sleep which does not arrive at sleep, which weighs down the eyelids without being able to shut them, and which unites in one and the same expression what one feels about both stupidity and repulsion on the down-turned corners of our mouths and at the edges of our discouraged lips. This is a sleep like that which futilely oppresses our body during the massive insomnias of the soul.

Only at the approach of night, do I feel in a certain way, not a sense of happiness, but rather a sort of relaxation which, since other moments of relaxation are pleasurable, that one is too, by an analogy of feeling. Then, sleep vanishes in a sort of confusion, a mental chiaroscuro, provoked by that sleep, fades away, becomes clear, almost shines with clarity. For an instant, there lives hope for something else. But that hope is short-lived. What follows is a boredom without sleep, without hope, the painful awakening of a man who has not managed to sleep. And, from the window of my room, wretched soul in an exhausted body, I stare at myriads of stars; then nothing, nothingness, but those myriads of stars . . .

❦

The sense of smell is an odd sense of sight. It evokes sentimental landscapes which the subconscious suddenly sketches. It is something I have often experienced. I walk down a street; I see nothing, or rather, as I look around me, I see as all the world sees. I know that I am walking down a street which exists with its two sides made up of different houses, built by human beings. I walk down a street. From the bakery, there floats the smell of bread, nauseating with its gentle smell; and my childhood surges up in front of me from a certain far-off neighbourhood, and another bakery surges up in front of me from out of that marginal kingdom composed of everything we have watched as it died. I walk down a street. Suddenly, it is redolent with the fruits displayed on the raking shelves of the narrow shop; and my brief sojourn in the country – I no longer know where or when – has trees at the end of it and offers peace to my heart, a child's heart beyond all doubt. I walk down a street. Unexpectedly, I am overwhelmed by the smell of packing cases in a carpenter's workshop. My dear Cesario, you appear before me and I am finally happy since I have regressed, through memory, back to the unique truth, that of literature.

❧

I have in front of me the two massive pages of a heavy accounting book; with livid eyes, I raise up from its raked angle on the old lectern a soul even more tired than my eyes. Beyond the nothingness all that represents, the shop aligns, as far as Douradores Street, its regularly spaced shelves and its employees equally regularly spaced out, human order and vulgar tranquillity. The noise of a different world bangs against the window, and the different noise is also vulgar, just like the tranquillity installed next to the shelves.

I lower fresh eyes on to the two white pages, on which my precise numbers have inscribed the company's balance-sheet. And, with a smile I keep to myself, I recall that life – which includes these pages covered with numbers and the names of drapery manufacturers, with their blank spaces, their ruled lines and their calligraphic handwriting – also includes famous explorers, major saints, poets of every era, all of them without a line in their memory, a vast people exiled by those who establish the values in this world.

In this very accounting book, covered by a cloth I do not recognize, open the gateways to India and to Samarkand, and Persian poetry, which belongs to neither country, produces from its quatrains, whose third lines do not rhyme, a distant panacea for my disquiet. But, avoiding errors, I inscribe and add up, and the writing continues line after line, as is normal for an employee in this office.

❧

We are loved by nobody after a sleepless night. Vanished sleep has carried off something which rendered us human. There is a latent irritation with ourselves which, one might say, even impregnates the surrounding, inorganic air. Finally, it is ourselves whom we upbraid, and it is between us and ourselves that the diplomacy of that mute struggle is deployed.

Today, I dragged my feet and my immense fatigue through the streets. My soul has been reduced to a tangled ball of wool, and, whatever I am or was, which is me, has forgotten its name. I do not know if I have a tomorrow. I have no ideas about anything except the fact I did not sleep, and the confusion of varying intervals produces long silences in my internal discourse.

Ah, spacious parks which belong to others, gardens so familiar to so many, extraordinary pergolas of those who will never know me! I stagnate between vigils, like one who has never dared to be superfluous, and what I reflect on twists and turns like sleep approaching its end.

❧

Clouds . . . I am aware of the sky today, for there are days when I do not look at it . . . living as I do in a city and not in the countryside which includes it. Clouds . . . Today they are the

46

principal reality and they preoccupy me as if the sky, by veiling itself, became one of the major dangers threatening my existence. Clouds ... they come in off the ocean towards St George's Castle, from west to east, in a tumultuous naked disorder, some tinted white, thinning out to favour some vanguard; other slower ones are almost medium-black, until the highly audible wind sluggishly disperses them: black shot through with a dirty white, until, as if longing to stay, they blacken with their passage rather than with their shadows the false space which the emprisoned streaks open up between the narrow rows of houses.

Clouds ... I exist without knowing it, and shall die without wanting to. I am the caesura between what I am and what I am not, between what I dream about and what life has made of me. I am the abstract carnal medium between things which are nothing – and myself who am nothing more. Clouds ... What anguish when I feel, what malaise when I think, what futility when I want. Clouds ... they continue to pass, some as gigantic as houses which do not permit us to judge if they are less big than they appear, you might well say that they were about to take over the whole sky; others are of an uncertain size, perhaps they are two clouds joined together, or one cloud about to split in two – they have no further meaning, up there in the tired sky; still others, extremely small, seem to be the toys of powerful entities, irregular balls of an absurd game, piled up in a heap on one side, solitary and cold.

Clouds ... I question myself without knowing myself. I have achieved nothing useful, shall never achieve anything I could justify. That part of my life I have not wasted in a confused interpretation of non-existent things, I have frittered away in writing prose-poetry, dedicated to untransmittable feelings, through which I make the universe mine. I am saturated with myself, objectively, subjectively. I am saturated with every-thing, and with the everything of everything. Clouds ... all of them, dislocated from the heavens, are the only real things today between the nullity of the earth and the non-existent sky; indescribable tatters of the weighty boredom I impose on them; fog condensed into menaces of absent colour; dirty wads of cotton from a hospital without walls. Clouds ... they are like me, a cramped passage between heaven and earth, tossed by an invisible force, whether accompanied by thunder or not, elating the world with their whiteness, or obscuring it with their blackness, fictions of the caesura and of error, they are far from earth's tumult but lack the silence of the heavens. Clouds ... they continue to pass, they always continue to pass, they will pass, they will pass for ever, furling and unfurling their ashen skeins, pulling into confusion their false undone sky.

❦

I have understood! My employer Vasquès is Life! Monotonous necessary Life, giving orders and being misunderstood. That trivial man represents the triviality of Life. He is everything to me, from the exterior, since Life is everything to me, from the exterior.

And if my office in Douradores Street represents Life for me, my flat on the second floor, where I live, also in Douradores Street, represents Art. Yes. Art living in the same street as Life, but in a different place. Art which provides a respite from Life without, however, providing a respite from living, and which is equally monotonous as Life – being simply in a different place. Yes, for me this Douradores Street contains the entire meaning of things, the solution to every enigma – except that of their very existence, since it is precisely that enigma which is not open to solution.

❦

No problem can be solved. Not one of us can undo the Gordian knot: either we all desist, or we all cut it. With one blow we solve, through our feelings, problems which are in the domain of intelligence, and we act in such a way either out of lassitude, or out of fear of drawing conclusions, or out of an absurd need to find a crutch for ourselves, or out of the gregarious instinct which drags us backwards towards others and life.

Never knowing all the elements of a problem, we can never solve it.

To attain truth, we would need sufficient data, and the intellectual processes with which to extract the interpretation from that data.

❦

There are feelings which are sleep, which blanket like a fog the entire expanse of our mind, which do not permit us either to think or to act, and which do not allow us a clear existence. It is as if we had not slept all night, yet there subsists in us something of the dream; there is a torpor of the day's sun coming to heat the stagnant surface of the senses. It is a drunkenness of being nothing, and desire is the bucket knocked over in the courtyard by the lazy movement of a passing foot.

One looks, but one does not see. The long street animated by human animals is a sort of horizontal shop-sign, on which the letters are shifting and making no sense. The houses are simply houses. We have lost the capacity of giving a sense to what we see but we see perfectly that which is, that we do.

The hammer blows at the carpenter's door echo with a strange proximity. They echo, well spaced out, each one provoking a futile resonance. The noise of the cars appears to be that of a day pregnant with a coming storm. Voices emerge from the air, not from the cars. Far off, the river limps along, exhausted.

What one feels is not boredom. Nor is it pain. It is the longing to go to sleep with another personality, to forget – with a raise in salary. One feels nothing except for an automatism down there in our body which causes the feet to echo on the pavements, feet which belong to us and which go forward, in involuntary steps, feet which we feel in our shoes. Perhaps one does not even feel that. All around our eyes and, as if our fingers were in our ears, there is a band screwed tight inside our head.

You might call it a soul cold. And with the literary image of

49

illness is born the desire that life must be a sort of convalescence, without walking; and the idea of convalescence evokes properties on the outskirts of the city, not in its centre, with their rooms far away from the street and the noise of wheels. No, one feels nothing. One walks on considering, while simply asleep, and in the impossibility of imparting a new direction to one's body, through the doors one must pass in order to enter. One goes everywhere. Where is our tambourine, you motionless bear?

Faint, like something about to begin, the salty smell of the breeze rises up from the Tagus and is dispersed, through the bottom streets of the Lower City. It was sickening with the tang, with the cold torpor of the tepid sea. I felt life in my entrails and my sense of smell changed into something else behind my eyes. High up, very high up, three clouds floated in the void, scattered and piled up on each other, in a greyness dissolving into a pseudo-whiteness. The atmosphere was a threat to the cowardly sky, just like an inaudible clap of thunder, which only produces blasts of air.

You felt the stagnation even in the seagulls' flight; they appeared to be things lighter than air, left there by somebody or other. Nothing suffocated. The day trailed away in a disquiet which was ours; intermittently, the air became cooler.

What wretched hopes are mine, born of a life I had been obliged to live! They are like this moment, this air, fogless fogs, shoddy threads of false storm. I want to scream, to rid myself of the landscape and of my thoughts. But my plan stinks of mud, it too, and the low tide in me caused to appear that blackish mire which is out there and which I only see because of its smell.

How inconsequential to want to be self-sufficient! What an ironic consciousness of imagined feelings! What a mixed up jumble of soul and feelings, of thoughts with the air and the river, in order to say that life pains me in my sense of smell and in my consciousness – not to know how to say, as in that simple, all-encompassing phrase in the Book of Job: 'My soul is tired of life!'

And finally, over the obscurity of the shining roofs, the cold light of a tepid morning lurks like an apocalyptic torture. Once again, the immense night of increasing clarity. Once again, the usual horror – day, life, factitious utility, inescapable activity. Once again, my physical person, visible and social, transmutable by words which mean nothing, capable of being used at others' whims, others' consciousness. Once again, me as I am not. At the onset of that gleaming darkness, which invades with grey incertitudes the slats of the shutters (far from being hermetic, by God!), little by little I feel that I will not be able to keep this refuge for much longer: to rest in bed, unasleep but capable of sleeping, ruminating freely without knowing if there is a truth and a reality, floating between the cool warmth of the sheets and ignorance – exception made for the sensation of comfort – of the fact I possess a body. I feel gradually slipping away from me the happy unconsciousness in which I enjoy my consciousness, the animal somnolence in whose depths I seek, between the eyelids of a cat sunning itself, the movements which describe the logic of my free-ranging imagination. I feel gradually fading away the privileges of the penumbra and the sluggish rivers under the trees glimpsed at the edges of my eyelids, and the soft sounds of waterfalls, lost between the slow pulsing of blood in the ears and the faint persistent rain. Gradually, I lose myself until I become alive.

I do not know if I sleep, or if I simply feel I sleep. I do not dream in a precise space of time, but I perceive, as if waking from a sleep I had not slept, the first murmurs of the City's life rising, like a flood, from the imprecise well, down below where the streets lead God knows where. They are happy sounds, filtered through the sadness of the falling rain, or perhaps of the rain which has already fallen – since for the moment I no longer hear it . . . Nothing but the excessive greyness of the striated light creeping forward, amid vague, luminous shadows, insufficient for this time of morning which I ignore. They are happy dispersed sounds and they pain the depths of my soul, as if they summoned me to an examination or to an execution. Every day I hear dawning from this bed, where I do not know, seems to me to be inevitably a vital day of my life which I shall not have the courage to face. Every day, I feel it getting out of its bed of shadows, with the sheets falling over streets and alleys, convoking me before a tribunal. On each new today, I will be judged. And the eternally condemned man in me clutches at his bed as if at the mother he had lost, and caresses his bolster as if his nanny could protect him from the world.

The happy siesta of the peaceful beast in the shade of the trees, the cool exhaustion of the scruffy gypsy in the tall grass, the sleepiness of the Negro during the damp and distant afternoon, the delight in yawning with weary, fluttering eyes, all that rocks with forgetfulness and gives sleep the tranquillity of mental repose arrives and gently leans, with one leg in front of the other, against the shutters of the soul, the anonymous caress of sleep.

To sleep, to be distant without knowing it, to be stretched out, to forget one's own body; to have the liberty of being unconscious, the refuge of a lost lake, stagnating under the tall foliage in the gigantic solitudes of forests.

A nothing which breathes on the outside, a light death out of which one wakes with regret and a new freshness, and where the tissues of the soul give way to the draperies of oblivion.

Ah, and here again, just like the counter-arguments of a man one has not convinced, I hear the abrupt clamour of the rain splattering away in a clarified universe. I experience a coldness reaching into my so-called bones, as if I were afraid. And hunched up, a nothing, a human being alone with himself in the little remaining darkness, I weep, yes, I weep because of loneliness and life, and my sorrow, as derisory as a car without wheels, lies at the roadside of reality among the scrap of my distress. I weep because of everything. I weep for the memory of the knees, where, as a young child, I took refuge, for the hand held out towards me, now dead, and then for the arms which I never knew how they must have held me, the shoulder against which I could never rest my head ... And the day which breaks definitively, the pain which appears in me like the harsh truth of the day, that which I dreamt of, that which I thought about, that which, in me, has forgotten – all that, that smagma of shadows, fictions and remorse swirl together in the wake where worlds toss and roll, and fall among the objects of life, like the skeleton of a bunch of grapes, gobbled up in secret by the boys who stole it.

The noise of the human day abruptly increases like the tolling of a church bell. At the far end of the house, there clicks softly the first latch of the first door opening on to the universe. I hear slippers in an absurd corridor leading to my heart. And with a violent gesture, like a man killing himself, I wrench off my rigid body the sheets and blankets of the deep bed which shelters me. I am awake. The sound of the rain fades away up there in the indistinct exterior. I feel more at ease. I have achieved something I ignore.

I get up, go over to the window, open the interior shutters with the decisiveness of a brave man. I see a day of clear shining rain flooding my eyes with a dull clarity. Next, I open the windows. The fresh air dampens my still warm skin. I want to refresh myself, to live, and I crane my neck towards life as if towards a gigantic yoke.

❦

Months have passed since I last wrote. I maintained myself in such a state of sleep that I have been quite an other in life. Often I have had a feeling of happiness, in the figurative sense, as it were. I have not existed. I have been an other, I have lived without thinking.

And, suddenly, I have become once again what I am, or what I imagine myself to be. It occurred at a time of great lassitude, after I had worked without stopping. I put my head in my hands, my elbows resting on the tall inclined writing desk. And, eyes shut, I found myself once again.

In an illusory and distant sleep, I recalled all that I had been, and it was with the clarity of a keenly observed landscape that there suddenly arose before my eyes, before or after everything, the long façade of my childhood house, in front of which, right in the middle of that vision, in turn was sketched out, empty, the area of clay.

I felt immediately that futility of life. To see, feel, remember, forget – all that was mixed up in me and melted together – that slight pain at the elbows – with the imprecise murmur of the neighbouring street and the thin notes of the calm, regular work in the tranquil office.

When, having rested my hands on the upper rim of the writing desk, I cast around me a glance which should have been of a lassitude filled by dead worlds, the first thing I saw – what is called seeing – was a fat blue fly (that faint murmuring which was not from the office!) sitting on my inkwell. I watched it from the depths of the abyss, anonymous and attentive. It had tints of green overlaid with blue-black, and its shining repugnant brilliancy was not ugly. A life!

Who knows for what superior forces, gods or demons of the truth, whose shadow envelops one straying foot, I am nothing but a glistening fly, squatting for a second under their gaze? An over-facile comparison? Something said a thousand times over? Philosophy bereft of thought? Perhaps, but I have not thought: I have felt. It is on a direct carnal level, with deep horror, that I made that laughable analogy. I was a fly when I compared myself to a fly. I was a fly when I imagined that I felt myself to be a fly. And I felt I had a fly's soul. I slept as a fly, I felt shut in as a fly. But the greatest horror was that at the same time I felt I was myself. Despite myself, I raised my eyes to the ceiling, in fear lest some supreme ruler came crashing down on me, exactly as I myself might have squashed that fly. Happily, when I lowered my eyes, the fly had disappeared without a sound. The amorphous office once again was devoid of philosophy.

❧

For a long time now – days perhaps, or months – I no longer register the slightest feeling; I no longer think, hence I no longer exist. I have forgotten who I am; I no longer know how to write, since I no longer know how to exist. By a sort of oblique liberation, I have been an other. To realize that I do not remember is to wake up.

I have passed a part of my life unconscious in a faint. I come back to my senses without the memory of what I have been, and the memory of what I was previously suffers from having been interrupted. I sense in myself a confused notion of an unknown pause, and a futile effort by one part of memory as it tries to meet the other. I am unable to reforge a link with myself. If I have lived, I have forgotten to notice it.

Not that this first day of a now perceptible autumn – the first day which is cold without being fresh, clothing the dead summer with a feeble light – gives me, with its distant transparency, the sensation of aborted energy or of illusory willpower. Not that I find again, in this interlude of lost things, the uncertain trace of a lost memory. It is, more painfully than that, the tedium of trying to remember what one does not recall, the discouragement in the face of everything that consciousness has been lost, has been drowned among the algae and rushes, on some river bank or other.

I note that the day, static and limpid, has a positive sky, blue less clear than deep blue. I note that the sun, slightly less golden than before, gilds with humid reflections the walls and shutters. I note that in the absence of any wind, or even of any breeze which evokes or denies it, one feels nevertheless a potential freshness sleeping over the indistinct city. I note all this, without thinking or desiring, and I want to sleep only in memory, to be nostalgic only in disquiet.

I begin a sterile, distant convalescence after an illness I never had. I prepare myself, alert after my waking up, for that which I dare not do. What sleep did not allow me to sleep? What caress did not wish to speak to me? How marvellous to be someone else, breathing in this cold gulp of vigorous spring! How marvellous to think at least of being an other, better than life itself, whereas, far off in the image conjured up by memory, rushes, untouched by any perceptible wind, are flattened down, glaucous with the river's reflections!

It happens so often to me – as I remember him who I never was – that I imagine I am very young and all the rest is forgotten! And they were different, those landscapes I never saw; and, without ever having existed, they are new, those landscapes I truly saw. What matter? I have faded away in a series of chances and interstices, and when the freshness of the day is that of the sun itself, down there sleep, frozen in a sunset I see without possessing, the sombre reeds of the river banks.

❧

After the heatwave had stopped, and the first light rain had thickened into audibility, there floated in the air a tranquillity which the overheated air had not had, a new peace in which humidity brought its own breeze. So clear and full of joy was that gentle rain, free of darkness and storms, that even those without umbrellas or raincoats – that is the majority – laughed as they talked and strode down the glistening streets.

In an indolent pause, I went over to the window (which the heat had caused to be opened, but the rain had not caused to be shut) and I contemplated, with that intense indifferent concentration, which is in my nature, that which I had just described with exactitude before ever having seen it. Yes, down there, I saw the banal gaiety of couples scurrying about, talking and smiling at each other beneath the fine rain, walking along at a rapid rather than hurried pace, in the limpid clarity of the already veiled day.

But abruptly, rolling out from a corner of a street which was already there, there sprang into view an old man, modest in appearance, poor but not destitute, who came on impatiently under the abated rain. That man, who visibly had no purpose, was at least lightly impatient. I stared at him not with that inattentive concentration one accords things, but with that analytical concentration one accords symbols. He symbolized *nobody*; that is why he was in a hurry. He symbolized those who have been nothing; that is why he was in pain. He belonged, not to those who feel smilingly the incompatible gaiety of the rain, but to the rain itself – an unconscious fellow, and so unconscious that he experienced reality.

It was not that, however, I wished to say. Between my observation of that passer-by (whom I immediately lost sight of, having ceased looking) and the nexus of these remarks, a certain mysterious inattention has slipped in, some haphazard thought has broken the thread of my thoughts. And at the bottom of that intimate confusion, I hear, without clearly hearing, the noise of the packing boys at the end of the shop, in the part where the shop begins, and I see, without seeing, the string they use to pack the parcels for the post, with double knots twice looped round the parcels with their heavy brown paper, on the table next to the window which gives on to the courtyard, between jokes and scissors.

To see is to have seen.

❦

I do not know any pleasure like that of books, and I read sparingly. Books are introductions to dreams, and there is no need of introduction when one begins, very naturally, talking with them. I have never been able to read a single book to which I gave myself over entirely; at each step, always, the incessant commentary of intelligence and imagination interrupted the thread of the narrative. After a few minutes, it was I who was writing the book – and what I wrote nowhere existed [. . .]

I read and abandon myself, not to reading, but to my own self.

❦

I was born into a generation of which the majority of young people had lost their faith in God, for the same reason that their ancestors had possessed it – without knowing why. And, as the human spirit has a natural tendency to criticize, because it feels instead of thinking, the majority of those young people chose Humanity as a successor to God. None the less, I belong to that category of mankind which always remains at the edge of what it belongs to, and who sees not only the multitude to which it belongs, but the vast spaces which exist on either side of it. That is why I did not abandon God as radically as they did, and that is why I never accepted the idea of Humanity. I thought that God, although highly improbable, might exist; hence, that it was conceivable to adore him; but that Humanity, a simple biological concept signifying nothing more than the human animal species, did not merit adoration any more that any other animal species. That cult of Humanity, with its rituals of Freedom and Equality, has always seemed to me to be a revival of antique religions, where animals were thought to be gods, or else the gods had animal heads.

So then, not knowing how to believe in God and incapable of believing in an agglomeration of animals, I remained, as people on the fringes of crowds, at that distance from what is commonly called Decadence. Decadence is the total loss of unconsciousness; since the unconscious is the basis of life. If it could think, the heart would stop.

For us (those few like me and myself), who live without knowing how to, what is left as a *modus vivendi* but renunciation, and contemplation as a destiny? Not knowing what religious life is, and incapable of knowing it, since faith is not acquired through reason, incapable of believing in that abstraction of mankind and not even knowing how to deal with it in relation to oneself – there remained for us, as a motive for having a soul, the aesthetic contemplation of life. Thus, strangers to the solemnity of all worlds, indifferent to the divine and contemptuous of the human, we gave ourselves over futilely to aimless feeling, cultivated in the bosom of a sophisticated Epicureanism, as was fitting for a cerebral nervous system.

Only retaining from science its central precept, that is that all is subject to inexorable laws against which independent reaction is impossible since our very reactions are provoked by the action of those laws; and realizing how well that precept is adapted to that other, more ancient, one: the divine fatality of things – we then renounced all future effort, as the feeble renounce the exertions of athletes, and we bent down over the book of feelings with an enormous scrupulosity of experienced erudition.

Taking nothing seriously, and imagining there could be no other reality as trustworthy as that of our feelings, we sought refuge in them and explored them, as if they were vast uncharted lands. And if we worked assiduously not only on aesthetic contemplation, but also on the way its forms and results were expressed, it is only because the prose or verse we wrote, stripped of any necessity to convince the mind or to influence the will of whomsoever, was almost as if we were reading out loud to ourselves in order to give total objectivity to the subjective pleasure of reading.

We knew full well that no work can be perfect, and that the least tenable of our aesthetic lucubrations would be the very ones we wrote about. But all is imperfect, there is no sunset so beautiful that it could not be improved on, no light breeze, lulling us to sleep, which could not bring us more peace and quiet. So, contemplating with an identical serenity mountains and statues, enjoying days like books, and, above all, dreaming about everything so as to convert it into our most intimate substance, we could simultaneously make descriptions and analyses which, once completed, would become alien to ourselves and which we could enjoy as if they had arrived during the late afternoon.

This is not a pessimist's attitude, like Vigny's, for whom life was a prison where he wove baskets to pass away the time. To be a pessimist is to take everything tragically, and such an attitude is at one and the same time both excessive and uncomfortable. Certainly, we have no value judgement we can apply to our own productions. We produce, it is true, to distract ourselves, but not at all like the prisoner making baskets to distract himself from Fate, but more like a young girl embroidering cushions for distraction, nothing more than that.

I consider life to be an inn where I am forced to stay until the arrival of the coach from the abyss. I have no idea where it will

59

take me, since I know nothing. I could consider that inn a prison since I am obliged to remain within its walls; I could consider it to be a friendly place, since I meet people there. However, I am neither impatient, nor do I have vulgar tastes. I leave all that to those who lock themselves up in rooms, amorphous, stretched out on a bed waiting sleeplessly; I leave all that to people who prattle away in drawing-rooms, out of which emerge voices and music which strike me as pleasant. I sit at the door and intoxicate my eyes and ears with the colours and sounds of the landscape, and I sing *sotto voce*, for myself alone, vague songs which I compose while waiting.

Night will fall and the coach will arrive for us all. I savour the breeze which I have been given and the soul I have been given to savour it with, and I ask no further questions. If what I leave behind inscribed in the hotel register can, read by others than myself, distract them too while they wait, so much the better. If they do not read it, or if they find no pleasure in reading it, then that too will be so much the better.

❧

An aesthetic quietism of life, thanks to which the insults and humiliations which constitute life, which the living inflict on us, cannot get any closer to us than the pathetic periphery of our sensibility, at the remote exterior of our conscious soul.

❧

I went among them as a stranger, but not one of them saw what I was. I lived among them as a spy, but nobody – not even myself – suspected what I was. All of them imagined I was one of their kinfolk, but not one knew that there had been a substitution at my birth. So I was like others without resembling them, brother of each and every one without belonging to any family.

I came from a prodigious land, out of landscapes finer than life, but I have never spoken about those places and I have never evoked those landscapes, seen only in dreams. My footsteps on the parquet and the flagstones were like theirs, but my heart was far away, even though it beat alongside them, the false master of an exiled alien body.

Nobody recognized me behind that mask of similarity, nor even knew I was wearing a mask, as nobody knew there were masked creatures in that world. Nobody even imagined that next to me was someone else who, ultimately, was me. I have always been considered identical to myself.

I was asked to their houses, I shook their hands, they saw me pass in the street as if I was there; but he who I am was never in those rooms, he who I live has no hands for others to grasp, he who I know myself to be has no streets to pass by in, unless it is a question of all streets, nor streets to be seen in, unless he himself is all the others.

We all live far from each other and anonymous; disquieted, we suffer, unknown. However, for some people that distance which exists between a being and himself is never apparent, for others, it flares up, in times of horror and suffering, with an unconstrained blaze; for still others, it is the constant, painful, daily factor of their entire lives.

To imbue ourselves with the conviction that what we are is none of our doing, that what we think, what we experience is always a translation, that what we want, we have never really wanted and that, perhaps, ultimately, has never been wanted by anybody else – to know all that at all moments, to feel all that in each and every feeling, is that not to be alien to one's very own soul, exiled in one's very own feelings?

But the mask which I looked at inert, which spoke on the corner to a man without a mask, this final night of carnival – finally has held out its hand and departed in laughter. The natural man has turned left, at the corner of the small street I was at. The mask – a charmless domino – went straight on, fading among the play of light and shadows with a definite goodbye, abstracted from what I was thinking about that very second. Only then did I realize that there was something else in the streets in addition to the glowing streetlamps, per-turbing the area they did not illuminate – a vague, occult and silent moonbeam, filled with nothing like life . . .

Abruptly, as if some quack doctor had operated on me for an ancient blindness with immediate results, I raise my head up from an anonymous existence towards the limpid knowledge of the manner of my being. And I see that all I have done, all I have thought, all I have been, is nothing but a sort of mirage and lunacy. I am appalled by all I have succeeded in not seeing. I am perturbed by all I have been and which in fact, I see now, I am not.

I scan, as if it were a huge area lit by a ray of sunlight stabbing through the clouds, my entire past life; and I take note, with metaphysical stupefaction, to what degree my most judicious actions, my clearest ideas, my most logical plans, have, after all, been nothing else but a congenital drunkenness, a natural folly, total ignorance. I have not even played a part: my role has been played for me. I have not been an actor either; I have merely been his gesticulations.

All that I have done, thought or been, is nothing but a mass of submissions, either to a fictive being which I believed to be me since I acted out of him towards the exterior, or else to the weight of circumstances I took to be the very air I breathed. I am, in this flash of insight, a being suddenly alone who discovers he is an exile from where he always believed himself to belong. Even in my most intimate thoughts, I have not been me.

Then, a sarcastic terror of life overwhelms me, a disarray which goes far beyond the limits of my conscious individuality. I know that I have been nothing but error and mistake, that I have not even lived, that I have only existed in the sense that I have filled up time with conscious thought. And the impression I have of myself is that of a man who wakes from a sleep peopled by real dreams, or of a man extracted, by an earthquake, from the penumbra of a cell to which he was accustomed.

I am crushed, truly crushed, by the weight, as if condemned to knowledge, of that sudden realization of my true individuality, that which has spent its time travelling, somnolent, between what it felt and what it saw.

It is so hard to describe what one feels the moment one feels

that one has a real existence, and that the soul is a real entity –
so hard that I ignore which human words could describe it. I
know not if I am feverish, as I think I am, or if the fever of being
a sleeper in life has dropped. Yes, I say it again, I am like a
traveller who suddenly finds himself in an unknown city,
without knowing how he got there; and I remember those
cases when people lose their memories and become somebody
else for a very long time. I myself was an other for a very long
time – since my birth and my consciousness – and I wake up
today in the middle of a bridge, spanning the river, and
knowing that I have a more solid existence than all I have been
up until now. But it is a foreign city, foreign streets, and pain
without remedy. So, I wait, leaning over the bridge, for truth to
leave me, and to abandon me once more – a fictive void,
intelligent and normal.

It lasted only a moment which has already passed. Once
again, I see the furniture surrounding me, the pattern on the
old wallpaper, the sun through the dusty window-panes. I saw
truth for an instant. I was conscious for an instant, as great
men are their entire lives. I recall their words and actions, and I
wonder if they too are tempted successfully by the Devil of
Reality. To ignore oneself is to live. To know oneself badly is
to think. But to know oneself abruptly, as in that lustral
instant, is abruptly to possess the notion of the intimate
monad, of the magical word of the soul. But a sudden clarity
consumes all, burns it all away. It leaves us naked, even
stripped of our being.

It lasted only a second, and I saw myself. After, I would not
even know how to explain what I have been. And, finally, I am
sleepy, since, without knowing why, I believe to feel is to
sleep.

THE AESTHETICS OF ARTIFICE

Life prejudices the expression of life. If I lived a great passion, I
would never know how to retell it.

I, myself, ignore if this me, which I regale you with in these sinuous pages, really exists, or if it is a false aesthetic concept I have forged of myself. Living myself aesthetically in an other, I have sculpted my life like a statue carved out of a substance akin to my being. There are times when I do not recognize myself, so much have I employed, in a purely artistic fashion, the consciousness I have of myself. Who am I, behind that irreality? I do not know. I must be someone. And if I attempt to live, act, feel, it is – believe me – to avoid damaging the already defiled characteristics of my supposed personality. I want to be him whom I wanted to be and who I am not. If I surrender, I would destroy myself. I want to be a work of art, at least in my soul, as I cannot be one in my body. That is why I sculpted myself in a calm, detached pose, placed in a greenhouse sheltered against over-cool breezes and too glaring a light – where my artificiality, like an absurd flower, can flourish in splendour.

Sometimes I dream how agreeable it would be, in my dreams, to create a second uninterrupted life for myself, where I would spend entire days with imaginary fellow travellers, totally fabricated people, and I would live, suffer, and take pleasure from that fictive life. In that world, sadness would happen, huge joys would fall on me. And nothing of me would be real. But everything there would possess a superb serious logic, all would dance to the rhythm of voluptuous falsehood, all would take place in a city made up out of my very soul, which would go and vanish away on the platform beside a peaceful train, far off inside me, very far off . . . And all would be clear, inevitable, the outside life, except the aesthetics of the Death of the Sun.

❧

It sometimes happens – and always unexpectedly – that right in the middle of my feelings there arises such a terrible lassitude for life that I cannot possibly imagine a way to overcome it. As a cure, suicide is not sure; death, even including unconsciousness, is still very little. It is a lassitude which desires not to cease existing – which may or may not be in the realm of the possible – but a deeper, more horrific thing: to cease from having ever existed, which is in no way possible.

Sometimes, I think I glimpse in the generally confused speculations of the Hindus something of that desire, more negative than nothingness. Yet, either there is a lack of sharpness of feeling which prevents them from expressing what they think, or it is a lack of acuity of thought which prevents them from feeling what they experience. The fact is that I no longer see what I glimpsed in them. The fact is that I think that I am the first person to put into words the sinister absurdity of that irremediable feeling.

And I cure it by writing about it. For there is no desolation, if it has profound truth, if it is not pure feeling but partly shared with intelligence, which ignores the ironic remedy of expression. When literature will no longer be of any other use, it will at least keep that one, even though destined for a minority.

Illnesses of the spirit, sadly, cause less suffering than those of feelings, and the latter, unhappily, less than those of the body.

I say 'unhappily' since human dignity preconizes the contrary. There is no anguished feeling of mystery which can hurt like love, jealousy or regret, which can choke like intense physical fear, which can bring about change like anger or ambition. Yet, it is equally true that none of those pains which destroy the soul are as real as a toothache, a stomach-ache or (I imagine) the pangs of childbirth.

We are made in such a way that our intelligence, which ennobles certain of our emotions or feelings, raising them up over others, also abases them if it extends its analysis as far as mutual compassion.

I write like one who sleeps, and my entire life is an unsigned receipt.

In the henhouse he will leave only to die, the cock crows hymns to liberty because he has been given two perches.

I have assisted, incognito, at the gradual defeat of my life, at the progressive shipwreck of all I would have liked to have been. I can say it, with that truthfulness which does not require flowers to realize it is dead, that there is not one single thing I wanted, or in which I put my hopes, if only for a second, or in which I put the dream of that second, which has not been smashed into smithereens under my window like a dust, like stone dust, falling from a flowerpot on the top floor. You might even say that Fate has always delighted first in making me want or desire that which it has already parcelled out in order that I realize, the following day, that I did not and would never have it.

Ironic spectator of myself, despite all, I have never given up, discouraged by the spectacle of life. And, since I know today, by anticipation, that each vague desire will undoubtedly be deceived, I suffer from the singular pleasure of enjoying the deception simultaneously with the hope, like a sweet-and-sour dish, which emphasizes the sweetness by contrasting it with the sour. I am a gloomy strategist who, having lost every battle in advance, outlines in his future battle plans, enjoying each detail, the precise order of his final retreat, on the eve of each new battle.

As if by a sly demon, I have been tracked down by the fate of never being able to desire anything without the knowledge that I will obtain nothing. If, for a second, I see in the street the nubile silhouette of a young girl and if, totally indifferent, I imagine for a moment what I would feel if she were mine – without fail, ten feet away from my dream, the young girl meets a man who I see immediately is her husband or her lover. A romantic would make a tragedy out of it; a stranger would live it as a comedy; but I, I mix them both since I am basically both a romantic and a stranger to myself, and I turn the page on another irony.

Some say life is impossible without hope, and others that with hope life is a void. For me, who today neither hopes nor despairs, life is merely an external frame which surrounds me and at which I assist as if it were a play devoid of any plot, created uniquely for the pleasure of the eyes – a ballet with no coda, leaves shaken by the wind, clouds where sunlight assumes shifting colours, a labyrinth of old streets, laid out by chance in the bizarre neighbourhoods of the city.

To a large extent, I am the very prose I write. I evolve in sentences and paragraphs, I read myself with punctuation marks and, with an unchecked plethora of images, I disquiet myself, like a child, as a king dressed up in newspaper or, as I create rhythms out of a series of words, I crown myself, like a lunatic, with dried flowers, perpetually alive in my dreams. And, above all, I am as calm as a clown who becomes conscious of himself, shaking his head from time to time, so that the ball perched on top of his pointed hat (which forms an integral part of his head) makes some sound or other – tintinnabulating life of a dead man, minimal warning to Fate.

How often, however, amid this peaceful dissatisfaction have I felt gradually rising in me, until it turns into a conscious emotion, the acute feeling of the void and the boredom of such thoughts? How often, like a man eavesdropping on the ebb and flow of conversation, have I not felt the essential bitterness of a life alien to human life – a life where nothing takes place except in its consciousness of itself? How often, waking up from myself, have I not glimpsed from the depths of my exile how much better it would be to be everybody's 'no one', the happy man who at least has a real bitterness, the satisfied man who feels tired instead of being bored, who suffers instead of imagining he suffers, who kills himself, yes, instead of allowing himself to die?

I have become a character in a novel, a real life. What I feel is not (despite myself) felt except to make me write that it was felt. What I think turns at once into words mixed with images which undo it, opening out into rhythms which are already something else. By pulling myself together, I have destroyed myself. By having thought of myself, I have become my very thoughts, but am no longer me. When sounding my depths, I dropped the probe; I spend my life wondering if I am profound or not, without another probe today except my gaze, revealing to me – clear against a black background in the mirror of the dizzying well – my own face, looking at me in the process of looking at myself.

I am a sort of playing card, an ancient symbol, the unique relic of a lost game. I make no sense, I ignore my value, I have no element of comparison to establish what I am, I have no useful quality whatsoever which might help me to recognize myself. And so, in the succession of images I employ to describe myself (not devoid of truth, but with the addition of a few lies), I ultimately recognize myself more in the images than in me. I say so forcefully to myself that I no longer exist, using my very soul as ink, which is good for nothing else but writing. But the reaction fades, yet again I am resigned. I return in my being to what I am, even if it is nothing. And something like tearless weeping burns my haggard eyes, something like non-existent anguish chokes my arid throat. But, alas! I do not even know what I might have wept over, if I had done so, nor for what reason I did not do so. Fiction follows me like my shadow. All I want to do is sleep.

❃

Everything confuses me. When I believe I remember, it is another thing I am thinking of: if I see, I ignore, and when I am distracted, I see extremely well.

I turn back to the greyish window with its panes cold to the hands which touch them. And I carry away with me – with the aid of the penumbra's spell – suddenly the interior of the old house, and the courtyard next door where the parakeet cackled on; and my eyes are invaded by sleep, beneath the ineluctability of having really lived all that.

It's been raining for two days now, and a special rain falls down out of the cold grey sky which, because of its colour, saddens the soul. Two days ... I am sad that I feel, and I think of it at the window, to the echo of dripping water and the falling rain. My heart is heavy and my memories change to anguish.

Not that I am sleepy, having no reason to be sleepy, yet I feel a gigantic urge to sleep. In the old days, when I was young and happy, there was, in a house in the next courtyard, the living voice of a speckled green parakeet.

Never, even on rainy days, did this cackling lose its enthusiasm, being well sheltered no doubt, proclaiming some constant feeling or other, which floated, in the ambiant sadness, like a primeval gramophone.

Did I think of that parakeet because I feel sad and my distant childhood dredged up that memory? No. I really thought of it because in the actual courtyard in front of me a parakeet's voice is oddly shrieking.

(And there you have an imaginative episode which we call reality.)

❧

I record day after day, in my ignoble and profound soul, the impressions which make up the external substance of my consciousness of myself. I note them down in errant words, words which, once written, desert me and go off by themselves over the slopes and meadows of images, through the alleys of concepts, down the paths of chimaeras. All that is no use to me, since nothing is of any use to me. But I feel relieved when I write, like a sick person who suddenly breathes more easily, without his illness having left him.

Some people, in moments of distraction, scribble down absurd doodles and names on their blotting-paper, in the chamfered corners. These pages are the scribblings of the cerebral unconsciousness I have of myself. I shape them with a sort of lethargy wherein I see myself, like a cat in the sun, and sometimes I read them over with a faint and belated surprise as if I suddenly recalled that which had been lost for ever.

When I write, I pay a solemn call on myself. I possess special salons, remembered by another person, in the interstices of the play in which I thrill myself by analysing what I do not feel and where I scrutinize myself like a painting in the dark.

I lost, before birth, my family castle. Before I came into existence, the tapestries from my ancestral palace were sold. My pre-life manor house has fallen into ruins, and it is only in those rare moments, when moonlight is born in me over the stems of the reeds in the river, that I am penetrated by the icy nostalgia of those places where the gap-toothed remains of walls are silhouetted, black against the dark blue of a sky tinted milky yellow white.

Sphinx, I unriddle myself with enigmas; and from the lap of the queen whom I miss, falls – like a scene in her futile needlework – the forgotten ball of wool which is my soul. It rolls under the marquetry chiffonier, and something in me follows it, like a regard, until the moment it is lost in a profound horror of the grave and of annihilation.

❧

Yet, the exclusion I imposed on myself from having aims and variations in life; the rupture, which I sought, from having any contact with things – all that led me to precisely what I wished to avoid. I did not want to experience life, nor to have any contact with things, knowing, thanks to the totality of my experience of my temperament having been exposed to the world's contamination, that the sensation was always painful for me. But, by avoiding that contact, I isolated myself and, by isolating myself, exacerbated my already excessive sensibility. If it had been possible for me to cut myself off entirely from any contact with things, my sensibility would have been perfectly all right. But total isolation cannot be achieved. No matter how little I do, I breathe and no matter how little I act, I move. To such a degree that, merely successful in exacerbating my sensibility by isolation, at the same time I have achieved the result that even minimal events, which formerly would have meant nothing, now affect me on a catastrophic scale. I chose the wrong type of flight. I escaped, via an uncomfortable detour, only to arrive at my point of departure, combining together the fatigue of the journey with the horror of living there.

I have never envisaged suicide as a solution because I hate life, precisely since I love it. It took me ages to realize what that lamentable misunderstanding is which consists of living with myself. Once I had grasped what a mistake that was, I became extremely angry, as always happens when I talk myself into something, because for me that is always the equivalent of losing an illusion.

I have slaughtered my will with analysis. If only I could return to my pre-analytical infancy, even if it was also the age of pre-will.

In my pasts I sleep dead in the somnolence of lakes beneath the sun at its zenith when insects' buzzing pullulates in the static hour and living overwhelms me, not like anguish but like a continually diffuse physical pain.

Far off palaces, pensive gardens, the narrowness of paths vanishing in the distance, dead beauty of stone benches made for those who have been: evaporated splendours, undone grace, lost glass beads. O forgotten desire, if only I could recuperate the acrimony with which I dreamt of you!

❦

When I first came to live in Lisbon, there was, on the floor above where we lived, the noise of piano scales, the mono-tonous apprenticeship of a little girl I never saw. Today, I discover by a process of infiltration I know nothing about still alive in the cellars of my soul, clearly audible if the bottom door is opened, the never-ending scales, endlessly misplayed, of the child now a woman or else dead and buried in a white place where the green cypresses produce black flames.

At the time, I was a child, today I am one no longer; despite everything, the sound in my memory is identical to the one it was, and preserves, immutably present, wherever it surges up out of where it was pretending to sleep, the identical fractured timbre, the identical rhythmic monotony. By thinking of it and perceiving it in that way, I am invaded by an ill-defined anguished sadness of my own.

I do not weep for the loss of my childhood; I weep because everything, my childhood included, is in the process of vanishing. It is the abstract flight of time – not the concrete flight of time which belongs to me – which agonizes me, in my physical brain, by the involuntary, incessant recurrence of the piano scales on the floor above, hideously anonymous and far

71

off. It is the entire mystery of the fact that nothing endures which hammers out, without cease, things which are not even music but are nostalgia in the absurd depths of memory.

Imperceptibly, in a gently swelling vision, I see the small salon which I never saw, where the young learner whom I never knew continues to massacre, note by note, with great care, the scales identical with what has already died. I see, I see better and better, I reconstitute because I see. And it is the whole apartment on the floor upstairs, nostalgic interior of today but not of yesterday, which surges up, fictive, out of my incongruous speculations.

I suppose I live all that in a figurative sense, that the nostalgia I feel is not really mine, nor entirely abstract, but the emotion plucked out of the air of some passer-by, for whom those emotions, which for me are literary, would be, as Vieira might have said, literal ones. It is with that hypothesis of feelings I torture and anguish myself, and those regrets, whose sensation fills my eyes with tears, are conceived and felt by me through imagination and otherness.

And still, with a continuity coming from the end of the world, a persistence which studies metaphysically, there echoes over and over again, the scales of a tyro at the piano, physically playing on the vertebral column of my memory. It is the old streets, peopled by other people, today the same but different streets; it is the dead who speak with me, through the transparence of their present absence; it is the remorse for what I have never done or been, the rushing of a nocturnal stream, sounds rising from the peaceful house.

I long to scream in my head. I would like to stop, to squash, to break the impossible accord resounding in me, alien to me and an intangible torturer. I want to command, to order my soul to be a car, to proceed without me and to leave me there. It drives me insane to be obliged to listen. And, in the end, I am me – in this atrociously sensitive brain, in this dermatological skin, in my flayed sinews – I am those badly played notes in never-ending scales on that abominable, particular piano of memory.

And again, yet again, as if a segment of the brain had a life of its own, I hear those echoing scales, from one end of the keyboard to the other, emerging from the first house in Lisbon I came to live in.

❧

In my eyes, all that is not my soul is nothing else, despite all my efforts, but scenery and decoration. A man, even though I can admit rationally that he is a living creature like myself, always has had – as far as that random most authentic part of me is concerned – less importance than a tree, provided it was a handsome one. That is why I have always experienced human events – the major collective historical tragedies, or what is made out of them – as if they were polychrome friezes, emptied of the soul of those who live through them. I have never been afflicted by what happened in China. It is a distant décor, albeit painted with blood and pestilence.

I recall, with ironic sadness, a workers' demonstration, how sincere it was I ignore (for I always have trouble in imagining sincerity in collective manifestations, since it is the individual, by himself, who really knows what he feels). It formed a compact, disorganized group of idiotic creatures who moved by bellowing out various slogans in the face of my alien indifference. I felt violently sick. They were not even dirty enough. They who suffer truly do not gather in vulgar crowds, do not form groups. They who suffer, do so alone.

What a deplorable agglomeration! What a lack of humanity and pain! They were real, hence unbearable. Nobody could have used them in a novel, in a descriptive passage, they flowed like refuse into a river, the river of life. Watching them, I felt sleepy, a supreme nauseous sleep.

❧

What produces in me, I think, this deep feeling I have of discordance with others is that most people think with their sensibility, and I feel with my thoughts.

For an ordinary man, to feel is to live, and to think is to know how to live.

It is odd to realize that, given that my capacity for enthusiasm is somewhat limited, spontaneously it is more stimulated by those with a character antithetical to mine than by those who belong to the same spiritual tribe. In literature, I admire nothing as much as the classics, with which, beyond all doubt, I have the least in common. If I had to choose one single writer, between Vieira and Chateaubriand, I would quickly opt for Vieira.

The more a man differs from me, the more real he seems, precisely because he is less dependent on my subjectivity. And that is precisely why my constant, careful study is focused on that very banal humanity which repels me and to which I feel so alien. I love it because I hate it. I love to watch it because I have to feel it. Landscapes, however admirable in paintings, usually make revolting beds to sleep in.

❧

Just as we all have, whether we know it or not, a metaphysical system, so whether we wish it or not, we all have a morality. I have an extremely simple morality – to do neither good nor harm to anybody. To harm nobody, because not only do I recognize for others, just as for myself, the right not to be bothered by anyone, but also because I find, as far as evil is necessary in the world, natural evils are amply sufficient. Down here, we all live aboard a ship sailing towards a port we do not know, and veering towards another port we ignore; we should have towards one another the good manners of travellers embarked on the same voyage. To do no good, since I do not know what is good, nor if I really do good when I believe I am doing it. Have I any idea of what evils I can provoke by giving alms? Have I any idea of what evils I can cure by education or instruction? When in doubt I abstain. And I think that even to help or to give advice is yet again, in one way, to trespass in the life of another. Goodness is a caprice: we do not have the right to make others victims of our caprices, even though they are caprices born out of humanity or tenderness.

Good acts are something inflicted on us: that is why, coldly, I execrate them.

If, out of moral scruple, I do no good, I do not exact either that good is done to me. If I fall ill, what bothers me the most is that I oblige someone to look after me, something I myself would neglect to do for somebody else. I have never visited a sick friend. And each time when I was ill, somebody came to visit me. I underwent each visit as a discomfort, an insult, an unjustifiable rape of my deepest privacy. I detest being given presents; people appear thus to force me to give them back in turn – to the same ones or to others, the importance is minimal.

I am extremely sociable, in an extremely negative way. I am the most inoffensive creature on earth. But I am not more than that; I do not want to be, I cannot be more than that. To all that exists I have a visual tenderness, an intellectual tenderness – nothing from the heart. I believe in nothing, hope in nothing, have charity for nothing. I abominate, shocked and sickened, the sincere ones of all sincerities and the mystics of all mysticisms, or rather, to put it better, the sincerity of all sincere people and the mysticism of all mystics. That nausea becomes almost physical when those mysticisms are active and when they pretend to convince others' intelligence, or to oblige others, against their will, to search out the truth or to reform the world.

I consider myself happy to have no more family. Thus I am not compelled (which would oppress me considerably) to love anybody. I have only literary regrets. I remember my childhood with tears in my eyes, but they are rhythmical tears shot through with prose. I recall it as an exterior thing, and through exterior things. It is not the peace of provincial evenings which touches me, in the memory of a childhood lived there – it is the place of the tea-table, it is the way the furniture was arranged in the room – it is the faces and gestures of the people around me. I am nostalgic about paintings. That is why my own childhood touches me just as much as anybody else's; both of them are – in a past which I know nothing about – purely visual phenomena which I see with an entirely literary

75

attentiveness. Doubtless, I am moved, but not by memory: by the vision.

I have never loved anybody. What I have loved the most are my feelings – states of conscious viscosity, impressions of a quick ear, smells which are a means, for the humility of the external world, to speak to me, to talk to me about the past (so easily recalled by smells), that is to provide me with more reality, more emotions than a mere loaf of bread cooking at the back of an old bakery, as on that distant afternoon when I was coming back from the burial of an uncle who loved me deeply, and when I felt the sweetness of a minor appeasement, from what I have no idea.

That is my morality, or my metaphysics, in other words, what I am: the ultimate Passer-by, of everything and even of my soul; I belong to nothing, desire nothing, am nothing – an abstract centre of impersonal feelings, a sensitive mirror fallen by chance and pointed towards the diversity of the world. After all that, I have no idea if I am happy or unhappy: it is of little or no importance to me.

IN THE FOREST OF DREAMING SOLITUDE

I know I am awake, and that I still sleep. My ancient body, mangled by the fatigue of living, tells me it is still very early. I feel remotely febrile. I oppress myself. I do not know why . . .

In a lucid lethargy, ponderously incorporeal, I stagnate between sleep and wakefulness, in a dream which is only the shade of a dream. My attention hovers between two worlds, and blindly sees the profundity of an ocean simultaneously with the profundity of a sky; and those depths interpenetrate, mingle, and I no longer know either who I am or what I dream.

A wind gravid with shadows blows away the ash of my dead projects over that part of me which is awake. Down from an unknown firmament falls a dew tepid with boredom. A massive inert anxiety manipulates my soul from inside and alters me confusedly, as the wind changes the contours of a tree line.

In my morbid and tepid room, this moment precursor of dawn outside, is a mere quivering of the penumbra. I am entirely tranquil confusion. Why has day to break? It pains me to know that daybreak will come, as if it required an effort on my part to cause it to appear.

I calm myself with a confused slowness. I make myself lethargic. I float in the air, half awake, half asleep, and here materializes another sort of reality with me in the middle, springing out of nowhere . . .

It comes – but without effacing what is most near, that tepid room – it comes, that strange forest. In my captive, attentive state the two realities coexist, like two plumes of smoke mingling together.

How well defined it is, in its own world and in the other, that transparent landscape!

And who then is that woman who, at the same time as I, gazes at that remote forest? Why should I, even for a second, have to ask? I am not even aware of wanting to know . . .

The equivocal room is a window through which, conscious of its existence, I see that landscape . . . and that landscape, I have known it for a very long time; for a very long time with that unknown woman I explore it, another reality, through irreality. I feel in me the centuries and centuries I have known those trees and flowers, those sprawling paths, as well as that distant me roaming about down there, old and ostensible under my gaze who, in order to know I am in that room, clothes myself with penumbra to see.

From time to time, in that forest where, from afar, I see and feel myself, a languid gust of air scatters the mist, and that mist is the obscure and clear vision of the room where I actually am, with its vague furniture, its curtains, and its nocturnal torpor. Then the gust of wind vanishes, and the landscape becomes complete and entirely itself, a remote landscape in that other world.

At other times, that narrow room is nothing but ashes of mist, on the horizon of that so different land . . . And there are moments when the ground we tread down there is this visible room.

I dream and I lose myself, a double of myself and that woman. A massive fatigue and a black fire which devours me . . . A gigantic passive anxiety is the false life which oppresses me . . .

O crushed happiness . . . O perpetual state of being at the crossroads! I dream, and, behind my concentration, someone else dreams with me . . . Am I not perhaps the dream of that someone else who does not exist . . .

Outside, dawn is far off! And the forest so close, beneath my other eyes!

And I who, when far from that forest, almost forgets it, since it is when I possess it that I feel the greatest nostalgia for it, it is when I explore it, I weep and aspire the most to find it again.

The bees! The flowers! The paths plunging into the undergrowth!

Sometimes we walk, arm in arm, under the cedars and the Judas trees, and neither of us dreams of living. Our flesh was a faint perfume, and our life the murmuring echo of a fountain. We took each other's hands and our unfocused gazes asked each other: what would it be like to be sensual beings, what would it be like to achieve, in the flesh, the illusion of love?

In our park there were flowers of every variegated beauty – roses with incurved petals, lilies whose whiteness was tinged with yellow, poppies which might have remained hidden if their redness had not betrayed them, violets sprinkled on the tufted edges of the slopes, minuscule myosotis, sterile camelias without any scent . . . And just like astonished eyes, over the tall grass, solitary sunflowers gazed at us – agape.

Our soul, entirely vision, caressed the visible freshness of the mosses, and we had, passing by the palm trees, the faint intuition of other lands . . . And our throats were tight at the memory, since even here, happy as we were, we were not . . .

Oak trees of knotty centuries caused us to stumble over the dead tentacles of their roots . . . Plane trees unexpectedly sprang into view . . . And through the nearby trees, you could see hanging in the distance, in the silence of the trellises, the blue-black reflection of bunches of grapes . . .

Our dream of living walked before us, and we had for it an identical remote smile, born in our twin souls without our having looked at each other, without either of us knowing anything of the other, apart from the presence of an arm leaning with abandoned attention on the other arm, which felt it.

Our life had no interior. We were on the outside and we were other. We did not know each other, and it was as if we had appeared to our souls at the end of a voyage through dreams.

We had forgotten time, and the immense space had diminished in our minds. Beyond the trees nearby, beyond the trellises far away, beyond the last hills on the horizon, was there anything real, worthy of that wide-eyed gaze one gives to things which exist . . .?

In the clepsydra of our imperfection, regularly spaced drips of dream mark off irreal hours . . . Nothing is worthwhile, my distant love, unless it is to know how sweet it is to know that nothing is worthwhile . . .

The static movement of the trees; the untranquil calm of fountains; the undefinable breath of the intimate rhythm of sap; the slow lateness of things, which appears to come from inside them and to give its hand, with total spiritual agreement, to the far-off sadness, far but so close to the soul, to the silence in the depths of the sky; the cadenced, futile falling of leaves, droplets of dreaming solitude, where the entire landscape comes to fill our eyes and turns sad in us like the memory of some homeland or other – all that, a loosening belt cinches us vaguely in.

We lived down there a time which did not know how to elapse, a space for which there was no possibility of measurement. A passage outside Time, an extension which ignored the modalities of reality in space . . . How many hours, my futile companion of boredom, how many hours of happy disquiet offered us their simulacrum in that country . . .! Hours of the ashes of the spirit, days of spatial nostalgia, internal centuries of an exterior landscape . . . And we never asked ourselves what use was all that, delighting in the knowledge that all had no use.

Down there, we knew, thanks to an intuition we certainly did not have, that this dolorous world in which we would be two, if it existed, would be situated far beyond the extreme horizon where mountains are no more than diluted forms, and beyond that horizon there was nothing. And it was the contradiction of that double knowledge which caused the moments lived down there to be as dark as a cave in the land of superstition, and our perception of those moments to be as bizarre as the profile of a Moorish city, silhouetted against a sky of autumnal dusk.

Shores of unknown seas resounded on the sonorous horizon of our hearing, beaches we would never see, and it was the acme of our joy to listen, until we saw it in ourselves, to that ocean on which, no doubt, cruised caravels with other aims than utilitarian goals and shore-based directives.

We noticed suddenly, as one notices when seeing, that the air was filled with birdsong, and that, as an ancient perfume impregnates satins, the rustling of the leaves impregnated us more than the very consciousness we had of hearing them.

And so, the trilling of the birds, the sussuration of the trees and the monotonous and forgotten background of the eternal sea placed above our abandoned life a halo of non-self-knowledge. We slept down there waking days, content to be nothing, to have neither desires, nor hopes, to have forgotten the colour of love and the taste of hate. We thought we were immortal . . .

Down there, we lived hours filled only by the presence of the other, living those very hours, of a vacuous imperfection, and so perfect for that same reason, and so splendid since they were diagonal to the rectangular exactitude of life. Imperial hours of deposition, hours clothed in faded purple, hours fallen down on the earth from another world more filled with pride at having more scattered anguish . . .

And it hurt us to enjoy that, it hurt us . . . For, despite the savour of calm exile, that entire landscape reminded us that we belonged to the real world, that it was entirely saturated with the humid pomp of vague tedium, sad, enormous and perverse, like the decadence of an unknown empire . . .

On the curtains of our room, morning is a shadow of light. My lips, which I know to be ashen, have for each other the taste of not wanting to live.

The air in our neutral room is as heavy as a baldaquin. Our attention, somnolent towards the mystery of all that, is as flabby as the train of a cloak, hissing over the floor during some crepuscular ceremonial.

No anxiety of ours has a reason to exist. Our concentration is nothing but an absurdity, granted to us by our winged inertia.

I ignore what oils of penumbra anoint the very idea of our body. The fatigue we experience is the shadow of a fatigue. It comes to us from far away, just as that idea that our life may exist somewhere . . .

Neither of us has a name or a plausible existence. If we could make sufficient noise to imagine ourselves laughing, we would certainly laugh at the fact that we believe ourselves to be alive. The tepid coolness of the street caresses (for you as for me) both our feet, each one of which senses the nudity of the other.

Let us detach ourselves, my love, from life, from its jaws and its illusions. Let us fly until we have the desire to be ourselves. . . . Let us not remove from our finger the magical ring which conjures up, when twisted, the fairies of silence, the elves of the night and the gnomes of oblivion.

And now, just when we were thinking of speaking of it, there arises, once again, before our eyes, the dense forest, but this time more perturbed than our perturbation and more sad than our sadness. Like a dissolving mist, our idea of the real world drifts away from before it, and I enter again into possession of myself in my errant dream of which that mysterious forest forms the frame.

The flowers! the flowers I have seen down there! Flowers which sight translated by naming them, by recognizing them, and whose perfume our soul plucked, not from them but from the melody of their names . . . Flowers, whose names were, repeated in libraries, orchestras of sonorous perfumes ... Trees whose verdant voluptuousness put shade and coolness into the way they were called ... Fruits whose name was as if one sunk one's teeth into the soul of their pulp ... Shades which were the relics of the once happy ... Clearings, clearings entirely clear, which were the frankest smiles of that landscape yawning close by ... O polychromed hours ... Instant-flowers, minute-trees, O time fixed in space, dead time covered with flowers and the perfume of flowers, and the perfume of the names of flowers ...!

Mad reverie in that dream silence!

Our life was the whole of life ... Our love was the perfume of love ... We lived impossible hours, filled with being ourselves. And that because we knew, with all the flesh of our flesh, that never would we be reality.

We were impersonal, husks of ourselves, some other thing ... We were that landscape seeping away in the consciousness of itself ... And just as there were two together – reality, but illusion too – so we were obscurely two, and neither one of us knew exactly if the other was not himself, if that uncertain other was alive ...

When we abruptly emerged in front of the stagnation of the lakes, we wanted to weep ... That landscape had eyes full of tears, staring eyes, saturated with the nameless boredom of being ... Yes, saturated with the boredom of being, of having to be something, reality or illusion, and that boredom found its homeland and its voice in the mute exile of the lakes. We continued to walk, without knowing or caring, yet it seemed that we tarried at the edge of those lakes, so much of us remained in them, inhabited them, was symbolized and absorbed by them.

And what a fresh and horrific happiness that no one was there! Not even we, who walked down there, had been there ... For we ourselves were nobody. We were absolutely nothing. We had no life which Death needed to kill. We were so tenuous and so insubstantial that the breath of becoming had left us to our futility and time had passed, caressing us like the breeze caresses the crest of a palm tree.

We had no epoch, no aim. All the finality of things and beings remained at the threshold of the paradise of absence. They had immobilized themselves to feel us feeling them, the rough soul of the tree trunks, the outstretched soul of the leaves, the nubile soul of the flowers, the sagging soul of the fruit.

That is how we died our life, so absorbed by dying it separately that we did not see we were a single entity, that each of us was the other's illusion, and that each of us was, in the interior of himself, the simple echo of his own being . . .

A fly buzzes, uncertain and minuscule.

Imprecise sounds dawn on my awareness, well defined and dispersed, and flood with the break of day the consciousness I have of our room. Our room? Ours for which couple, since I am alone? I know no more. Everything fades away and nothing remains, half-burned, but a fog-reality in which my dark incertitude and my understanding of myself, cradled by opiates, goes to sleep.

Morning has irrupted, like a waterfall, down from the pale summit of the Hour . . .

They have burnt to cinders, my love, in the hearth of our life, the logs of our dreams.

Let us renounce hope, since it betrays, love, since it tires, life, since it calms without invigorating, and even death, since it brings us more than we want and less than we hope.

Let us renounce, Veiled One, our own boredom, since it ages by itself and since it does not dare to be all the anguish it is.

Not to weep, not to hate, not to desire.

Cover, Silent One, with a sudarium of fine linen the rigid and dead profile of our Imperfection.

OUR LADY OF SILENCE

It occasionally happens to me – whenever I feel so diminished and depressed that even the strength to dream loses its leaves and dries up, and the only remaining dream for me is to think of my dreams – then it happens that I flip through them, as a book one continues to flip through although it does not contain anything more than inevitable words. It is at that moment that I wonder who you can be, figure passing through all my sluggish visions of differing landscapes, bygone intentions, in the luxurious ceremonial of silence. In all my dreams, you appear to me as a dream, or you accompany me as a fake reality. I visit with you regions which are perhaps part of your dreams, countries which are perhaps part of your body, formed out of absence and inhumanity, your essential body thinned down into the tranquil plain and coldly profiled mountains in the garden of some secret palace. Perhaps, I have no other dream but you and it is perhaps in your eyes, my face pressed against yours, that I shall read those impossible landscapes, those false boredoms, those feelings which live in the shadow of my lassitudes and the grottoes of my disquiets. Who knows if the landscapes of my dreams are not my way of dreaming of you? I know not who you are, but do I truly know who I am? Do I know what it is to dream, to know what my dream means when it summons you? Do I know if you are not a part of me, perhaps the most important and real part? And do I actually know if it is not me who is the dream and you the reality and I one of your dreams and not you a dream which I dreamed?

What sort of life do you have? What way of seeing is the way I see you? Your profile? It is never the same, but it never changes. And I say this because I know it, without knowing, however, that I know it. Your body? It is identical naked and clothed, and it maintains the same position whether seated, prone, or upright. What does that signify which signifies nothing?

⁂

My life is so sad and I do not imagine crying over it; my time is so false and I do not dream of the gesture of discarding it.

How not to dream of you? How not to dream of you?

Our Lady of the Passing Hours, Madonna of stagnant waters and dead algae. Tutelary Goddess of open deserts and landscapes black with sterile rocks . . . free me from my youth.

Consolatrix of those who have no consolation. Tears of those who never cry. Hour which never dreams – free me from happiness and felicity.

Opium of all silences. Lyre never to be plucked, stained-glass window of remoteness and abandon, make me hated by men and incarnated by women.

Symbol of Extreme-Unction, Gesture-less Affectation, Dove dead in the shadow, Oil of hours passed in sleep, free me from religion as it is sweet, and from incredulity as it is strong . . .

Iris saddening the afternoon, Coffer of faded flowers, Silence between prayer and prayer, fill me with the nausea of living, with the hatred of being sane, with the disdain of being young.

Make me useless and sterile, Asylum of all vague dreams; make me pure for no reason to be so, and false for no love of being it, Rushing Water of Living Sadnesses; that my mouth be a landscape of ice, my eyes two dead lakes, my gestures a slow waving of ancient trees, Litany of disquiets, Raped-Mass of Exhaustions, a Corolla, a Liquid, Ascension . . .

What pain to pray to you as a woman and not to love you as a man, and to be unable to raise the eyes of my dreams like Dawn – contrary to the irreal sex of the angels who will never enter heaven!

❧

Your sex is that of dream forms, the non-sex of imprecise forms.

Sometimes a mere profile, sometimes a mere pose, other times a slow difficult gesture – you are moments and poses which spiritualize themselves by becoming mine.

In my dreams of you, there is no latent sexual fascination, below your cloak of a madonna, only interior silences. Your breasts are not those one might think of kissing. Your body is wholly flesh-soul, but is not soul, it is body. The substance of your body is not spiritual but is spirituality. (You are woman prior to the Fall.) . . .

My horror of real women with a sex constitutes the path I followed to find you. Those earthly women, who must support the wriggling motion of a man – how can one love them without love being immediately mangled by the anticipated vision of pleasure in the service of sex? How to respect the Wife without being obliged to see her in another coital position? How not be revolted by having a Mother, by the idea of having been vulvar at one's origin, and having been birthed in such a revolting fashion? What disgust have we not been subjected to by the idea of the carnal origin of our soul – of that corporal maelstrom out of which our flesh is born; and, however beautiful it may be, our soul is disfigured by its origin, and revolts us by its birth.

False idealists of real life write poems to the Wife, they genuflect before the idea of the Mother. Their idealism is a cloak which conceals, not a dream capable of creation.

You alone are so pure, Our Lady of Dreams, that I can conceive of you as a mistress without conceiving stains, because you are unreal. You. I can think of a mother and adore you, since you have never allowed yourself to be soiled either by the nightmare of fecundation or by the horror of childbirth.

How not to adore you as you are the only adorable one? How not to love you, if you alone are worthy of love?

Who knows if, by dreaming of you, I do not create you, real in another reality; if you must not, down there, be mine, in a different pure world where we could love without tactile bodies, with other gestures to embrace each other, and with other essential positions to possess each other? Who even knows if you do not exist already and if, far from creating you, I have not simply seen you, with another pure interior vision, in a different perfect world? Who knows if dreaming of you was not simply meeting you, if to love you was not the fact of thinking-of-you, if my disdain for the flesh and my disgust for love were not an obscure desire with which, without knowing you, I anxiously awaited you, and a vague aspiration with which, without knowing anything about you, I wanted you?

Who even knows if I have not already loved you, in an imprecise somewhere else, the nostalgia for which perhaps is the root of my boredom? You are perhaps a nostalgia of mine, body of absence, presence of distance, female for other reasons, perhaps, than those who cause one to be so.

I can think of you virgin and mother as well because you are not for this world. The baby you hold in your arms was never so young for you to have worried about carrying him in your womb. You have never been other than what you are and, consequently, how could you not be a virgin? I can love and adore as well, since my love does not possess you and my adoration does not distance you from me.

Be Eternal-Day and let my sunsets be the rays of your sun, possessed in you.

Be Invisible-Dusk and let my desires, my disquiets be the colours of your indecision, the shadows of your incertitude.

Be Total-Night, become Unique Night and let me lose and abolish myself entirely in you, and let my dreams shine forth, stars, on your body of remoteness and negation.

Let me be the folds of your mantle, the jewels of your diadem, the other gold of the rings on your fingers.

Ash of your hearth, what matter if I am dust? Window of your room, what matter if I am space? Hour of your clepsydra, what matter if I drip through since, belonging to you, I shall remain if I die, since, belonging to you, I shall not die, if I lose you, if by losing you I find you?

Creator of absurdities, spinner of phrases without connections, let your silence cradle me and lull me to sleep. Let your pure-being caress me, soothe me and comfort me, Lady of the Beyond, Empress of Absence: Virgin-Mother of all silences, Refuge of frigid souls, Guardian-Angel of the abandoned, human landscape, totally unreal with sadness, eternal Perfection.

You are no woman. Nothing inside of me evokes anything I feel as feminine. It is when I speak of you that the words call you female and the expressions delineate you as woman. Because I need to speak of you with tenderness and loving dreams, words find a voice only by treating you as feminine.

But you, in your vague essence, are nothing. You have no reality except a reality which is yours alone. In fact, I do not see you, nor do I feel you. You are like a feeling which is its own object and entirely belongs to the most intimate part of itself. You are always the landscape which I was on the point of being able to see, the hem of the jacket which I nearly missed seeing, lost in an Eternal Now, just beyond the bend in the road. Your profile is to be nothing, and the contours of your unreal body undoes, each pearl separately, the necklace of the idea of a contour. You have already passed, and already have been, and I have already loved you – to feel you present is to feel that.

You occupy the gap in my thoughts and the interstices of my feelings.

Moon of memories lost over a black landscape, shining with vacuum and my imperfection of understanding itself. My being feels your return movement, as a belt would feel you yourself. I lean over your white face, in the depths of the nocturnal waters of my disquiet, knowing full well you are the moon in my heaven in order to provide it, or else a bizarre submarine moon in order, I know not how, to simulate it.

How I long to create the New Look with which I could see you, the New Thoughts and Feelings thanks to which I could think and feel you!

I want to touch your mantle, and my phrases exhaust themselves with the sketchy gestures of their outstretched hands, and a stiff painful fatigue freezes my words. It is why birds' flight, which seems to approach and never arrives, curves around all that I would like to say about you, but the material of my sentences does not know how to imitate the sound of your footsteps, or the slow passage of your gaze, or still further the vacant sad colour of the curve of gestures you have never made.

And if it turns out that I speak to a distant being, and if, today cloud of the possible, tomorrow you truly rain on the earth, never ever forget your divinity which originated in my dreams.

Let your vocation be that of being superfluous, your life your act of looking at it, also your act of being looked at, never identical. Never be anything else.

Today you are nothing but the invented profile of this book, a time become flesh and different from other times. If I was certain of your existence, I would construct a religion on the dream of loving you.

You are what is lacking in all things. You are what is lacking in everything for us to be able to lose it always. Lost key of the Temple doors, hidden way into the Palace, Distant Island eternally hidden in the mist.

THE RIVER OF POSSESSION

That we are all different is an axiom of our nature. We resemble each other distantly and in the proportion, by consequence, that we are not ourselves. Life, then, is made for the undefined: those who can only agree that they will never be defined, and who are neither one nor the other, strictly nobodies.

Each of us is two, and when two people meet, become close, and are linked, it is extremely rare that the four of them can be in agreement. The dreaming man at the bottom of every man of action, and who already is in conflict with himself, how can he struggle against the man who acts and the man who dreams, both of which are present in the Other.

We are forces because we are lives. Each one of us sails towards himself and uses the others as ports of call. If we have sufficient respect for ourselves to find ourselves interesting, every approximation is a conflict. The Other is always an obstacle for the one who seeks. Only the non-seeker is happy; for only the non-seeker can find, since he already has, and to have, whatever else it may be, is to be happy (exactly as non-thinking constitutes the major part of being rich).

I look at you inside me, my imaginary fiancée, and already, long before you come into existence, misunderstanding has occurred. My habit of dreaming with clarity provides me with an accurate notion of reality. He who dreams too much, reads to give some reality to his dream. He who gives his dream some reality, is obliged to give to his dream the equilibrium of reality. He who gives to his dream the equilibrium of reality suffers from the reality of his dream as much as from the reality of life (and from the irreality of dream as much as from irreal life).

I await you, in my delirium, in one room with twin doors; I dream you come near me and, in my dream, you enter through the door on the right; if, when you come, you enter through the door on the left, that creates a distinction between you and my dream. All human tragedy is contained in that small example, of how those at whose sides we dream are never those we dream about.

Love loses its identity in difference, which is already impossible logically, and even more so in real life. Love wants to possess, to make his what should remain outside him so that he may know what he cannot either make his, or be that, which he loves. To love is to deliver oneself up. The greater the gift, the greater the love. But the greatest gift is to offer oneself up to the other's consciousness. The greatest love is then death, or oblivion, or renunciation ...

On the ancient terrace of the palace, overhanging the sea, we meditate on the difference between us. I was the prince and you the princess, on the terrace over the sea. Our love was born out of our meeting, as beauty is created from the meeting between the moon and the waves.

Love wants to possess, without knowing what it means. If I am not me, how could I be yours, or you mine? If I do not possess my own being, how could I possess another's? If I myself am different from him whom I resemble, how could I resemble him from whom I differ?

Love is a mysticism which longs to be practised, an impossibility only dreamt about in order to be realized.

I am metaphysical. But the whole of life is obscure metaphysics, like a confused noise of the gods and the lack of the knowledge that one path is the only one.

The worst trick my decadent spirit played on itself is my love for health and clarity. I have always found that a beautiful body and the felicitous rhythm of a young person's gait is more effective in the world than all the dreams I have in me. It is with the contented mood of a man aged by spirit that I follow sometimes – without jealousy or desire – casual couples meeting at the end of the day and who walk, arm in arm, towards the conscious unconsciousness of youth. I enjoy them like I enjoy a truth, without asking myself if it applies to me or not. If I compare myself to them, I go on enjoying them, but this time like a truth which wounds me, joining to the pain of the wound the consciousness of having understood the gods.

I am the opposite to Platonic Christians for whom every being and each event are the shadow of a reality of which they themselves are but a shadow. Instead of being a point of arrival, each thing for me is a point of departure. For occultists everything is achieved in everything; for me, everything begins in everything.

I proceed, like them, by analogy and proposition, but the cramped garden which suggests to them the order and beauty of the soul, only reminds me of a vaster garden, where there can be, far from mankind, a happy life which cannot exist. Each thing suggests to me not the reality of which it is the shade, but the reality towards which it is the path.

The garden of Estrêla in the late afternoon, evokes for me an ancient park, planned centuries prior to the insatisfaction of the soul.

ANTE-EROS – THE VISUAL LOVER*

I have a superficial and decorative notion of profound love and its correct usage. I am subject to visual passions. I preserve intact a heart given over to more unreal destinies.

I do not remember ever having loved, in someone, anything else but 'the painting', or the pure exterior – where the soul

---

* Anti-Eros is also a possible reading.

does not enter into play, except to animate that interior – and so to differentiate it from paintings made by painters.

That is how I love: I freeze an image I find beautiful or seductive or, for one reason and another, lovable, of a woman or a man – there where there is no desire, there is no sexual preference – and then that image obsesses me, captivates me, invades me utterly. Then, I want nothing else but to see it, and would detest nothing more than the possibility of knowing and speaking to the real person who has their apparent manifestation in that image.

I love with my regard and not with my imagination. Since I imagine nothing about the image which seduces me, I do not imagine myself linked to it in any other way. It does not interest me to know who it is, what it does, what the creature thinks, who is presenting me with its exterior aspect.

The immense series of people and things who form the universe is for me an endless picture gallery, whose interior does not interest me. It does not interest me because the soul is monotonous, always identical in each person; only individual manifestations differ, and the best part is that which spills over into dreams, into the allure and gestures, and so enters into the painting which captivates me . . .

So I live, with pure vision, the exterior animated by things and beings, indifferent, like a god from another world, to their spirit-content. I do not plumb the being itself, except obliquely, and, when I really desire profundity, it is in me and my conception of things that I look for it . . .

THE DEATH OF THE PRINCE

Would not all be an entirely different truth, without gods, men, reasons? Would not all be something which we could not even conceive of conceiving: a mystery entirely from another world? Why should we not all be – men, gods and the universe – dreams which someone else dreams, thoughts which someone else thinks, placed eternally on the exterior of that which exists? And that someone else who dreams or thinks, why should he not be someone who neither dreams nor thinks, he himself captive of the abyss and of the fiction? Why should everything not be something else, or nothing at all, and that, which is not the unique thing which exists? Where am I then to see that all this might be possible? Over which bridge do I cross to be able to see down there, from such a great height, the lights of all the cities in this world and in the other world, and the clouds of scattered truths turned to dusk which float above them, and all of them searching, as if they searched for something which could be embraced?

I am scared, deprived of sleep, and I see without knowing what I see. All around, then the vast plains, and rivers in the distance, and mountains ... But, at the same time, nothing of that exists, and I am with the commencement of the gods, terrified by the idea of leaving or of staying, and of where I am and of what I am, and this room too, where I hear you watching me, is something which I know and which I think I see; and all these things are mingled and separate, and not one of them is that other thing which I am striving to see.

Why have I been given a kingdom to hold if I may never possess anything finer than this house, during which time I am between that which I have never been and that which I shall never be?

❦

In this world there will always be strife, without any victory or decision, between the one who loves what is not, because it exists, and the one who loves what is, because it does not exist. Always, always there will be the abyss between the one who denies mortality because he is mortal and the one who loves mortality since he hopes never to die. I see which one I was in childhood, in that moment when the boat I had been given sank in the garden pond, and there is no philosophy which can replace that instant, nor reasons which can explain to me why it happened. I remember, and I live; what better life do you have to give me?

'Not one, not one, since I too remember.'

'I too remember well! It was in the old house at tea-time; after the mending and sewing, came the tea and toast and that wonderful sleep I was about to have. Give it me over again, just as it was, with the clock tick-tocking in the background, and keep for yourself all the gods. What is for me an Olympus which does not have for me the aroma of that bygone toast? What do I have in common with gods who do not love my old clock?'

Perhaps everything is but symbol and shadow, but I do not like symbols and I do not like shadows. Give me back the past and keep the truth. Give me one more time my childhood, and carry off God.

'Your symbols! If I weep at night, like a scared child, none of your symbols will come and caress my shoulder and rock me to sleep. If I lose my way, you have no better Virgin Mary to come and take my hand. Your transcendentalisms strike me cold. I want a hearth in the Beyond. Do you believe anybody is thirsty in his soul for metaphysics, and mysteries and lofty truths?'

'Thirsty for what is one's soul?'

'For anything resembling our childhood. For dead toys, old departed aunts. Those things are reality, even though dead. What has the Ineffable to do with me?'

'One thing . . . Did you have old aunts, and an old country house and teas and a clock?'

'I did not. I should like to have had them. And have you lived on the beach?'

'Never. Didn't you know?'

'I knew it, but I believed you. Why not believe in what is proposed.'

'Don't you know that this is a dialogue in the Palace Gardens, a lunar interlude, a spectacle during which we amuse ourselves, while for others the hours pass?'

'Of course, but I was thinking that . . .'

'Why not? I wasn't. Reason is the worst type of dream since it carries me into the dream of the regularity of life which does not exist, that is to say, it is doubly nothing.'

'But what does that mean?'

Putting my hand on the other's shoulder and holding him in my arms, 'Aïe, my son, what does anything mean?'

✺

Where then is God even if he does not exist? I long to pray and weep, to repent for the crimes I have not committed, to enjoy being forgiven with a not entirely maternal caress.

A bosom to cry on, but an enormous bosom, with no shape, as capacious as a summer night, and yet very close, warm, feminine, next to some fire or other ... To be able to weep there for unthinkable things, faults whose nature I ignore, tenderness for inexistent things, and mighty tense doubts about some future or other ...

A new childhood, an old nanny once again, and a small bed in which I end up by falling asleep, between fairy stories which I can just hear, my concentration turning into warmth, and which are rife with perils penetrating a child's hair as blond as wheat ... And all that very massive, very eternal, defined for always, with the unique statue of God, down there in the sad, somnolent background of the ultimate reality of things ...

A bosom, or a cradle, or a warm arm around my neck ... A voice singing softly which seems to want to make me cry ... The crackling of the fire in the hearth ... Heat in the winter... The dull ebbing of my consciousness ... And later, noiselessly, a tranquil sleep in a huge space, like the moon rolling among the stars ...

When I set aside and arrange in a corner, with a care full of tenderness – longing to kiss them – my toys: the words, the images, the sentences – then I end up feeling so small and so inoffensive, so alone in such a big sad room, so profoundly sad!

After all, who am I when I do not play? A wretched orphan abandoned in the streets of feeling, shivering with cold on the windy corners of Reality, forced to sleep on the doorsteps of Sadness and to beg my bread from Imagination. As for my

95

father, I only know his name; I have been told he was called God, but that name evokes nothing in me. Sometimes at night, when I feel too alone, I call for him and I cry. I try to form an idea of him which I could love ... But ... I reflect that I do not know him, that perhaps he is not like that, perhaps he will never be the true father of my soul ...

When will all that end, these streets through which I drag my misery, and those steps where I curl up my cold, feeling the cold hands of the night slipping under my rags? If only one day God came for me and took me home, providing me with warmth and affection ... I think about it sometimes, and I cry with joy at the very idea of being able to think it. ... But the wind loiters in the streets and the leaves tumble down on the pavements ... I raise my eyes and see the stars, which make no sense ... In the middle of all that, there remains only me, a wretched abandoned child, whom no Love wanted as an adopted son, and no Friendship as a playmate.

I am so cold. I am so exhausted, so tired of this solitude. Wind, go and find my Mother. Take me by Night to the house I never knew ... Silence, give me back my nanny, my cradle and my lullaby with which I fell asleep.

I never sleep. I live and I dream or, to put it better, I dream in life as in sleep, which is also life. There is no break in my consciousness: I feel what surrounds me if I am not yet asleep, or if I sleep badly; and I begin to dream the second I really go to sleep. Hence, what I am is a perpetual unrolling of coherent or incoherent images, always feigning to come from the outside, the latter interposed between mankind and light if I am awake, the former between ghosts and that non-light if I am asleep. I do not really know how to distinguish one from the other, and I would be incapable of stating that I am not asleep when awake, or that I am awake even when asleep.

Life is a ball of wool tangled by someone else. It has a sense if one unravels it and pulls it straight, or winds it up properly.

But, such as it is, it constitutes a problem without a real knot, a tangle with no middle.

I feel that, which I shall write down afterwards, since I imagine already the sentences to say it when, during the night of semi-sleep, I perceive, conjointedly with the landscapes of imprecise dreams, the sound of the rain outside which renders them all the more imprecise. They are the riddles of the void, quivering gleams of the abyss, and through them filters, futile, the external complaint of the incessant rain, teeming minutiae of the landscape of the ear. Any hope? Nothing. Down from the invisible sky falls with a keening sound the rain driven before the wind. I continue to sleep.

It was, beyond all doubt, in the paths of the park where the tragedy which resulted in life was played out. They were two, they were beautiful, and they longed to be something else; love kept them waiting in a future boredom and nostalgia for that which had to happen, becoming already the daughter of a love they had not yet enjoyed. So, under the lunar clarity of the nearby woods, through which filtered the moon, they went, hand in hand, without desire and hope, into that particular desert of unkempt paths. They were totally children since they really did not exist. From path to path, from tree to tree, they wandered criss-crossing, silhouettes of paper cut-outs, in a décor belonging to nobody. And so they vanished by the lakes, each time nearer and more apart, and the faint sound of the rain is that of the jets of water towards which they went. I am the love they felt and that is why I leave them in the depths of the night when I do not sleep, and it is why I also know how to live with unhappiness.

❦

Some work out of boredom; and in the same way I write sometimes from having nothing to say. The reverie in which a man, who does not think, loses himself, I lose myself in by writing, since I know how to dream in prose. And there is a lot of sincere feeling and legitimate emotion which I extract from the very fact that I feel nothing.

97

There are times when the vacuity of feeling alive arrives at the consistency of something positive. In the case of great men of action, that is to say saints – for they act with total emotion and not just with a part of it – that intimate feeling that life is nothing leads to the infinite. They drape themselves with garlands of night and stars, anointed with silence and solitude. As for great men of inaction, among whose number I humbly count myself, the identical feeling leads to the infinitesimal; one pulls at sensations like elastic bands in order to see the pores of their ersatz and flaccid continuity.

And both of them, at such moments, love sleep, exactly like the vulgar man, who knows neither how to act or not to act, a mere reflection of the generic existence of the human species. Sleep is fusion with God, it is Nirvana, however you may define it; sleep is the slow analysis of sensations, whether it is employed as an atomic science of the soul or slept as a music of the will, a slow anagram of monotony.

I write, tarrying over words as in front of shop windows where I see nothing, and what remains behind for me are half-feelings, quasi-expressions, like the stuffs of which I only noticed the colours, glimpsed harmonies composed out of I know not what objects. I write cradling myself, like a mad mother cradling her dead child.

One find day, I found myself in that world – which one I ignore – and previously, since the moment when, quite clearly, I was born, up until now, I have lived without feeling anything. When I asked where I was, everybody misled me, contradicting each other. If I asked what I should do, everybody tried to mislead me by answering in a different way. If, not knowing where to go, I stopped on the way, everyone was astonished either that I chose the road which led nobody knew where, or that I did not retrace my steps – I, who, awakened at the crossroads, ignored from where I had come. I saw that I was on the stage and I did not know the text which the others immediately began to declaim, without knowing it either. I saw myself dressed as a page, not having been given my queen whom I was blamed for not having. I saw myself holding in my hands the opening message, and when I told them that the paper was blank, they laughed at me. And yet I do not know if they laughed because all papers were blank or because all messages have to be divined.

Finally, I sat down on the stone at the crossroads as if at the hearth I had lacked. And I began, all by myself, to make paper boats out of the lies I had been given. Nobody wanted to believe me, even that I was a liar, and I myself had no lake with which to prove the truth.

Otiose words, lost words, suave metaphors, which a vague anguish chained to shadows . . . Vestiges of better times, lived out in ignored paths . . . Extinguished lamp whose gold shines in the obscurity via the memory of the snuffed-out light . . . Words given, if not to the wind, to the bare earth, let slip by the non-grasping fingers, like dry leaves fallen on them from an infinitely invisible tree . . . Nostalgia for the ponds in distant gardens . . . Tenderness for what has never been . . .

To live! To live! And the continuing suspicion that even in Proserpine's bed I would not sleep well.

❦

I re-read, in one of those dreamless somnolences in which we discuss intelligently without intelligence, a few of the pages which make up, all together, my book of erratic impressions. And there comes wafting up from them, like the smell of something very familiar, an arid impression of monotony. I feel, even when saying I am always different, that I have endlessly repeated the same thing; that I am more like myself than I should like to admit; at the end of the road, I have neither the exaltation of winning nor the emotion of losing. I am a non-entry in my own balance-sheet, a lack of spontaneous equilibrium which both amazes and enfeebles me.

All that I have written is greyish. It might well be said that my entire life, including the cerebral one, has been nothing but a day of languid rain, composed out of non-events and penumbras, empty privileges and forgotten *raisons d'être*. I sadden myself wrapped in scraps of silk. I ignore myself in light and boredom.

My humble effort to say at least who I am, to register like a nervous machine the most insignificant impressions of my subjective and hyper-sensitive life – all that has suddenly been spilt like an overturned bucket of water, wetting the soil like all water. I have created myself out of false colours – and the result is a cardboard empire. This heart, into whose hands I had given the major events of living prose, seems to me today, described in these distant pages which I re-read with another soul, to be an ancient pump in a provincial garden, set up by instinct and used by necessity. I have been shipwrecked without even a storm in a sea in which I could stand.

And I wonder what is left to me of consciousness, in this confused series of gaps between non-existent things, what use was it to fill so many pages with sentences I believed in, holding them to be mine, with feelings I felt as thoughts, with the flags and standards of armies which turned out finally to be nothing but bits of paper stuck together by the saliva of a beggar's daughter sheltering by the threshing-floors.

I ask what is left of me, what purpose do these useless pages serve, consecrated to dross and trash, lost before they even existed in the crumpled papers of Destiny.

I ask myself and I go on. I write down my question. I envelop it with new sentences, the disentanglement of fresh emotions. And tomorrow I shall go back to writing down, in order, in my idiotic book, the daily impressions of my lack of conviction as coldly as possible. They follow on just as they are. Once the game of dominoes is over – whether lost or won – the pieces are turned over face down and the board is black.

❦

When one lives constantly in the abstract – whether the abstraction of thought, or that of the thought sensation – it soon happens that, contrary to one's very thoughts and desires, we turn into phantoms up to and including things of real life which, according to our nature, should be the most sensitive for us.

Whatever friendship I may feel towards someone, and

however genuine it may be, to learn that that friend is sick or dead only produces in me a vague, blurred, semi-erased impression, which shames me. By living in the imagination, one's capacity to imagine has been exhausted, and above all that of imagining reality. By force of living in the mind that which is not, nor cannot be, one ends up by being incapable even of dreaming of what might be.

Today, I was told that one of my old friends had just gone into a hospital to be operated on. I had not seen him for a long time, but I always think of him, utterly sincerely, with what I imagine to be real affection. The only impression I got from that piece of news, the only clear and positive impression, was that of the unavoidable tedious duty which awaited me: to visit him, or, the ironic alternative, if I had not the courage to go and see him, the remorse I would feel over it.

Nothing else . . . By living with shadows, I have turned myself into one – in what I think, feel, and am. The throbbing guilt of the normal human I have never been inundates the very substance of my being. But it is merely that, and only that, which I feel, I do not really feel pain for my friend upon whom they are about to operate. I do not really feel pain for all the people who are about to be operated on, all those who suffer and struggle in this world. I only feel the pain of being someone incapable of feeling it.

And, in a flash, I am irresistably in the process of thinking about something else, seized by some compulsion or other. And, as if I were delirious, there comes to mingle with what I have been unable to feel, unable to be – a rustling of trees, a murmur of water running down towards the lakes, a non-existent park . . . I struggle to feel, but I do not know how one feels. I have turned into a phantom of myself, a phantom to which I have ceded my being. In opposition to Peter Schlemihl in the German tale, I have not sold my shadow to the devil, but my real substance. I suffer from not suffering, not knowing how to suffer. Do I live or pretend to live? Am I asleep or entirely awake? A casual breeze, which brings coolness in the heat of the day, causes me to forget everything. My eyelids agreeably droop . . . I feel that that same sun gilds meadows where I am not, and do not want to be ... From the noises of the city emerges a great silence ... How sweet it is ... But how much sweeter, perhaps, if I could feel ...

❀

I sometimes think with a bisected satisfaction of the future possibility of a geography of the consciousness we have of ourselves. In my way of seeing, the future historian of our very sensations might perhaps reduce to an exact science his own attitude towards the consciousness he will have of his own spirit. For the moment, we are merely on the threshhold of this difficult art – and art it is: a chemistry of feelings, still at the level of alchemy. Tomorrow's expert will have a particular care for his own interior life. From out of himself, he will create the instrument precise enough to reduce it to analysis. I see no particular difficulty in the fabrication of such a precision instrument, destined for auto-analysis, uniquely utilizing the steel and bronze of thought. I am talking not of steel and bronze which are truly bronze and steel, but those of the mind. And it should be fabricated in such a way. Perhaps one should create for oneself the concept of a precision instrument by representing it for oneself materially, so as to be able to proceed with a rigorous analysis. And naturally the spirit should be reduced to a sort of real substance provided with a sort of space where it could exist. All that depends on the hyper-acuteness we apply to our interior feelings, which, pushed to their extreme capacity, would reveal without doubt, or would create in us a real space identical to that which exists there where there are real things, and which, in addition, is irreal as any thing.

I wonder if even that interior space will not merely be a new dimension of the other. Future scientific research will perhaps succeed in discovering that all realities are dimensions of the same space, which therefore would be neither material nor spiritual. Perhaps we live in one body, in one dimension; in another – in one soul. and there exist perhaps other dimensions where we also live other aspects just as real of ourselves. There

102

are times when I take pleasure in allowing myself the gratuitous speculation as to the farthest limit where those researches may end.

Perhaps we shall discover that what we call God and what is in all evidence on a different plane than logic, or spatial and temporal reality, is, in fact, a human way of existing, a feeling of ourselves in another dimension of being. It does not seem impossible to me. Dreams too might well be, perhaps, either yet another dimension in which we exist, or else the meeting point of two dimensions: just as a body exists in its length, breadth and width, perhaps our dreams in exactly the same way live in the ideal, the ego and in space. In space because of their visible representation; in the ideal, because they appear to us in a different way than matter; finally, in the ego because of that intimate dimension which derives from the fact that they are ours. The Ego itself, which belongs to each of us, is perhaps a divine dimension. All this is complex and doubtless will be defined at the right time. Present-day dreamers may be the great forerunners of the ultimate science of the future. I should like it to be understood that I do not believe in any ultimate science of a future. But that has nothing to do with it.

I sometimes create this sort of metaphysics, with the scrupulous and deferential attention of a man who really works and is engaged in scientific work. As I have already pointed out it could be really true, the essential is not to become too proud of it, for pride is prejudicial to impartial exactitude and scientific precision.

EDUCATION SENTIMENTALE

Whenever life is extracted from dreams and the hot-house cultivation of our feelings turns into a religion and a political attitude, then the first step, that which sears our soul with the brand of making the first step, is to experience the most minimal things in the most extraordinary and extreme fashion.

That is the first step and nothing more than the first step. To know how to put in a teacup the essence of extreme voluptuousness which a normal person can only find in the supreme joy of a suddenly realized ambition, or in nostalgic regrets abruptly erased, or still further in the final carnal acts of love; to be capable of finding in the contemplation of the setting sun or in a decorative detail that exacerbated feeling which is generally provided, not by what one sees or hears, but only by what one breathes in or tastes – that proximity of the felt object which only carnal feelings (touch, taste, smell) manage to sculpt – is our consciousness; to be able to render the interior vision, the dream hearing – all the imagined feelings including those of the imagination – receptive and tangible like senses orientated towards the exterior: I choose those (and the reader can imagine others which are similar) from among the ones which an amateur, who cultivates the art of feeling himself, arrives at, after practice, pushing to their paroxysm – so that they communicate a concrete idea and an idea sufficiently close to what I wish to express.

However, to arrive at this intensity of feeling pre-supposes for the amateur the corresponding weight and physical onus he feels by correlation with that identical conscious exacerbation which is painfully imposed on him from the exterior, and at times from the interior, in exchange for each given instant of concentration. It is when he thus realizes that excessive feeling, if this sometimes signifies to enjoy excess, can also signify limitless suffering; and it is because he is brought to such a realization, that the dreamer is led to take the second step in his ascension towards his self.

I leave to one side the step which he might or might not make and which, depending on whether he could or not, might determine such and such an attitude or even the speed of his progress, corresponding to the levels he might attain – I mean to say that according to whether he was able or not to isolate himself completely from real life (whether he will be rich or not – it comes to that). I imagine in fact that when he has read between the lines of my thesis and has understood that his lesser or greater capacity for isolation is in direct correlation to his possibilities of concentrating on the self with a greater or lesser intensity, then the dreamer should focus on his major task: to rouse morbidly the functions of his impressions of things and dreams. If one is obliged to live an active life among mankind and to see it the whole time – and one can in fact reduce to a minimum the forced intimacy with people (for it is intimacy and not mere contact with people that is unhealthy) – then one should freeze the entire surface of contact with the other so that any cordial or brotherly gesture made towards us slides off our backs without any penetration or any sign of its presence. That seems already a great deal, but it is only a small thing. It is easy to keep people at a distance, it is enough to avoid approaching them. In brief, I pass over that and return to the argument I was in the process of expanding

In order to forge a finesse and immediate complexity out of our simplest, most inevitable emotions implies, as I said above, a moderate increment in the pleasure derived from feeling, but equally a disagreeable augmentation of the suffering which it also provokes. For that reason, the dreamer's second step should consist in avoiding suffering. He should not avoid it like a Stoic or an Epicurean of the first step – by un-nesting himself as thus he hardens himself against pleasure as well as pain. On the contrary, he should extract pleasure from pain and then practise feeling false pain, in other words, whenever he feels pain, feeling some pleasure or other. There are several means to this end. One of them consists in analysing suffering in an excessive way, having previously prepared his mind, and, in the presence of pleasure, not to analyse but to feel; it is the more facile alternative – for superior men naturally – than it appears by simply stating it. To analyse suffering and to enure oneself by submitting suffering to analysis – each time it appears until one does so instinctively, without thinking – adds to any pain the pleasure of analysis. By exaggerating the capacity and instinct of analysis, suffering is reduced to an indeterminate substance, submitted to analysis.

Another method, more difficult and more subtle, consists of accustoming oneself to incarnate pain in an ideal form. To create another Ego which takes on the load of suffering, which suffers what we suffer. Then to create an internal sadism – entirely masochistic – capable of enjoying its own suffering as if it were that of another. This method, which, at first sight, seems impossible to apply, is not easy to follow, but it poses no major difficulty as soon as one has graduated as a master in the art of lying to oneself. It is, on the contrary, eminently possible. And then, once you have got so far, with whatever taste of blood and sickness, with whatever bizarre bitterness of distant decadent pleasure, pain and suffering cover themselves up, pain becomes closer to that anxious rending paroxism of certain spasms. To suffer – that long slow suffering – takes on that yellow hue which is the colour, at its most intimate, of the vague happiness of a profoundly lived convalescence. And a refined lassitude, redolent with disquiet and morbidity, approaches closer to that complex feeling of anxiety caused by pleasures linked to the idea of their own disappearance, and to the morbid taste which voluptuousness extracts from the pre-lassitude which is born of thinking about the lassitude which it will provoke.

There is a third method of translating pains into pleasures and of making a feather-mattress out of our doubts and anguishes. It consists in giving to our torments and sufferings, thanks to an exacerbated application of our concentration, such an intensity that this very excess provides us with the pleasure of all excesses, and so, by its very violence, it is capable of suggesting to a person who, through education and habit of the mind, devotes and consecrates himself to pleasure – pleasures which cause suffering since the pleasure is extreme – an exaltation in the taste of blood because we have been wounded. And whenever, since it happens to me as well – I who refine false refinements, I, the architect, who constructs himself out of feelings, purified by the exercise of intelligence, by the abdication of life, of analysis and of pain itself – whenever these three methods are used simultaneously, whenever a pain, instantaneously experienced so allowing no breathing-space to elaborate an intimate strategy, is analysed and wrung dry, situated in an Ego so exterior it is almost

tyranny, and lodged in my recesses to its paroxysm of pain –
then I feel myself to be a true hero and victor. Then my life
stands erect and art grovels at my feet.

All this merely constitutes the second stage which the
dreamer must reach in order to attain his dream.

The third stage, the one which leads to the luxurious
threshhold of the Temple, that one, who else apart from me
has known how to arrive there? It is the expensive one as it
exacts an interior effort infinitely more difficult than an effort
in life, but which offers compensations to the soul which life
has never been able to offer. That third step, once all the
foregoing has been achieved, all has been simultaneously
executed in its entirety – yes, once my triad of subtle methods
has been employed, fully used – consists in directly filtering
feelings through pure intelligence, sieving it through superior
analysis in order to sculpt it into a literary form and to give it
shape and relief. Then indeed I have fixed it once and for all.
Then I have made the real unreal, provided the inaccessible
with an eternal pedestal. Then, inside me, I have been crowned
Emperor.

For do not believe that I write to be published, nor for
writing's sake, nor even to create art. I write because it is the
ultimate, the supreme confinement, the temperamentally
illogical refinement, of my cultivation of the states of my soul.
If I can take any of my feelings, and unravel it until I am able,
with it, to weave into interior reality what I can name: *The
Forest of Dreaming Solitude* or *The Unaccomplished Voyage*, I
truly believe that it is not a matter of producing clear,
sparkling prose, nor even taking pleasure in prose – even
though I want to do that as well, adding this novel and added
refinement, like a splendid final curtain on my dream décors –
but actually in order that the prose endows what is interior
with a total exteriority, that so it realizes the unrealizable,
conjugates opposites and, returning to the exterior dream,
confers on it the maximum capacity for pure dreaming – I, the
stagnator of life, the etcher of inexactitudes, the sorrowing
page of my soul Queen, reading at dusk, not the poems in the
book of my life, opened up on my knees, but the poems I

tirelessly construct and pretend to read, and she pretends to listen to, while the Evening somewhere outside edulcorates, set against the metaphor, erected in my recesses as Absolute Reality, the thin ultimate light of a mysteriously spiritual day.

❧

And so I am, futile and sensitive, capable of violent and absorbing impulses, good and bad, noble and vile, but never of a feeling which lasts, never of an emotion which continues, and penetrates the substance of my soul. Everything in me can be summed up as an urge to be immediately something else; an impatience of the soul with itself, like an importunate child; a disquiet which is always on the increase and always identical. Everything interests me and nothing retains my attention. I apply myself to everything by continually dreaming; I pin down the slightest details of the facial expressions of the person I am talking to. I register the intonations down to the last millimetre of what he expresses; but, even listening, I do not hear him, since I am in the process of thinking about something else, and what I remember least about our conversation is precisely what was said – by one or the other. So, very often, I repeat to people what I have already told them, I ask over again a question to which they have already replied; but I can describe, in four photographic words, the facile expression which they employed to say what I no longer remember, or this tendency to listen only with the eyes to the story which I do not remember having told them. I am two – and both of them keep their distance, Siamese twins linked by nothing.

❧

… Hyper-acuity, perhaps of feelings themselves, or perhaps of their expression, or perhaps, more accurately, of the intelligence which is situated between both of them and which creates, out of the purpose of expressing them, a fictive

108

emotion which only exists to be expressed: perhaps it is not in me simply the apparatus of the revelation of what I am not.

The sensation of convalescence, particularly of the preceding illness concentrated on the nervous system, has a melancholy happy aspect. Emotions and thoughts know a sort of autumn or, perhaps better, one of those onsets of spring which, apart from falling leaves, are similar, both in atmosphere and in the skies, to autumn.

Fatigue can be pleasurable and that pleasure hurts us somewhat. We have the sensation of being on the fringe of existence, even though we are part of it, as if craning over the balcony of the house of life. We are contemplative without thinking, we feel without any identifiable emotion. The will relaxes since it is unnecessary.

It is the moment when certain memories, certain hopes, certain vague desires sluggishly climb the ramp of consciousness, as if they were just perceptible travellers seen from the top of a mountain. We recall futilities, hopes without importance in their non-realization, desires bereft of violence either in their nature or in their expression, and which were never even capable of wanting to exist.

When the day adjusts itself to those feelings, like today which, even in midsummer, is half-veiled by blues, and a faint breeze which, instead of being hot, is almost cold, then this state of mind is accentuated by the fact that we think, feel and live these impressions. It is not that the memories are any clearer, or the hopes and desires we once had. But they are more strongly felt, and the ill-defined mass weighs down lightly, in an absurd way, on our heart.

In this moment, there is a distant something in me. I am really on the balcony of life, but not exactly on the one of this life. I am above it, and look down on it from where I am. It stretches out before me, descending in slopes and terraces, like another landscape, down to the smoke floating over the white houses of the villages in the valley. If I shut my eyes, I continue to see since I do not see. If I re-open them, I see nothing more, since I did not see. I am entirely a vague

nostalgia for the present, anonymous, prolix and misunderstood.

❀

For me, intensity of feeling has always been more feeble than
intensity of its consciousness. I have always suffered more
from my consciousness of pain than from the very suffering of
which I was conscious.

My emotional life has chosen, from the outset, to install
itself in the salons of thought, and the emotional knowledge of
life has lived always more expansively there.

And as thought, when it shelters emotion, becomes more
demanding with it, the regime of consciousness, in which I
decided to live what I felt, has made my way of feeling more
day-to-day, more titillating, more epidermal.

❀

I am one of those souls whom women say they love, and whom
they never recognize when they meet them; one of those
whom, if they recognized them, even then would never
recognize them as such. I painfully support the finesse of my
feelings with a disdainful concentration. I possess all those
qualities for which romantic poets are admired, up to and
including the absence of those same qualities which enable
one to be a true romantic poet. I find myself (partially)
described in various novels as the protagonist of various plots;
but the essential part of my life, identical to that of my soul, is
destined never to be a protagonist.

I have no clear idea of myself; not even the one which would
consist of a lack of an idea of myself. I am a nomad of
consciousness of myself. Since the first watch, the flocks of
my intimate richness have strayed away.

The unique tragedy is to be incapable of conceiving oneself
as tragic. I have always clearly seen my coexistence with the
world. I have never clearly felt my lack of coexistence with it;
for that reason, I have never been normal.

To act is to relax.

All problems are insoluble. By definition, the existence of a problem pre-supposes that there is no solution. To look for facts signifies that no facts exist. To think is not to know how to exist.

❦

I re-read, with lucidity and without haste, bit by bit, all I have written. And I discover that all is vanity and it would have been better never to have written at all. Realized things, whether phrases or sentences, constitute, because they have been realized, the worst sides of real things which are the knowledge that they perish. However, it is not that I feel which affects me during these long hours I re-read myself. What really afflicts me is that the writing is not worthwhile and that the time lost in doing it I have only gained through the illusion, now destroyed, that it was worthwhile.

Whatever we search for, we do because of an ambition, but that ambition is either never achieved, and we are paupers, or we create a belief in one achievement, and we are simply rich and mad.

What afflicts me is that the best is bad, and the rest, if it exists, that other part I dream of, could have been far better written. All that we do, in art or in life, is the imperfect copy of what we imagined we were doing. It gives the lie not only to an external perfection but also to an interior perfection; it lacks not only what is missing from the canon of what ought to be, but also from the canon of what we believed it might be. We are husks, not only on the inside but on the outside, pariahs of promised anticipation.

With what vigour of the solitary soul I wrote page after page, living syllable by syllable the false magic, not of what I wrote, but of that I imagined I had written! Under what charm of ironic sorcery did I believe myself to be a poet of my own prose, in the winged moments in which it was born in me, fleeter than the movements of my pen, with a falacious revenge on life's faults. And, finally, today, re-reading myself, I see my puppets disembowelled, their straw seeping out of the holes, emptying themselves without ever having been ...

%

Given the penchant I have for boredom, it is odd that I have never taken the trouble, until today, to ask myself what it consists of. Truly, today, I am in that intermediary mood where one has no desire either for life, or for anything else. And I employ this sudden idea – never to have reflected on what was boredom – to dream, at the whim of semi-impressionistic thoughts, about the analysis of what it could mean, despite the fact it must always be somewhat factitious.

I truly do not know if boredom is simply the wakened equivalent of a vagabond's somnolence, or if, in fact, it is something more noble than lethargy. I am frequently bored, yet its appearance – in as much as I realize and pay attention to it – does not conform to any precise rules. I can spend an inert Sunday without the slightest boredom; I can feel it suddenly like a cloud outside, just at the very time I am working as hard as I can. I do not succeed in establishing a link between boredom and my good or bad health; I do not succeed in recognizing there the effect of causes lodged in the most overt part of my being.

To say that it is a mask of metaphysical angst, that it is a sort of unknown disillusion, that it is the deaf poetry of the soul, disabused, tangental, at the window of life – to say things like that, or similar ones, may colour boredom as a child colours a drawing whose contours they overrun and efface, but it brings me nothing except the echo of empty words clanging away in the cellars of thought.

Boredom ... To think without anything in us thinking, but with the exhaustion from thought; to feel without anything in us feeling, but with its anxiety; not to desire, without anything in us refusing to desire, but with the nausea of non-desire – all that is part and parcel of boredom without being it, and is nothing more than paraphrase or metaphor. It is, as far as our feelings are concerned, as if, over the moat encircling the castle of our soul, the drawbridge was suddenly raised and there remained nothing between the castle and the adjoining land but the possibility of looking at both of them without being able to cross from one to the other. There is in us an alienation from ourselves, but an alienation in which what separates us is equally stagnant as ourselves, a ditch of dirty water girding our intimate dis-agreement.

Boredom ... To suffer without pain, to love without desire, to think bereft of reason ... It is like being possessed by a negative devil, a useless enwitchment. It is said that sorcerers, or minor witches, depict us in images which they then maltreat, so obtaining, owing to some sort of astral transfer, that the injuries are deviated on to us. It seems to me that boredom, by a sensitive transposition of that image, is like the evil reflection of the spells of some demon from Hades which acts, not on my image, but on its shadow. It is on to the most intimate shadow of myself, on the outside of the inside of my soul, that scraps of paper are being stuck, or pins are being pricked.

Boredom ... I work very hard. I fulfil what the moralists of action call my social duty. I fulfil this duty, or this destiny, without any major effort, without any flagrant non-intelligence. But, sometimes in the middle of my work, sometimes plumb in the centre of my repose which, according to those same moralists, I truly have merited and which should be pleasant, my soul overflows with the bile of inertia, and I am exhausted, not by the work or the rest, but by my self.

Why by my self, unless I was thinking of me? For what other reason, unless I was thinking about that? By the secret of the universe which finds itself devalued in my calculations or in my nonchalance? With the universal agony of living which abruptly assumes a distinct character in my sorcerer's soul? It is a sensation of emptiness, a hunger with no appetite, as noble as the simple sensations of the brain, and of the stomach, which are caused by heavy smoking or bad digestion.

Boredom ... It is perhaps, finally, the dissatisfaction of the intimate soul which we have not endowed with belief, the affliction of the unhappy child we intimately are, since we have not bought him his divine toy. It is perhaps the anguish of a being who needs no guidance, but who only feels, along the sombre path of profound feeling, the night and the silence of its incapacity to think, the empty road and its incapacity to feel . . .

Boredom . . . The man who has Gods is never bored. Boredom is the lack of mythology. If one has no beliefs, even doubt is impossible, even scepticism lacks the strength to doubt. Yes, boredom is that: the loss for the soul of its capacity to deceive itself, the lack for thought of that inexistent staircase up which it can securely arrive at the truth.

※

Between the end of the summer and the onset of autumn, in that still summery interval when the air weighs down on us and colours lose their intensity, the ends of the day wrap themselves in the fugitive garb of false glory. They may be compared to those tricks of the imagination in which our regrets float unfocused, extending themselves for ever like the wakes of boats creating their ever repeating unbroken serpents.

On such afternoons, I feel myself sated, like the sea at high tide, by a feeling worse than boredom but for which there is no more suitable name – a feeling of desolation in some undefined space, a sensation of a shipwreck of the entire soul. I feel I have lost a compassionate god, that the marrow of all things is dead for ever. And, for me, the sentient universe is a corpse which I loved when it was alive, but all has been transformed into nothingness in the still torrid light of the last shimmering clouds.

My boredom takes on a horrifying aspect; my lassitude one of terror. It is not my sweat which is icy but the consciousness I have of it. It is not a physical malaise, but a malaise of the mind, so pervasive that it penetrates into the pores of my entire body and, in turn, freezes them.

This disgust is so powerful, and the terror of living so strong, that I can imagine nothing which might serve as a palliative, an antidote, or a soothing lotion – or even an oblivion of it. To sleep seems totally monstrous to me. To die seems totally monstrous to me. To go forward or to halt constitute one and the same impossibility. Hope and incredulity both lead back to coldness and ashes. I am a shelf of empty bottles.

And yet! What potential regrets if I abandon to vulgar eyes the dead salutation of the luminous, ebbing day! What a grandiose burial of hope as it silently advances through the gilded spaces of inert skies, what a cortège of words and nothingnesses filters away in the rufous blues, already paling through the vast spaces of an idiotic space!

I know not what I want nor do not want. I have ceased wanting, knowing how to want, or recognizing the emotions or the thoughts which usually lead us to know what we want, or what we want to want. I know not who I am, nor what I am. Like someone buried beneath a wall which has collapsed on him, I lie prostrate under the collapsed void of the entire universe. And I go on, following my own wake, until night finally arrives, and brings me the caress of feeling different, flowing like a breeze over these stirrings of my impatience with myself.

And this full moon high in the sky, during these calm nights, soaked with faint anguish and disquiet! Sinister peace of this celestial beauty, cold irony of this horrid air, blue-black, redolent of moonlight and bashful of the stars.

❧

I went from studying metaphysics to more violent tasks of the mind as regards one's nervous equilibrium. I wasted nights of terror poring over tomes of mystics and cabalists, which I was never patient enough to read in their entirety except with an intermittent trembling and . . .

The rites and tenets of the Rosicrucians, the symbolism of the Cabbala and the Templars . . . I suffered from their proximity for a long time. And they feverishly inundated my days of poisonous speculations, with demoniacal logic of metaphysics – magic . . . alchemy – and I extracted a false vital stimulus of painful, prescient feelings of always being on the edge of discovering a supreme mystery. I lost myself in secondary systems, made hysterical by metaphysics, in systems full of disturbing analogies, of leaps for lucidity, which have in their possession mysterious landscapes in which reflections of the supranatural awake mysteries on their fringes.

I was invaded by feeling . . . I washed myself in the enjoyment of thought . . . And my life turned into a metaphysical fever, perpetually discovering hidden feelings in things, playing with the fire of cryptic analogies, pushing into the background the integrality of lucidity, normal synthesis . . .

I fell into a complex cerebral indiscipline, full of indifferences . . . Where to run to? I have the impression that I took refuge in a non-place. I gave myself over to I know not what.

❦

I compressed and circumscribed my desires in order to hone them more acutely. To attain infinity – and I truly believe it can be attained – we need a safe harbour, only one, and to depart from there for the Undefined.

I am today an ascetic in my own religion. A cup of coffee, a cigarette, and my dreams can easily replace the sky and its stars, work, love and even the beauty of glory. I have, so to speak, no need of stimulants. My opium I find in my soul.

What do I dream about? I do not know. I have deployed all my efforts in order to reach a point where I no longer know what I am thinking of, what I am dreaming about, or what my visions are. It seems to me that I dream of something always more distant, and more and more vague, imprecise, unenvisageable.

I do not elaborate theories about life. I do not ask myself if it is good or bad. In my eyes, it is cruel and sad, and interspersed with delicious dreams. What advantage can there be for me in knowing what it means to others?

The life of others is simply of use to me in order to live for

them, for each of them, the life which appears to suit them best
in my dreams.

❦

[. . .] There are days when there surges up in me, as if from an
alien soil towards my own head, a distaste, an anguish for life
which only the fact of seeing myself withstanding it prevents
me from finding intolerable. It is the strangulation of life
within me, a desire to be someone else in every pore of my
skin, a brief foretaste of my end.

What I feel most of all is lassitude, and that anxiety which is
the twin sister of anxiety whenever it has no other *raison
d'être* but precisely that of existing. I experience an intimate
fear of the gestures I must make, an intellectual timidity
towards the words I must pronounce. Everything seems
doomed to failure.

The unbearable distaste for all those faces, made equally
stupid by intelligence as by a lack of it, and so nauseatingly
grotesque by being happy or unhappy, revolting because they
exist – that distinct morass of living things to which I remain
alien.

❦

We are dead. That which we imagine to be life is the sleep of
real life, the death of what we really are. The dead are born,
they do not die. For us, the two worlds are inverted. When we
believe we live, we are dead; we begin to live when we are
moribund.

This relationship which exists between sleep and life is
identical to the one which exists between what we call life and
what we call death. We are in the process of sleeping and this
life is a dream, not in a metaphysical or poetical sense, but in a
true sense.

Everything we dream to be superior in our actions shares in
death, everything is death. What does ideal mean except that
life is useless? What is art but the negation of life? A statue is a

dead body, sculpted in order to fix death in incorruptible matter. Even pleasure, which seems to us to be a deep immersion in life, is far more an immersion in ourselves, a destruction of the links binding us to life, a quivering shadow of death.

The very act of living implies death, since we never live a day more in life without it becoming, *ipso facto*, a day less.

We people dreams, we are errant shades in the forests of the impossible, whose trees are houses, customs, ideas, ideals and philosophies.

Never to find God, not even to know if God exists! To go from one world to another, from incarnation to incarnation eternally lost in the chimaera which seduces us, in the error which flatters us.

Truth never, rest never either! Never union with God! Never completely in peace, but only somewhat in peace and that unceasing longing for it!

THE FUNERAL MARCH FOR LUDWIG II OF BAVARIA

Today, more haltingly than ever, Death came selling on my doorstep. In front of me, more haltingly than ever, she unrolled the carpets, the silks and damasks of her oblivion and consolation. She smiled in front of them, a laudatory smile, and cared not that I saw that. But when I tried to buy, she replied that they were not for sale. She had not come for me to lust after what she showed me, but, by what she had brought, to make me lust after her. And, about her carpets, she explained they were like the ones walked on in her distant palace; about her silks, that they were the only ones worn in her castle of shadow; about her damasks, that those which covered, as altar-cloths, the retables of her mansion beyond the world were far better.

She undid with a tender gesture the visceral attachment binding me to my naked threshold. 'Your hearth,' she said, 'has no fire: why then do you want a hearth?' 'Your house,' she said, 'is without bread, what use then is a table to you?' 'Your life,' she continued, 'is without a friend's presence: with whom then can your life seduce you?

'I am,' she said, 'the fire of extinguished hearths, the bread of bare tables, the devoted companion of hermits and the misunderstood. Glory, which is lacking in this world, is the ceremonial in my black and sombre kingdom. In my empire, love never tires, for it is not sick with possessivity; it does not wound, since it never tires, never having possessed. My hand comes to rest lightly on the heads of men who think, and they forget; I watch cradled on my breast men who hoped in vain, and they recover confidence at last.

'The love one bears me knows not consuming passion; no errant jealousy; no tarnished memory. To love me is like a summer's night, where beggars sleep under the stars and appear to be stones at the roadside. From my mute lips no song swells up like that of sirens, nor any melody like that of trees and springs; but my silence welcomes, as undefined music, and my peace caresses like the torpor of some breeze.

'What then do you have,' she said, 'to link you to life? Love does not haunt you, glory does not pursue you, power does not know where to find you. The house you inherited had fallen into ruins. The first fruits of the acres handed down to you were already burnt by the frost and the sun had devoured their promise. You have never seen the well in your garden other than dry. The leaves had rotted in your lakes before you ever saw them. Rampant weeds had roofed over the paths and alleys on which your feet had never trod.

'But in my empire, where night alone rules, you would find consolation, as you would never have hope; you would possess oblivion, since you would never desire; you would have rest, since you would not have life.'

And Death showed me how sterile was the hope of better days, when one had not been endowed, at birth, with a soul capable of recognizing the better ones. She showed me how dreams cannot console us, as life afflicts us even more on awakening. She showed me how sleep cannot bring repose, since it is haunted by ghosts, shades of things, vestiges of our actions, dead embryos of our desires, flotsam of the shipwreck of life.

And, as she spoke, more languidly than ever, she rolled up her carpets which had captivated my eyes, her silks which my soul had coveted, the damasks of her retables on which only my tears had fallen.

'Why try to be like others, condemned as you are to be yourself? Why try to laugh since, when you laugh, your sincere happiness is false, born as it is of your forgetting who you are? What point in crying since you feel it is of no use, and you weep rather because your tears no longer console you than for the consolation they might provide?

'If you are happy when you laugh, your laughter is my victory; if then you are happy not to remember what you are, how much happier will you be with me, there where you shall no longer remember anything at all. If you are able to rest comfortably, and even sleep without the slightest dream, what rest will you not enjoy in my bed, where sleep is ignorant of the faintest reverie. If you come to your feet in a moment in the presence of Beauty, forgetting both life and yourself, how will you not spring to your feet in my palace, whose nocturnal beauty suffers no discussion, no ageing, no comparison; in my halls, no wind flutters the draperies, no dust sprinkles the armour, no light causes to fade, little by little, the tissues and velvets, and no time yellows the whiteness of the empty walls.

'Give yourself up to my tenderness, which knows not how to vary; give yourself over to my love, which knows not how to stop! Drink from my cup, which never empties, the supreme nectar which provokes neither nausea, nor bitterness, nor disgust, nor drunkenness. And contemplate from the window of my castle not the brightness of the sea and the moon, which are beautiful things, hence imperfect, but the vast maternal night, the unfissured splendour of the gigantic abyss!

'In my arms, you shall forget even the painful path which brought you there. On my breast, you shall not even feel the love which impelled you to seek it out! Come sit next to me on my throne – and you become once and for all the unexpugnable emperor of the Grail and of the Mystery, you shall coexist with gods and destinies, if, like them, you are nothing, you possess neither more nor less, you feel no need for excess or lack, nor even for mere sufficiency.

'I shall be your maternal spouse, your twin sister refound again. And as soon as all your anxieties are wedded to me, as soon as is reserved for me all that you sought in yourself and never possessed, then you shall confound yourself in my mystical substance, in my negative existence, on my breast where the very gods faint away.'

O King of Detachment and Renunciation, Emperor of Death and Shipwreck, living dream who wanders, sumptuous, in exile over the roads and ruins of this world!

O King of Despair and pomp, painful lord of palaces which no longer satisfy him, maestro of feasts and processions which no longer suffice to efface life!

O King erect among the tombstones, who came in the night, under the bright light of the moon, to recount your life to other lives, page of leafless lilies, imperial herald of icy ivories.

O Shepherd King of Vigils, errant knight of Anguish, *sans* glory or a lady in the lunar clarity of the roads, lord of forests overhanging cliffs, mute profile, visor down, who traverses valleys, misunderstood by villages, mocked in towns, despised in cities.

O Lord King whom Death has anointed for her own, pale and absurd, forgotten and unknown, ruling over tarnished stone-work and dilapidated velvets, on a throne at the limits of the Possible, surrounded by an unreal court, sitting in a circle of shadows and guarded by a phantasmagorical militia, mysterious and insubstantial.

Pages, bring – virgins, bring – serving boys and girls, bring on the cups and garlands for the feast at which Death is present! Bring them, dressed in black and crowned with myrtle.

Let mandragora be served in your cups . . . on your salvers, and let the garlands be woven from violets and flowers evocative of sadness.

The King goes off to dine with Death, in his ancient palace

on the lake shore, between the mountains, far from life, distant from the world.

A thrill of excitement races through the wings of the palace.

Here he comes, escorted by Death whom no one sees and who never arrives.

Heralds, sound your trumpets! Give due honour!

Your love of things dreamt was nothing but your disdain for things lived.

Virgin-King who has spurned love.

Shadow-King who has disdained light.

Dream-King who did not want to live!

Beneath the leaden thudding of cymbals and drums, Shade proclaims you Emperor!

Your coming shines in the sunset, towards those regions where Death rules absolute.

You have been crowned with mysterious flowers of unknown hues, a ridiculous circlet as fitting for you as for a deposed god.

. . . your cult purple with dreaming, luxurious antichamber of Death.

. . . impossible hetairas of the abyss.

Sound your trumpets, heralds, from the heights of the battlements, to greet this grandiose dawn.

The King of Death arrives in his kingdom!

Flowers of the abyss, black roses, carnations of lunar whiteness, butterflies of a redness exuding light.

❦

Abstract intelligence implies a certain fatigue, the worst type of all fatigues. It is not oppressive like physical fatigue, not disturbing like that born of our emotions. It is the weight of the consciousness of the world, it is the incapacity to breathe with the soul.

Then, just as clouds driven by the wind, all those ideas which constitute the foundations of life, all the ambitions, all the noble purposes on which we erected our hopes for its continuity, are torn apart, melt away and fade, ash and mist, tatters of what has never been, can never be. And, at the rearguard of this rout, appears, without a stain, the black and implacable solitude of the empty, starred sky. The mystery of life murders and terrorizes us in many ways. It approaches sometimes like a pale ghost, and our soul quivers with the most awful horror – that of seeing monstrous non-being take shape. On other occasions, it appears behind us, only visible to those who turn to look, and it is truth in its entirety which unveils its fathomless terror – that of remaining unknown to us.

But the horror which paralyses me today is less noble and even more corrosive. It is a desire not even to want to think, an urge to have never been anything, a conscious despair in every single cell of the body and of the soul. It is the abrupt sensation of finding oneself cloistered in a cell without limits. What use of trying to escape, since the cell itself is all?

And then the desire possesses me (overflowing, absurd, a sort of satanic pre-Satanism) to find one day – a day stripped of living substance – an exit open to allow an escape from God, and to see the deepest part of us finally cease, I know not how, to belong to being or to non-being.

PAINFUL INTERMEZZO

Everything exhausts me, even that which does not exhaust me. My happiness is as painful as my pain.

How I long with God's grace to be a child who makes boats out of paper on the pond of a country house with a rustic gatehouse closed by an elaborate iron grille which casts curlicues of light and green shade on to the murky shadows of the shallow water.

Between life and me, a thin sheet of glass. It matters little that I see and understand life clearly, I cannot touch it . . .

My dreams are an idiotic refuge, like using an umbrella to ward off lightning.

I am so inert, so pitiful, so stripped of active gestures. No matter how deep I plunge into myself, all the paths of dream take me back to the clearings of anguish.

Even I, who dream so much, experience intermittently periods when dreams quit me. Then things seem clear. The mist I wrap myself in vanishes. And the invisible thorns scratch the flesh of my soul. All the seen harshnesses wound me with the knowledge I have of their harshness. All the visible weights of objects oppress the interior of my soul.

My life is a history of assault and battery.

To live a dispassionate and cultivated life, full of whimsical ideas, reading, dreaming, and thinking about writing, a life sufficiently dilatory so as to be always on the fringes of boredom, sufficiently thought out so as never to fall into it. To live out that life far from emotions and the emotions in ideas. To stagnate in the sun, gilded all over, like an obscure lake edged with flowers. To possess, in the shade, that nobility of individuality which consists in insisting on nothing in life. To be in the revolving worlds like pollen blown about by an unknown wind rising in the late afternoon, and which the lethargy of the falling night lets fall haphazardly, undistinguishable, in the midst of vaster things. To be that with a certain knowledge, neither happy nor sad, but thankful to the sun for its brilliance and to the stars for their remoteness. To be nothing more, to have nothing more, to desire nothing further . . . The music of the starving beggar, the song of the blind man, the relic of the unknown vagabond, the hoof-prints in the desert of an unladen camel without a point of arrival.

Nobody has yet defined, in a language comprehensible to those who have never experienced it, what boredom is. What some people call boredom is nothing but the brute fact that they are bored; or else it is merely a type of malaise; or else, they are describing exhaustion. But although boredom forms one component of exhaustion and malaise, the fact of being bored is only a component, just as water is made up of the hydrogen and oxygen which compose it. It contains them without being identical to them.

If some give such a restrictive and incomplete sense to boredom, others give it a connotation which in some ways transcends it – defining boredom as that personal and entirely spiritual distaste, which is provoked by the diversity and incertitude of the world. That which causes us to yawn is the product of being bored; that which causes us to change positions is a malaise; that which prevents us from moving is exhaustion – none of these constitutes boredom; but neither is it also the profound feeling of the vacuity of things, through which frustrated aspirations free themselves; the anxiety of disillusion comes to the surface and forms in the soul the seeds out of which mystics and saints are born.

Boredom is well and truly a blasé distaste for the world, the malaise of being alive, the exhaustion of having lived; indeed, boredom is the fleshly sensation of the prolix vacuum of things. But boredom is, to a greater extent, the distaste for other worlds, whether they exist or not; the malaise of being obliged to live by being an other, an other in a different fashion, in another world; the exhaustion dates not only from today and yesterday, but from tomorrow as well, from eternity, if there is one, from nothingness if that is eternity. It is not only the vacuum of things and beings which pains the soul when it feels bored; it is also the vacuum of some other thing, which is not things or beings. It is the vacuum of the very soul feeling the void, and which feels itself to be void, and is disgusted by and repudiates that feeling in itself.

Boredom is a physical sensation of chaos. It is the feeling that chaos is all. The bored one, the ill-tempered one, the exhausted one have the feeling that they are locked up in a narrow prison cell. The man revolted by the narrowness of life feels himself to be exposed in a big prison cell. But the man who knows boredom feels himself to be a prisoner deprived of normal freedom of action in an infinite prison cell. On the one who yawns out of boredom, on the one seized by a malaise, on the one worn out with exhaustion, the prison cell can come crashing down to bury them. The man revolted by the pettiness of the world can see his chains falling off and can escape; or he may also be in agony because he cannot cast them off; and, thanks to his pain, can live again without self-hatred. But the walls of the infinite cell cannot bury us, since they do not exist; and the pain of the chains cannot bring us back to life, since our hands have always been free.

And that is what I feel, comforted by the tranquil beauty of this never-ending evening as it fades away. I look up towards the clear deep sky, where vague rosy entities, like the shadows of clouds, form the intangible down of a distant winged life. I look down on the river, where the water, simply ruffled by faint ripples, is of a blue which seems to be reflected off a deeper sky. Once again, I look up in the sky, and already there floats among the vague colours overtly trickling away in the invisible air, a glacial tonality of wishy-washy whiteness, as if some part of things, that where they are the most high and ordinary, also had a specific tangible boredom, an incapacity of being what it is, an imponderable body of anguish and desolation.

What then? What is there in the upper air but upper air which is nothing? What else is there in the sky other than a colour which is not its own? What is there in those fluffy apologies for clouds, about which I already have my doubts, other than a few refractions of light, materially incidental, from an already setting sun? What is there in all that but me? Ah, but boredom is that, only that. It is the fact that in all which exists – sky, earth, world – in all that, there is nothing but me!

❧

The emblem I prefer today to define my frame of mind is that of a creator of indifferences. Above all, I should like my way of acting in life to be an attempt at educating others to feel at one time more deeply for themselves and at the other less in conformity with the dynamic law of the collectivity.

To mould them to this spiritual antisepsis, thanks to which all vulgar contamination may be avoided, seems to me the most stellate destiny *par excellence* of the intimate pedagogue I would like to become. That all who read me may learn – even though step by step as is necessary with such a subject – not to experience any feeling at all under the gaze of others, confronted by others' opinions – that is the result which would crown to perfection this scholastic stagnation in my life.

The incapacity to act in my case has always been a sickness which should be defined in terms of metaphysical purpose. To accomplish a gesture has always constituted, in my experience of things, a perturbation, a de-doubling, in the world outside; the mere fact of moving myself has always given me the impression that it could not leave the stars intact nor leave the skies unchanged. For that reason, the metaphysical importance of the slightest gesture acquires an astonished contour inside me. I have, faced with action, acquired scruples of transcendental honesty which prevented me, from the moment it became rooted in my consciousness, from having an over-close relationship with the palpable world.

AESTHETICS OF INDIFFERENCE

In the face of every thing, what the dreamer should strive to acquire is the limpid indifference which, as far as possible, it provokes in him.

To know, with an immediate instinct, how to extrude from each object that which it can contain of dreamworthiness, leaving for dead in the Outside World all that it contains which is real – that is what the sage should attempt to realize in himself.

Never to experience sincerely his own emotions, and to

raise his pallid triumph to the point where it can with indifference look on his own ambitions, anxieties and desires; to ignore his joys and his pains, as people pass over those who are of no interest to them ...

The greatest control of oneself is indifference towards oneself, one's being, one's body and soul, like the town house and country house where fate decided we should pass our lives.

To handle our own dreams and intimate desires magisterially, *en grand seigneur*, making it a point of intimate finesse not to notice them. To be bashful about oneself; to perceive that we are alone in our presence, witnesses of ourselves, and for that reason to act in front of ourselves as we would before a stranger, with a serene and studied exterior tactic, indifferent as an *hidalgo*, and cold since indifferent.

To avoid being held in lower esteem, it suffices to enure ourselves to not having either ambitions, or passions, or desires, or hopes, or compulsions, or disgust. To achieve that, may we always remember that we are in our own presence, that we are never so alone that we can entirely relax. And so we shall eliminate our tendency to experience passions and ambitions, since passions and ambitions are chinks in our armour; we shall have neither desires nor hopes, since desires and hopes are servile and inelegant attitudes; we shall have neither compulsions nor excitation, since haste is indelicate in others' eyes and impatience is always vulgar.

An aristocrat is a man who is incapable of forgetting that he is never alone; that is why etiquette and protocols are attitudes of the aristocracy. Let us interiorize the aristocrat by wrenching him out of his salons and his gardens, let us transport him into our soul and our consciousness of being. Let us face ourselves relentlessly, with respect for etiquette and protocols, so performing studied gestures made-for-others ...

Each one of us is a small group, like the life in a *quartier*; nevertheless, we should render the life of one *quartier* elegant and distinguished, doting the halls of our feelings with dignity and refinement and stamping the galas of our thoughts with restrained good manners. All around us, other creatures might well construct poor, insalubrious slums; let us demark clearly where our *quartier* begins and ends and, from the lofty façade of our buildings until the secret rooms of our shyness, ensure that all is noble and serene, with discreet sculptural ornamentation, and, as if subreptitiously, without self-aggrandizement. Let us allow each of our sensations to find its gentle auto-realization. Let love be reduced to the shadow of a dream of love, a pale quivering interval between the crests of two ripples, highlighted by the moon. To render desire a futile and inoffensive thing, like the gentle smile of the soul in communion with itself; and to make of it an object which never dreams of accomplishment, nor of expression. To drug hatred into sleep like a tame snake, and to tell fear to retain nothing, out of its manners, but the anguish behind every look, and only behind the look of our soul, the unique attitude compatible with aesthetics.

PAINFUL INTERLUDE

Not even in pride do I find any consolation. What have I to be proud about since I am not my own creator? And even if I had something to be proud of, equally there would be something – to a greater extent – not to boast about.

I live out my life prostrate. And, even in dreams, I am unable to accomplish the gesture of getting to my feet, so far have I been emptied, in my soul, by the effort of making an effort.

Artisans of metaphysical systems, fabricators of psychological explorations know far greater pain. To systematize, to explain is nothing but construction. And all that – the arranging, the setting in place, the organization – what is it but a finalized effort – which is to say, pathetically, that it constitutes life!

I am no pessimist. Happy are those who succeed in translating their sufferings into universality. As far as I am concerned, I ignore if the world is good or bad, and it is a matter of the utmost indifference to me, since others' pain is both a bore and non-important. From now on, let them refrain from weeping and wailing (which irritates and annoys me), I could not give a damn for their suffering – so heavy and weighty is my disdain for them.

But, I am one of those who believes life to be half-shade, half-light. I am no pessimist. I never complain about life's tribulations. I complain since the only important thing in my eyes is the fact that I exist, that I suffer, and that I cannot even dream that I am entirely exterior to my painful sensations.

Happy dreamers are pessimists. They sculpt the world in their image and so always manage to feel at their ease. What pains me the most is the ditch separating the gay hubbub of the world from my sadness, from my silence charged with boredom.

Life, with all its sorrows, apprehensions and comings-and-goings, ought to be good and happy, like a trip in a coach in good company.

Nor can I imagine any element of Greatness in my sufferings. I do not know what they are. But I suffer from such petty things. I am hurt by such banalities that I do dare to insult with that hypothesis the other hypothesis, that of my possible genius.

The glory of a marvellous sunset, with all its beauty, saddens me. Before such a sight, I often say to myself: how happy is the man who feels content to be such a thing!

And this book is an entire jeremiad. Once written, the poems from *Alone* will no longer be considered to constitute the saddest Portuguese book.

Next to my pain, all other sufferings seem false or derisory. They are the sufferings of the happy ones, or of those who live and complain. These are those of a prisoner of life, of a very different creature.

Between life and me. . . .

In such a way that I see all that is anguish. And I am totally insensible towards everything which produces happiness. In addition, I have noticed that pain the more it is visible, the less it is felt, whereas it is the opposite in the case of happiness. For by abstaining from thinking and seeing, it is possible to achieve a certain satisfaction, exactly like the one possessed by mystics, gypsies and petty crooks. But, finally, everything makes an entrance through the window of observation and the doorway of thought.

APOCALYPTIC FEELING

Considering that every incident in my life was a contact with the horror of Novelty, and that every new person I met was a new living fragment of the unknown, which I placed on my table for a daily horrified contemplation, I decided to abstain from everything, to aim at nothing, to reduce action to a minimum, to withdraw as far as possible from contact either with men or with events, to refine abstinence and to byzantinize abdication. So much does life revolt and torture me.

To make decisions, to achieve something, to exit out of doubt and obscurity, these are things which conjure up for me images of catastrophies and universal cataclysms.

For me life is apocalypse and cataclysm. Every day, my incapacity to sketch the slightest gesture increases, to conceive of myself in situations which are both real and well-defined.

Others' presences – always so disturbing to me – become day by day more painful and ridden with anxiety. To speak to others sends shivers down my spine. If they show any interest in me, I take to my heels. If they stare at me, I put space between us.

I am perpetually on the defensive. I importune both life and others. I can not face life head on. The very sun undoes and desolates me. Only at night, at night alone with myself, alien, forgotten, lost – unattached to reality and not part of utility – do I find myself and give myself consolation.

I am frozen by life. All my existence consists of dank caves and dusty catacombs. I am the headlong rout of the last army to defend the last empire. I know myself to be at the termination of an ancient dominant civilization. I am alone and abandoned. I who, in some ways, gave the orders. I am without a friend, without a guide, I, who always served as a guide for others.

Something in me eternally pleads for compassion – and I bewail myself as if mourning for some dead god, stripped of altars and rites, when the white horde of barbarians appears at the borders, and life comes to demand a reckoning from the empire of what it has done with its happiness.

I am eternally suspicious of what people say about me. I have failed in everything. I have not even dared to dream about becoming something; as for thinking that I might wish to be something, that too was out of the question, even in dream, since even in dream I saw myself as incompatible with life, up to and including my visionary state of pure dreaming.

No feeling can cause me to raise my head from this bolster in which I plunge it because I cannot stand my body, nor the idea that I live, not even the very idea of life itself.

I do not speak the language of reality, and among things of life I totter about like a bedridden sick person who gets up for the first time. Only in bed do I have the impression of leading a normal life. When I have a high temperature, I am relieved as it is a natural event for a chronically sick person like me. I shake and quiver like a flame in the wind. Only in the moribund air of closed rooms do I breathe in and out the normalcy of my life.

I have not the slightest nostalgia for sea snails on beaches. I have likened myself in my soul to a cloister in order to avoid being for myself anything but an arid autumn in the expanses of the desert, with no other life but a living reflection like a fading light over the misty obscurity of lakes, with no other effect or colour but a violet splendour – the exile of the final rays of a sunset on the mountain peaks.

When all is said and done, no other pleasure except the analysis of pain, no other voluptuousness except that of the liquid and morbid calibration of fragmentary decomposing feelings – light steps in an imprecise shadow, soft to the ear, and for which one does not even turn back to see to whom they belong, vague songs in the distance whose words one does not even bother to listen to, but by which we are more than soothed owing to the lack of clarity of what they are saying and the incertitude of where they come from; fragile secrets of pallid waters, which gently fill from afar the spaces of the night; the tinkling of carriage bells in the distance, returning from who knows where, carrying off with them who knows what laughter, which is inaudible from where we are, drowsy in the tepid torpor of the afternoon when summer drifts away into autumn's oblivion ... The flowers in the garden are dead and, as they fade, turn into other flowers – more old-fashioned, more noble and, with their faded yellow, more contemporary with mystery, abandon and silence. The water-snakes sinuously swimming in the lakes have their *raison d'être* in dreams. Distant croaking of frogs, dead lakes in my depths! Rustic tranquillity lived in dream! And my life futile as that of a peasant who does not work and sleeps at the roadside, with the scent of the fields pervading his soul like mist, like a fresh translucid sound, deep and yet fraught with the meaning that nothing is connected to anything – nocturnal, ignored, nomadic and exhausted under the cold compassion of the stars ...

I follow the train of my dreams, using images as so many steps towards newer images, and unfolding, like a fan, the metaphors haphazardly born from large paintings of an interior vision; I detach life from myself and set it to one side, like clothing which is too tight. I hide among the trees, far from the roads. I get lost. And I manage, for a few fleeting seconds, to forget love for life, to abolish both light and agitation, and to liquidate myself consciously and absurdly into the stream of my sensations, like a ruined empire bleeding with anxiety, like a victorious entry, amid the drums and standards, into a vast lost city where I would regret nothing, desire nothing, and ask for nothing, not even from myself – except to live.

This bluish surface of lakes created by my dreams – what agony. Mine is the paleness of the moon I glimpse over forest landscapes. Mine is the exhaustion of the autumn of stagnant depleted skies which I do not remember having seen. All my dead life weighs down on me, all my vain dreams, all that was mine without belonging to me, in the blue of my internal skies, in the visual lapping of the rivers of my soul, in the huge unappeased quiet of these fields of wheat which I see without seeing.

A cup of coffee; a cigarette one smokes and whose aroma transperces us, eyes half-shut in the darkened room . . . I want nothing more from life than my dreams and that . . . If that is too much to ask? I don't know. Do I really have any idea of what is too much and too little?

How I long to be an other on this summer afternoon . . . I open the window. All is so soft out there, but it pains me like an imprecise duet, like a vague feeling of discomfort.

And there is a final thing which hurts me, racks me, tears my whole soul apart. That fact that I, at the moment, at this window, face to face with these gentle and sad things, I ought to be a handsome aesthetic creature, like a figure in a painting – and I am not. I am not even that . . .

Let this moment pass, fade away.

Let night come and let it increase, falling on everything, and never end. Let this soul be my eternal grave, the acme of darkness, and may I never ever dream of living, feeling or desiring anything at all in the world any more.

❧

The habit and gift of dreaming is primordial for me. The circumstances of my life – I have been tranquil and solitary since childhood – other elements perhaps which have had a remote influence on me, via the play of obscure heredities, in accordance with this sinister moulding, have made my spirit a constant stream of deliriums. All that I am can thus be summed up, and even that which apparently in my case seems the least likely to produce a dreamer belongs in fact, without any hesitation, to a soul which does nothing else but dream, thus elevated to the highest degree.

I seek, for my own pleasure in self-analysis and, in the

measure it still affords me satisfaction, to set out little by little, in words, the mental processes forming an entity in me – that of an entire life devoted to dreaming, that of a soul completely moulded for dreams.

If I look at myself from the exterior (and it is how I normally see myself), I am a man incapable of action, ill at ease with the very idea of making a movement, of beginning something, clumsy in my speech with others, deprived of that interior lucidity which would allow me to amuse myself with anything costing a mental effort, without any physical propensity at all to give myself over to some mechanical activity, so providing myself with distraction as I worked.

It is normal! I am like that. It is understood that a dreamer should be like that. All reality perturbs me. Others' discourse drowns me in an incommensurate anxiety. The reality of others' souls endlessly surprises me. The vast network of the lack of consciousness, which is every action I see, seems an absurd illusion without any plausible coherence, a nothing.

Yet, if you imagine I misunderstand the fabric of human psychology and I have no clear notion of the most intimate motivations and thoughts of my peers, you would be hugely mistaken about the sort of person I am.

Since I am no dreamer, unless I am exclusively a dreamer, the habit of dreaming, uniquely of dreaming, has furnished me with an internal vision of extraordinary clarity. Not only do I see in astounding and sometimes disturbing relief the person-ages and décors of my dreams, but I also see, in similar relief, my abstract ideas, my human feelings (what is left of them), my hidden compulsions and my psychological attitudes towards myself. I affirm that, as for my abstract ideas, I see them inside me, I see them with a real internal vision in an interior space. And, so, the slightest oscillations become more visible for me in infinitesimal detail.

For this reason, I have complete knowledge of myself and, because of this total knowledge, I know the whole of humanity intimately. There is no base impulse, just as there is no noble intention, which has not flashed through my soul; I know all their exterior manifestations. Beneath the masks, employed by evil ideas, good ideas or indifferent ones, including those inside us and in our gestures, I know them for what they are. I recognize what in us strives to lead us astray. And so, I know the majority of people surrounding me better than they know themselves. Often enough, I attempt to probe them in order to make them mine. I vampirize every psyche I can explain, since for me to dream is to possess. And so it is entirely normal that, despite the fact I am a dreamer, I am also the analyst I claim to be.

That is why, among the rare things I like reading, I particularly esteem plays. Every day, different plays are acted out in me and I have complete knowledge of the way one can project a soul in Mercator's projections. However, it is only moderately amusing for me, since playwrights' errors are so huge and numerous. No drama has ever totally satisfied me. As I have explored the human psyche with the precision of lightning, probing in one flash all the corners, I am incensed by the crudity of the constructions made by playwrights, and the rare plays I see repel me like an ink-blot in the middle of a written page.

Things are the material of my dreams; that is why I consent a distracted but most precise attention to certain details of the Outside.

To provide my dreams with relief, I need to know how real landscapes and personages from life provide us with the impression of relief. For the vision of the dreamer differs from the vision of the man who actually sees things. The veritable reality of an object is but part of itself; the remainder is merely the extortionate tribute it pays to matter for the privilege of existing in space. Just so, there exists the reality in space for certain phenomena, which in dreams have a true and palpable reality. A real sunset is fixed and eternal. He who knows how to write is the one who knows how to see dreams with clarity (that is the truth) or to see life in dreams, to see life immaterially, to photograph it with the camera of delirium, on which the light beams of the past, of the futile and of the circumscribed, have no effect and turn out black on the spiritual plates.

As for me, this attitude, which inveterate dreaming has encysted in me, has always made me grasp the fact of reality which is dream. My vision of things always suppresses in them that which my dreams cannot use. So I live eternally in dreams, including when I live in real life. To contemplate a sunset inside myself or inside the Outside is one and the same thing, as I see them in the same way since my vision adjusts itself equally to both.

For that reason, the idea I have of myself is an idea which could seem mistaken to many people. In one way, it is. Yet I dream myself to myself and I select in me what is dreamable, and I compose and recompose myself in every possible way until I obtain a satisfactory image, capable of facing up to what I demand that I am and am not. Sometimes the best way to see an object is to annihilate it, but it still subsists, how I have no idea, made out of the very matter of the negation and abolition; I proceed in such a way with whole segments of my real being which, once suppressed in my image of myself, transfigure me in my reality.

How then can I not err as concerns my intimate processes of self-illusion? Why does the process which embodies a reality more real than real, an aspect of the world or a dream image, also embody, in order that it may be more real, an emotion or a thought; it strips them, therefore, of all their trappings of nobility and purity when, as is nearly always the case, they are not. It should be remarked that my objectivity is absolute, the most absolute of all. I manage to create the absolute object, doted with qualities of absoluteness despite its concrete character. I have not truly eloped from life to find a soft bed for my soul; I have simply altered it and have discovered in my dreams the identical objectivity as in life. My dreams – I study them further on – arise independently of my will and very often shock or hurt me. Very often, what I find in myself disturbs me, fills me with shame (perhaps because of a remnant of humanity remaining in me – what then is shame?) and terrifies me.

In me, uninterrupted delirium has replaced concentration. I have arrived at superimposing on seen things (including those seen in dreams) other dreams which I carry away with me. Already sufficiently inattentive to be able to achieve what I call seeing in dreams – I continue, since that inattention was caused by perpetual dreaming and by an even (though not too concentrated) preoccupation about the errance of them, to superimpose that which I dream on the dream itself which I see, and to bisect reality, already despoiled of matter by an absolute immateriality.

A consequence of that is the ease I have acquired in following several ideas at once, in observing things around me and, at the same time, in dreaming about totally different things; to find myself in the process of dreaming about a real sunset, over a very real Tagus, and, at the same time, dreaming about a morning on an interior Pacific Ocean; and both dreamt things mesh, without mingling and without creating a true amalgam of anything else except the varying emotional states which each one separately evokes in me; and it is as if somebody saw passing in the street a large crowd and simultaneously felt himself inside each and every individual – which could only take place in a communality of feeling – at the same time as I saw the different bodies – I would have to see them separately – passing each other in the street, full of uncountable feet.

THE COMMANDER

Nothing else reveals to me so intimately, interprets so exhaustively the substance of my congenital unhappiness as the sort of delirium which I really cherish the most, the lotion I most often choose in secret to soothe my anguish of existing. The synopsis and quintessence of what I long for is that: to sleep through life. I love life too much to be able to want it to be lived; I love not living life too much to be able to experience an incommensurate desire for life.

That is why what I am about to describe is my favourite

dream. Sometimes, in the evening in the house, peaceful because the inhabitants have gone out or else remain silent, I close the windows and close the inside shutters . . .; in an old suit, I snuggle deep down in my armchair and lock myself in the dream of being a retired major in a provincial hotel, sitting, after dinner, with another more sober resident, a slow fellow-diner who stays there for no reason.

I imagine I was born like that. I have no interest in the retired major's youth, nor in the ranks he has risen through to arrive at my longing. Independently of time and of life, the major I imagine myself to be has not been granted a previous existence, has no family, and has never had one; he lives out eternally the life of that provincial hotel, bored already by telling the anecdotes which follow one after the other told by his friends in order to pass the time.

❧

There is no burden like the affection of others – not even others' hatred, since hate is more intermittent than affection; as it is a painful emotion, the one who feels it instinctively tends to love less often. But both hatred and love are equally oppressive; both seek us out and pursue us, never leaving us in peace.

My ideal would be to live everything as if it were a novel, relaxing in life itself – to read my emotions, to live my disdain for them. For whosoever has a highly delicate imagination, the adventures of a protagonist in a novel are a specific and sufficient emotion, and, even more so since they are his and ours. No greater adventure exists than having loved Lady Macbeth with a true uncomplicated passion; when one has so loved, what else can one do, in order to have peace, but never love anybody else for the rest of one's life?

I ignore the direction of this journey I have been forced to take, between one night and another, in the company of the entire universe. I know that reading distracts me. I consider reading to be the most subtle way to make this journey, like the other one, more agreeable; and, from time to time, I raise my eyes from the book where I experience true feeling and see, like a stranger, the landscape flashing by – plains, cities, men and women, affects or regrets – and all that means nothing else to me but an episode of my tranquillity, an inert distraction where I rest my eyes from pages, read over time and time again.

We are truly only what we dream, since the remainder, the moment it is realized, belongs to the world and to the world in its entirety. If any dream were to be realized, I would be jealous of it, because it would have betrayed by allowing that to happen. I have realized all that I ever wanted, says the idiot, and it is a lie; the truth is that I have prophetically dreamed all that life has made of itself. We realize nothing. Life tosses us in the air like a stone and we go on repeating up there: 'Look how I move.'

Whatever the intermezzo played under the sun's spotlight and the stars' spangles, it is certainly not a bad thing to know that it is an intermezzo; if what lies beyond the stage-door is life, we shall live; if it is death, we shall die, and the play has nothing to do with all that.

That is why I never feel so close to the truth, so delicately initiated, as on those rare occasions I go to the theatre or the circus; then I know that at last I am watching the exact representation of life. And the actors and actresses, the clowns and the magicians are important and futile things like the sun and the moon, love and death, plague, hunger and war for humanity. All is theatre. Well then, I want the truth? I shall go on with my novel . . .

❦

Life is an experimental journey, involuntarily accomplished. It is a voyage of the mind through matter and, as it is the mind which travels, it is in it that we live. Hence, there are contemplative souls who have lived in a more intense, extended, and tumultuous fashion than others who have lived life on the outside. It is the result which counts. What has been felt is what has been lived. One can return exhausted from a dream as much as from a visible task. I have never lived so much as when I thought a very great deal.

He who is in the corner of the ballroom dances with all the dancers. I see everything and, since I see it, I live it. As everything in its ultimate elementality is a feeling of ours, so the contact with a body is its vision as well as its mere remembrance. So I dance when I see dancing. I say, like the English poet to the storyteller who watched, sprawled in the grass, three men reaping: 'There is a fourth man reaping, and it is I.'

All this is a direct result, whether spoken or felt, of a huge lassitude, which has suddenly come over me (apparently for no reason). I am not merely exhausted but in agony, and that agony too is unknown. My anxiety is such that I am on the verge of weeping – not with tears which fall but with expressed tears, tears of the sickness of the soul which have no tangible pain.

I have lived so much without ever living! I have thought so much without ever thinking. Worlds of static violence, motionless adventures heavily oppress me. I am sated with what I never had nor will ever have, annoyed by non-existent gods. I wear the scars of all the battles I avoided fighting. My muscular body is exhausted from the effort I have not thought of making.

Dulled, silent, nothing . . . The sky high up there is a dead, unfinished summer sky. I look at it, as if it were not there. I sleep what I think, I am prostrate when walking, I suffer without feeling anything. That immense nostalgia I have is nothing, it *is* nothing, like the high heavens which I do not see and which I stare at impersonally.

❦

The idea of travelling nauseates me.

I have already seen that which I have never seen.

I have already seen that which I have not yet seen.

The boredom of constant novelty, the boredom of discovery, lurking underneath the fallacious distinction between things and ideas, the perennial sameness of everything, the absolute similarity between the mosque, the temple and the church, the equality between the hovel and the palace, the self-same body which is the caparisoned being and the naked savage, the stagnation of all that I live which vanishes at the slightest movement.

Landscapes repeat themselves. During an ordinary train journey, I am torn, in a futile anguished fashion, between my disinterest in the landscape and my disinterest in the book which could conceivably distract me if I were another. I feel a slight nausea towards life, and each and every movement accentuates it.

The is no boredom uniquely in landscapes which do not exist, in books I shall never read. For me, life is a somnolent state which does not reach my brain. I keep my brain free in order to be sad in it.

Let those who do not exist, travel! For them there is nothing, like a river whose current should constitute life. But all those who think and feel, those who are fully awake, for them the horrific hysteria of trains, cars, boats neither allows them to sleep nor to awaken.

Even from the shortest journey, I return as if from a sleep gravid with dreams – a confused torpor with my sensations glued together, drunk with what I have seen.

In order to rest, I need a healthy soul. In order to move, I need something between a soul and a body; what I feel seeping away from me is not the movements but rather the desire to make them.

Very often it occurred to me to cross the river, a ten-minute trip between Terreiro do Paço and Cacilhas. And almost always I have been intimidated by all those people, by myself and by my idea. Once or twice I have crossed over, always feeling oppressed, only putting a foot on *terra firma* once I was back.

When one's feelings are overwrought, the Tagus is a nameless Atlantic, and Cacilhas another continent, even another universe.

Why travel? It is sufficient to exist to travel. I go from day to day, as if from station to station, in the train which is my body or my destiny, leaning over to watch the streets and the squares, the faces and the movements, perpetually identical and perpetually dissimilar just as, finally, all landscapes are.

'Any road, even this road from Entepfuhl, will take you to the end of the world.' But the end of the world, once the world has achieved a gyration, is precisely that Entepfuhl from which one departed. In reality, world's end like world's beginning is a conception of ours. It is in us that landscapes find a landscape. For this reason, if I imagine them, I create them; if I create them, they exist; if they exist, I see them like I see the others. What use in travelling? In Madrid, Berlin, Persia, China and at both Poles, where will I be except in myself, and locked in the typical mould of my sensations.

Life is what we make of it. Journeys are journeys. What we see is not what we see, but what we are.

❧

In knowledge, there exists an erudition which is rightly called erudition, and, in understanding, there is an erudition which is what is called culture. But there is also an erudition of sensitivity.

The erudition of sensitivity has nothing to do with the experience of life. Experience of life does not teach us anything, just as history does not provide us with information. True experience consists in reducing contact with reality and in intensifying the analysis of that contact. So sensitivity can develop and deepen, since in ourselves there is everything; it is enough to seek it out and to know how to search.

What is travel and what use is it? All sunsets are sunsets; there is no need to go and see one in Constantinople. The feeling of freedom engendered by travel? I can feel that by going from Lisbon to Benfica, and I feel it more intensely than someone who travels from Lisbon to China, since, if the feeling of freedom does not exist in me, it does not exist for me anywhere at all. 'Any road,' said Carlyle, 'even the road of Entepfuhl takes you to the end of the world.' But the road of Entepfuhl, if one follows it to the end, returns to Entepfuhl; in such a way that Entepfuhl, where we were, is the same end of the world which we set out to find.

Condillac begins his famous work, 'No matter how high we rise, or how low we fall, we never quit our sensations.' We never disembark from ourselves. We never attain an other except by othering ourselves by an imagination sensitive to our very selves. Real landscapes are the ones we ourselves create, as so, being their gods, we use them as they truly are, which is how we created them. Not one of the seven parts of the world actually interests me, nor can I truly see them; it is the eighth part which I explore and which is mine.

The man who has criss-crossed every ocean has merely criss-crossed the monotony of his self. I have criss-crossed more seas than any man alive. I have seen more mountains than most on this earth. I have been through more cities than exist and over the mighty rivers of non-existent worlds which flowed, absolute, under my contemplative gaze. If I were to travel, I would only find the pale copy of what I had already seen without travelling.

Those countries which others visit are found by them to be anonymous and alien. In the countries I have visited, I have been not only the occult pleasure of the unknown traveller, but the majesty of the king who rules them, the villagers who normally inhabit them and the entire history of that nation and its neighbours. The landscapes, the identical houses I have been because I saw them created in God by the substance of my imagination.

Renunciation is freedom. Power is not to love.
[. . .]
Basically, our experience on earth is composed of two elements: the universal and the particular. To describe the universal is to describe what every human being has in common and the entirety of human experience – the vast heavens with day and night appearing in them; the flow of rivers – all made from the fresh sisterly water; seas, quivering

extended mountain ranges, which preserve the nobility of height in their secret depths; fields, stations, houses, people, gestures; the costumes and the smiles; love and wars; gods, finite and infinite; shapeless Night, mother of the origin of the world; Hades, the intellectual monster which comprises everything... To describe this, or some universal thing like it, I use to speak to my soul the primitive and divine tongue, the idiom of Adam, intelligible to all. But what chopped-up tongue of Babel do I employ to describe the Funicular of Santa Justa, Reims Cathedral, Zouaves' baggy trousers, the way Portuguese is prounounced in the Tràs-os-Montes region? Those things are surface accidents; they can be experienced by going there but not by feeling them. What is universal in the Funicular of Santa Justa is its machinery which makes everyone's life easier. What is truth in Reims Cathedral is not the cathedral at Reims, but the religious majesty of those buildings consecrated to the knowledge of the profundity of the human soul. What is eternal about Zouaves' baggy trousers is the coloured fiction of their uniform, a human language which creates a social simplicity, itself in its way a novel type of nudity. What is universal about local differences in pronunciation is the familiar intonation of people spontaneously living out the diversity of communal life, the polychrome procession of ways of being, the differences between villages and the vast multiplicity of nations.

Eternal transients in ourselves, there is no other landscape but what we are. We possess nothing since we do not even possess ourselves. We have nothing since we are nothing. What hands could I stretch out towards the universe? The universe is not mine: I myself am the universe.

UNFINISHED JOURNEY

It was the fault of a vaguely autumnal dusk which caused me to start off on this journey which was never accomplished.

145

The sky – of which I retain an unreal memory – was a violet relic tinged with sad gold, and the agonized mountain line, vivid, itself hemmed in with a death-dyed halo, slid off, by softening them, into the subtlety of its contours. From the rails on the other side of the boat (it was colder and darker on this side of the canvas) the ocean throbbed away to where the eastern horizon slumped in madness, and where, scattering night shadows over the liquid and obscure edge of the extreme sea, there floated a wisp of a mist like a cloud on a very hot day.

The sea, I recall, had sombre tonalities, mingled with fugitive flights of vague light – and everything was as full of mystery as a mournful idea in a moment of happiness, precursor of who knows what.

I did not leave from a known port. Nor today do I know what port it was, since I never went there. Equally, the ritual aim of my journey was not to go either on a quest for non-existent ports – which would have been reduced to nothing but entries-to-ports, forgotten river deltas, squashed between cities of an irreproachable irreality. No doubt, as you read, you imagine my words are absurd. It is because you have never journeyed like me.

Did I leave? I could not swear to it. I found myself in other lands, in other ports, passing through towns which were not this one, even if neither this one nor that one were towns at all. You swear that I really left, I and not the landscape, that it was I who crossed other countries and not they who crossed me – I myself would not swear to that. I who, not knowing what life is, ignore if it is I who live it or if it is life which lives me (whatever arbitrary meaning the verb 'to live' may have), certain that I shall never swear anything.

I travelled. I believe it futile to explain to you that I have not taken up either months or days, or any quantifiable period of any time, in travelling. I travel in time, that is obvious, but not on this side of time which we measure in hours, days and months; it was on the other side of time I travelled, where it is not measured with any ruler. It passes without any means of measuring it. In some ways, it is more rapid than the time we have seen ourselves live. I am sure that you others are wondering if these sentences have any meaning. Avoid making any such mistake. Rid yourself of that puerile habit of asking the meaning of things and words. Nothing has any meaning.

On what boat did I travel? On the steamship *Whatever*. You laugh. I too, and at you perhaps. Which of you can say to us, both to you and to me, that I do not write in symbols for the gods to understand?

It is of no matter. I left at dusk. I still hear ringing in my ears the clanking noise as they raised the anchor. In the raking light of my memory, I still see the slow motion ending in the position 'at rest' of the arms of the crane which for hours had brutalized my view by its perpetual to-ings-and-fro-ings with barrels and crates. They abruptly shot up, bound in chains, over the gunwhale against which they scraped and banged, until swinging, they let themselves be manoeuvred, rushed along until they were suspended over the open hatch where they crashed down heavily with a deep wooden thud, before going off to roll and crash violently in some obscure corner of the hold. Then, the noise of screeching as the chains were removed; at last, the chain swung up, clanking away, and it all started up over again in apparent futility.

Why do I tell you all that? It is absurd to tell it to you, since it is about one of my journeys which I wish to tell you.

I have visited New Europes, and other Constantinoples have welcomed my arrival by sail, on the backs of false Bosphoruses. You interrupt: my arrival by sail? Yes, indeed, it was exactly as I tell you. The steamboat on which I left arrived at port as a sailing ship. Impossible, you say? That is precisely why it happened to me.

Aboard other steamboats, we heard news of dream wars in impossible Indias. And, hearing about those places, we had inopportune regrets for our own country, which remained so distant behind us – who knows if it was even in this world.

❄

And so I hide behind the door, in order that Reality, when it enters, will not see me. I hide under the table, where suddenly I startled Possibility. In such a way that I hid myself, as if from the two arms of a hug, from the two major boredoms which throttled me – the boredom of only being able to live the Real, the boredom of only being able to conceive the Possible.

So I triumph over the whole of reality. Sandcastles, my victories? Made out of what essential divine substance are those castles not made out of sand?

How do you know if, travelling in that way, I did not obscurely follow myself?

Infantile in my absurdity, I relive my childhood and I play with the ideas of things like tin soldiers, with which, as a child, I made things which clashed with the very idea of a soldier.

Drunk on my mistakes, for a few seconds I lose the feeling of being alive.

❧

For the majority of mankind, life is a crashing bore, lived without any attention being paid to it, a sad object punctuated by happy intervals, something like the pauses for jokes which embalmers make to break the tranquillity of the night and their duty to keep vigil. It has always seemed to me to be inane to consider life as a vale of tears: it is a vale of tears, yes, but how rarely are tears shed in it. Heine says that, after the great tragedies, we always end up with a handkerchief. As a Jew, and so universal, he saw with clarity the universal natural side of humanity.

Life would be intolerable if we were conscious of it. Happily, we are not. We live with the same unconsciousness as animals, in the same futile vain way, and if we think in advance about death (which they, in all probability, without being dogmatic, do not do), we think about it through the veils of so many oblivions, so many distractions and meanderings, that it can hardly be said we think about it at all.

So we live, and it is hardly a justification for imagining ourselves to be superior to animals. The unique thing which differentiates us from them resides in the external detail that we speak and write, that we possess an abstract intelligence to distract ourselves from possessing our concrete intelligence, and that we imagine impossible things. All these things, however, are accidents of our basic organism. To know how to speak and to write adds nothing new to our primeval instinct of living without knowing why. Our abstract intelligence is only useful for building systems, or ideas which are quasi-systems, which in animals is resumed by sleeping in the sun. Even our faculty of imagining the impossible perhaps is not exclusively ours as I have seen cats gazing at the moon, and perhaps it really was the moon they longed for.

The entire world, the whole of life is a vast network of the unconscious which operates via individual consciousnesses. Just as when you pass an electric current through two gases you obtain a liquid, so with two consciousnesses – the one of our concrete being and the one of our abstract being – by passing life and the world through them, you obtain a superior unconsciousness.

Happy, then, is he who does not think as he realizes by instinct and organic destiny that which we should realize by following a bias and a destiny, whether inorganic or social. Happy is he who is nearest to the animals, since without forcing himself, he is what we are after an imposed labour; for he knows the way to the house, which we do not find by taking imaginary paths, or, because, deeply rooted as a tree, he belongs to the landscape and consequently to beauty, and is not, like us, myths from the past, walk-on bit-part actors, costumed in uselessness and forgetfulness.

❧

The vulgar man, no matter how hard his existence may be, at least has the advantage of never thinking about it. To live life passing through it on the outside, like a cat or a dog, as do ordinary men, is to live life as life should be lived if it is to comprise the satisfaction of the cat and dog.

To think is to destroy. The very system of thought indicates this by thought itself, since to think is to decompose. If mankind knew how to meditate on the mystery of life, if it knew how to feel the myriad complexities which lie in ambush for the soul at each step of every deed, it would never act, nor would it even dare to live. Men would likely as not commit suicide from terror, like those who kill themselves to avoid being guillotined the following day.

❧

The persistence of instinct in the human race, filtered through the semblance of intelligence, is for me one of the most intimate and constant spectacles. The unreal camouflage of consciousness only throws into relief in my eyes that unconsciousness which wears no camouflage.

From birth to death, men live as slaves of the very exteriority of themselves, as do animals. Throughout their entire lives, they do not live, they vegetate, to a greater degree and with an added complexity. They follow certain guidelines without even knowing if they exist or not, nor that they follow them, and their ideas, feelings, acts are all unconscious – not that consciousness is lacking in men but because they do not have two consciousnesses.

Hazy intuitions about a lazy illusion – that is the lot, and no more, of the greatest men.

I follow, allowing my thoughts to roam at will, the banal history of banal lives. I see to what extent they are slaves of a subconscious temperament, of alien external circumstances, of the compulsions of familiarity, and which, in their very contact, by it and because of it, clash together like the empty shells of nuts.

How many times have I heard them repeating the same phrase which symbolizes all the absurdity, all the nothingness, all the verbal ignorance of life. It is the phrase they use in regard to some material pleasure: 'that's all one gets out of life...' Gets out of? In order to do what? To take it where? How sad it would be to wake them up from the dark with such a question. Only a materialist can utter such a phrase, as each

and every man who uses such language is, albeit unconsciously, a materialist. What does he imagine he is getting out
of life, such a man, and in what manner? Where does he think
he is going to carry off his pork chop, his red wine, and the girl
he picked up? Towards which heaven in which he does not
believe? To which land, where he will take with him only the
rottenness which was his larval life? I do not know any other
phrase so tragic, nor so openly revelatory of human humanity.
Plants would speak like that, if they could know that they
enjoyed the sun. Animals, inferior to men in their powers to
express themselves, would speak like that about their
somnambulistic pleasures. And who knows if I myself, who
speak at this time, and who write these lines with the vague
impression they may last – who knows if I, too, do not only
believe that the memory of having written them is that which
'I shall get out of life'. And, just as the useless corpse of the
common man is lowered into a common grave, so the corpse,
equally useless, of my tailor-made prose is lowered into
oblivion. The pork chop, the red wine, the pick-up of the other
– why then should I make fun of it?

Brothers in a shared ignorance, two differing issues of the
same blood, diverse types of the same inheritance – which of
us could repudiate the other? One can repudiate one's wife, but
not one's mother, father or brother.

❧

We never love anybody. We simply love the idea we have of
somebody else. What we love in the end is a concept forged by
us which is ourselves.

This is true for all types of love. In sexual love, we seek our
own pleasure vehiculed by another's body. In non-sexual love,
we seek our own pleasure vehiculed by one of our ideas. The
onanist is abject but, in perfect logic, he is the perfect logical
expression of the lover. He uniquely does not cheat either the
other or himself.

The relationship between one soul and another, via such
uncertain things as our usual language and gestures, is a

subject of bizarre complexity. In our own act of self-knowledge, we mislead ourselves. Both say 'I love you', or they think it, and feel it reciprocally, and each one wishes to express a different idea, a different life, perhaps even a different colour or perfume, in that abstract mass of impressions which constitutes the activity of the soul.

I am today as lucid as if I did not exist. My thought has a skeleton's clarity, without the casual rags which give the illusion of expression. And these thoughts, which I have only to abandon them, have been born out of nothingness – in any case out of nothing visible on the stage of my consciousness. Perhaps that deception which the accountant had with his girlfriend, or a sentence read in the love stories newspapers print, taken from foreign ones, or perhaps even some vague distaste which torments me and I do not manage to rid myself of physically . . .

He was wrong, that scholiast of Virgil. It is above all of understanding that we tire. To live is not to think.

❧

I do not believe out loud in animals' happiness, except on the occasions it amuses me to speak of it in order to underline a feeling to which that hypothesis gives some relief. To be happy, it is necessary to know what happiness means. There is no happiness in dreamless sleep, but, on awakening, when one realizes that one has slept without them. Happiness is found outside happiness.

Happiness does not exist without knowledge. But the knowledge of happiness is in itself unhappy; for to know oneself to be happy is also to see oneself having moments of happiness and to be obliged, consequently, to leave them behind us immediately. To know is to kill, in happiness as in all the rest. And yet, not to know is not to exist.

Only Hegel's absolute has managed, at least in his writings, to be both things at the same time. Being and non-being neither mingle nor commingle in the feelings and rationality of life: they are mutually exclusive by means of an inverted synthesis.

What's to be done? To isolate the moment like an object, and to be happy in the present, at the very instant we experience happiness without thinking beyond what we feel, excluding the rest, all the rest. To imprison our thought in feeling . . .

The open maternal smile of the fecund earth, the opaque splendour of a misty sky . . .

There you have my afternoon's opinion. Tomorrow morning it will be different since, tomorrow morning, I shall be an other. What opinions shall I hold tomorrow? I have no idea, since, to know that, it would already have to be tomorrow. Even that eternal God, in whom I believe today, will never know it, either tomorrow or today, for today I am and perhaps tomorrow he will never have existed.

The more we advance in life, the more we convince ourselves of two truths which, however, are contradictory. The first one is that, faced with reality, all the fictions of art and literature turn pale. Certainly, they provide us with nobler pleasures than those of real life; after all, they are like those dreams during which we experience feelings we do not have in life and we see an intermingling of forms which do not occur in life; all things taken into consideration, they are dreams out of which we wake, leaving us neither those memories nor those regrets with which we later live a second life.

The other idea is that, as every noble soul aspires to run the entire distance of life and to experience all things, all places, all feelings susceptible of being lived and, since that is not possible – then life in its entirety can only be lived subjectively and only by negation can it be lived entirely.

It is impossible to reconcile these two truths. The wise man will abstain from attempting to conjugate them, and equally from rejecting either one or the other. Nevertheless, he will be obliged to opt for one or the other, with eternal regrets towards the one he did not choose; or else he will have to reject both of them by lifting himself up into a private nirvana.

Happy those who ask no more from life than that which it

spontaneously offers and follow the example provided by the feline instinct, looking for the sun when it shines, and in its absence for warmth wherever it can be found. Happy are those who renounce their personalities for imagination and create their joys from the spectacle of others' lives, living out not its impressions but its totally exterior representations. Happy, finally, is he who renounces everything, and from whom, since he has renounced everything, nothing can ever be taken away or subtracted.

The peasant, the reader of novels, the pure ascetic – those three know happiness, since all of them abnegate their personalities: the first one as he lives by instinct, the second as he lives by imagination, which is oblivion, the last as he does not live and, without being dead, sleeps.

Nothing satisfies me, nothing consoles me and I am sated with everything – whether it has existed or not. I do not want to have a soul and I do not want to renounce having one. I desire that which I do not desire and renounce that which I do not possess. I am the bridge spanning that which I do not love and that which I do not want.

❧

To recognize reality as a form of illusion, and illusion as a form of reality is equally vital and equally futile. Contemplative life, if it wants to have an existence, must look on objective events as being the scattered premises of a conclusion which remains inaccessible to it; but, simultaneously, it should consider the contingencies of dreams as being worthy, up to a certain point, of the attention we pay them and which consequently renders us contemplative.

Everything may be thought of as either a wonder, or as a bore, as an entirety or as nothingness, as a path or as a preoccupation. To consider these things each time in a different fashion is to renew them and to multiply them by their own factor. That is why a contemplative spirit, which has never left its village, has notwithstanding the entire universe as its beck and call. Infinity can be found either in a cell or in the desert. We may sleep a cosmic sleep with our heads resting on a stone.

However, during our reflections, it occurs – as it occurs to anyone who has the slightest thoughts – that everything seems to us to be wasted, old, seen over and over again even if we have never seen it in our lifetime. The reason is that, however intensely we may think about something, transforming it by our thoughts, we shall never ever transform it into anything else but the object of our meditation. At that moment, one feels a violent desire for life, a longing to know otherwise than by knowledge, to think only with our senses, and to think on a tactile or sensory level from the interior of the object under consideration, as if we were the water and it the sponge. Then we have also our night, and the fatigue of every emotion is more intensified than when it is a question of the emotions of thoughts, which are already profound enough. But it is a night without rest, without a moon, without stars, a night where it seems that the universe has been turned inside out – the infinite restricted and pent up, the day transformed into the black lining of an unknown garment.

It is better, yes indeed, better always to be a human slug which loves in ignorance, the leach which is repellent without knowing it. Let life be ignorance! Let oblivion be feeling! So many events lost in the green-white wake of sunken ships, like the icy spray off the lofty rudder which stands in for a nose below the eyes of the ageing cabins!

The entire life of the human soul is a movement in the shadow. We live in the chiaroscuro of consciousness without ever finding ourselves in agreement with what we are or what we are supposed to be. The best ones among us harbour the vanity of something, and there is an error whose orientation we ignore. We are something which takes place between the acts of a play; from time to time we may glimpse through certain doors that which might not always simply be the décor. The whole world is in confusion like voices lost in the night.

I have just re-read and questioned these pages on which I have annotated my life with a clarity which is perpetually there. What is all this? What use is it? Who am I, when I feel? What thing am I in the process of dying, since I am?

As a man from a great height might attempt to distinguish living creatures below in a valley, so I contemplate myself from the top of a mountain peak, and I am, like all the rest, a confused and indistinct landscape.

It is during these hours when an abyss gapes wide in my soul that the most insignificant detail manages to depress me like a letter of *adieu*.

I find myself perpetually to be on the point of waking up, I suffer the envelopment of my self, smothered by conclusions. I would gladly shriek, if my wailing reached somewhere. But I am plunged in a profound sleep which slithers from one feeling to another like a succession of clouds – those clouds which sprinkle green and sun colours over the grass spotted by the shadows of never-ending prairies.

It might be said that, on tip-toe, I am looking for an object hidden I know not where and which nobody had told me anything about. We are playing at hide-and-seek with no one. Somewhere else exists a transcended subterfuge, a divinity both fluid and only audible.

Yes, I re-read those pages which represent pathetic hours, some small moments of relaxation or illusion, mighty hopes deviated towards a landscape, sadnesses similar to rooms into which no one enters, certain voices, an immense fatigue – the gospel which has to be written.

Each one of us has his own vanity and that vanity consists of forgetting that others exist and have souls like ours. My vanity is these scanty pages, a few passages, the odd doubt ...

I re-read? I lie! I do not dare to re-read. I am incapable of re-reading. What point in re-reading? He who is here is an other. Already, I understand nothing further. . .

My head aches and the universe with it. The pangs of physical pain are more acute than moral pain – causing, by their reflections in our soul, tragedies alien to them. They provoke a generalized impatience, which, encompassing everything, does not even exclude a solitary star.

I do not subscribe, never have, and never will I imagine, to the mongrel idea according to which, by our quality of possessing souls, we are the result of some material thing called the brain, which, since our birth, is situated in another equally material thing, called the skull. I am unable to be a materialist which is apparently the label attached to those ideas, since I cannot establish any clear relationship – any visual relationship, if I may so put it – between a visible mass of grey matter or of any other colour, and that thing which, behind my eyes, can see and think sky, or even can imagine skies which do not exist. And yet, even if I shall always avoid falling into the trap of believing that one thing can simultaneously be another, for the simple reason they are both in the same place (like a wall with my shadow on it), or to conceive for myself that the dependence of the soul on the brain is anything but my own dependence, as regards the journey I intend to make, on the vehicle which transports me; despite all, I consider that there exists between that which is pure mind in us and that which is equally the mind of the body, a relationship of a shared life in which disputes can arise. And, as a general rule, it is the more vulgar side which aggresses the other.

I have a headache today, perhaps one which pains me from the stomach. But that pain, proposed by the stomach to my head, is in the process of interrupting the thoughts which I have at the back of my head. What blindfolds me does not blind me it merely prevents me from seeing. And just so, because of the fact that I have a migraine, I act out without competence or nobility the spectacle, momentarily absurd and monotonous, of that external object which I have difficulty in imagining to be a world. I have a headache which means that I am conscious of the harm done to me by material things and which, like all harmful actions, goads me into a foul temper with all the world, including those in my immediate environment who have done me no harm.

I really long to die, at least temporarily, but, as I said, it is only because I have a migraine. And, abruptly, it crosses my mind that a great writer would phrase that in a far nobler way. He would develop, in sentence after sentence, the anonymous suffering in the world; before his eyes which create paragraphs would emerge suddenly, in their diversity, the human dramas played out on the earth, and, beneath the throbbing of his fevered brow, he would construct on paper an entire meta-physical system of unhappiness. But I, doubtless, have no nobility of style. My head aches because I have a headache, the universe pains me because my head causes me pain. But the universe which really causes me pain is not the real one, the one which exists since it ignores my existence, but the other, my universe which, if I run my hands through my hair, gives me the impression that each and every single hair suffers with the unique aim of making me suffer.

❧

Sometimes, I do not know why, I feel brushed by a presentiment of death. Whether it is an ill-defined sickness not concretized in pain and so tends to be spiritual, or whether it is an exhaustion so profound that it necessitates such deep sleep that mere sleeping is not sufficient – what is certain is that I have the impression of being a sick patient whose condition has taken a turn for the worse and who, at the last moment, relaxes unviolently and without regrets his feeble hands which clenched the counterpane as if it too was provided with feelings.

So then I ask myself what is this thing we call death. I do not mean the mystery of death which I cannot enter into, but the physical sensation of ceasing to live. Humanity fears death, but in a confused way; the normal person defends himself quite well in practice; the normal man, whether ill or old, rarely contemplates in horror the abyss of nothingness which he attributes to that very same abyss. All that is a lack of imagination. It is equally sordid, on the part of a thinking being, to believe that death is sleep. Why on earth should it be, since it has nothing in common with it? The essence of sleep is that one wakes up out of it, whereas nobody, it seems, wakes up out of death. But if death resembles sleep, we could imagine then that we might wake up out of it. It is not at all that, despite everything, which the normal person imagines in fact, he imagines death to be a sleep from which no one wakes, which is a non-sense. As I said, death does not resemble a sleep out of which nobody wakes, as in sleep one is both alive and asleep; and I wonder how death can be compared to anything at all, since we cannot have either any experience of it, or have anything to compare it to.

In my case, when I see a dead body, death seems to me like a departure. The corpse gives me the impression of a suit one has left behind. Someone has departed without feeling the need to take with him his one and only suit of clothes.

❧

I have no idea of what time is. I ignore its true dimensions, if indeed it has any at all. I know that clock-time is wrong, dividing time spatially from the exterior. Emotional-time is wrong too: dividing not time but the impression of time. Dream-time is erroneous as well: in dreams we caress time, either in slow motion or at top speed, and what we live in them is fast or slow in accordance with a secret ebbing and flowing whose nature I ignore.

Sometimes, I believe everything is wrong, and that time is nothing more than the moulding framing what is alien to it. In my memories of my past life, time was disposed on absurd levels and planes, and I find myself being younger in such and such an episode when I solemnly celebrated my fifteenth birthday than in another episode from my infancy when I sat among my toys.

My consciousness is all confusion whenever I think about such things. I foresee a hitch somewhere, but I do not know where it is. It is as if I were watching a conjuring trick, before which I am fully aware that I am being fooled without being able to guess the machinery of the mechanism which fools me.

Then, absurd ideas fill my mind and I cannot get rid of them. And yet, I am incapable of seeing them as totally absurd. I wonder if the man who has sluggish thoughts in a fast-moving car, is actually going slowly or quickly. I wonder if both speeds would be equal in the case of a man committing suicide by leaping into the sea, and the man who lost his balance on the quayside. I wonder if those movements which occupy the same space of time are truly synchronous – for example, those during which I smoke a cigarette, write this page and have obscure thoughts.

Let us imagine two wheels on the same axis: it is possible to conceive that one is always ahead of the other, if only by a fraction of a millimetre. Under a microscope, that difference would be blown up to an incredible degree, even to an impossible degree, except that it is real. And why should the microscope not be right rather than my eyes? Are these futile considerations? I know them very well to be so. Speculative illusions? I grant you that. However, what is this thing which measures us without proportion and which kills us without existing? And it is in those moments when I ignore if time exists, that I feel like a human being and want to go to sleep.

No man understands another man. As the poet says, we are islands in life's oceans; between us flows the sea, defining and separating us. A soul might well try to know what another soul is, it will never know anything except what a word says – an amorphous shadow cast on the floor of its understanding.

I love expressions as I know nothing about what they express. I am like the Master of Santa Marta, I am content with what I am given. I see, and that is already a lot. Who is capable of understanding?

It is perhaps owing to my scepticism about what is intelligible that I regard in the same way a tree and a face, a poster and a smile. (All is natural, all is artificial, all is identical.)

What I see is for me that which is uniquely visible, whether it is a deep-blue sky, pale green with the approaching dawn, or whether it is the grimace deforming the face of someone publicly enduring the death of a loved one.

Dolls, engravings, pages which exist and revolve. My heart is not in them and my attention scarcely engaged by them; it is enough to walk over them from the exterior like a fly across a sheet of paper.

Is it that I only know if I feel, if I think, if I exist? None of that: nothing more than an objective scheme of colours, shapes, expressions of which I am the quivering mirror, not worth a penny.

❦

If there is one thing which this life offers us, and for which, apart from life itself, we should thank the gods, it is well and truly the gift constituted by our ignorance: since we ignore ourselves, and each one of us ignores the other. The human soul is a sombre, viscous abyss, an unused well on the earth's surface. Nobody could love himself if he really knew himself; and if vanity, the life-blood of spiritual life, did not exist, we would all perish from an anaemia of the soul. No man knows another, and it is all to the good, for, if he knew him, he would recognize in the other – whether it was a mother, wife or child – his personal metaphysical foe.

We understand each other because we ignore ourselves. What would happen to all those happy couples if only they could see into each other's souls, if they were capable of understanding each other, as the Romantics claim, who ignore the danger – even though it is a futile one – of what they are saying. Every married couple in the world is a badly married one, since each partner hides away, in the hidden recesses where our soul belongs to the Devil, the subtle image of the desired one who is not that other, the shifting image of the sublime woman which the other does not represent. The happiest ones do not perceive those frustrated compulsions in themselves; the less happy are conscious of them but do not, for all that, know them any better, and sometimes only a clumsy bout of enthusiasm or a vaguely brutal word can fortuitously bring to the surface of gestures and words the occult Demon and the antique Eve, the Knight and the Sylph.

The life we live is a fluid lack of comprehension, a joyful middle way between greatness, which does not exist, and happiness, which does not know how to exist. We are content because, even when thinking and feeling, we are capable of not believing in the soul's existence. In that masked ball where our life takes place, the pleasure in our costumes does not suffice, whereas at the ball they are all-important. We are slaves of colours and of lights, we enter the dance as if it were the truth, and there is for us – unless left aside we do not dance – no knowledge of the glacial cold of the outside night, of our mortal body underneath the rags which will outlive us, of everything which, alone by ourselves, we believe to be essentially us, but in the end is nothing but the intimate parody of the truth we ignore.

All that we may say and do, all that we may think or feel, wears exactly the same fancy dress. We can try to strip ourselves of our costumes, yet we shall never succeed in being naked, for nudity is a phenomenon of the soul and not a mere taking off of clothes. So, clothed with a body and soul, with our various costumes still sticking to us like feathers to birds, we live happy or unhappy, or without even knowing who we are, during that short span of time which the gods allow us for their amusement, like children playing grown-up games.

One or the other of us, free or damned, suddenly sees – and yet it is a rare occurrence – that all we are is precisely that which we are not, that we are in error in our most solid reasoning. And the man who, during a short time, sees the universe stripped bare, then creates a philosophy or dreams up a religion; and the philosophy spreads and the religion is propagated, and those who believe in the philosophy begin to wear it like an invisible coat, and those who believe in the religion begin to wear it like a mask of what they have forgotten.

And we continue on, in our ignorance of ourselves and of

others, and we get on happily with each other, using the rituals of the dance or of tranquil discourse, futile humans, seriously playing in tune with the huge orchestra of the stars, under the contemptuous, distracted gaze of the organizers of the spectacle.

Only they know that we are prisoners of the illusion they created especially for us. But the type of that illusion, and the reason why it exists, that or any other, or why for them too that illusion exists, even when giving us the fate which that illusion imposed on them – that, doubtless, they themselves ignore.

MAXIMS

To have definite, sure opinions, instincts, passions and a stable and known personality – all that leads to this appalling realization: that our soul is converted into a fact, a material, externalized object. To live is a sweet fluid state of ignorance of things and of oneself (it is the unique way of life which is fitting and which animates a sage).

– To know how to interject oneself unfailingly between objects and one's self constitutes the acme of wisdom and prudence.

– Our personality should be impenetrable, even for ourselves, hence our duty to dream ceaselessly, and to include ourselves in our dreams, in order that it will be possible for us to hold any opinion whatsoever about ourselves.

And above all we should avoid any invasion of our personality from the exterior. Any alien interest in us is an unqualifiable lack of delicacy. That which prevents the vulgar greeting – 'How are you?' – from being an unforgivable lack of manners is that in general it is entirely without meaning and insincere.

– To love is to be bored with being alone: it is therefore a type of cowardice, and a sort of betrayal towards ourselves (it is of the utmost importance not to love).

– Giving good advice is an insult to the faculty of ambiguity which God has granted to the other. And, above all, others' actions should keep the advantage of not being ours as well. It is more understandable to ask others for advice: in order, by doing the opposite, to achieve knowledge that we are precisely ourselves and in total disagreement with Otherness.

– The only advantage of study is to luxuriate in how little has been said by others.

– Art is isolation. Every artist must attempt to isolate himself from the others, and to give them the desire for solitude. The ultimate triumph of an artist occurs when, reading his works, the reader prefers to possess them but not to read them. It is not because that helps to consecrate them, it is because that is their finest attribute.

– Lucidity consists in being ill-disposed towards oneself. When one looks inside oneself, the state of mind one should legitimately discover is that one we experience when looking at our nervous indecisions.

– The only intellectual attitude worthy of a superior being is a tranquil and frigid compassion towards everything which is not himself. Not that such an attitude is in the least truthful or accurate, but it is so enviable that one should assume it entirely.

❧

The country is there where we are not. There, and there alone, are real shadows and real trees.

Life is a hesitation between an exclamation and an interrogation. In doubt there is a full stop.

Miracles are God's lethargies, or rather the lethargy we ascribe to him by inventing the miracle.

Gods are the incarnation of what we can never be.
This lassitude of all hypotheses ...

❦

Liberty is the possibility to isolate oneself. You are free if you can distance yourself from mankind without being obliged to search it out for financial reasons, or out of a gregarious compulsion, or from love, glory, curiosity, all of which can only find nourishment in solitude and silence. If it happens that you are unable to live alone, you were born a slave. You can possess every possible grandeur of the mind or all those of the soul: you are still a noble slave or an intelligent valet; you are not free. And that tragedy is not yours since the tragedy that you were born like that is not yours but Fate's, exclusively that of Fate. It is your curse, nevertheless, if life's oppressive quality, that very thing, compels you to be a slave. It is your curse if, having been born free, capable of being self-sufficient and distant from mankind, penury obliges you to live among men. That, yes, is your tragedy and you carry it with you.

To be born free is the ultimate greatness of man; that which makes a hermit superior to kings, and even to the gods, who are self-sufficient in strength, but not in their disdain for it.

Death is a liberation since to die is no longer to need anybody. The wretched slave sees himself liberated, by force, from his pleasures, from his afflictions, from his uninterrupted and yearned-after existence. The king sees himself freed from his dominions which he did not wish to renounce. Those who have scattered love everywhere see themselves liberated from the triumphs they adored. Those who have conquered see themselves freed from the victories to which their lives had been consecrated.

For those reasons, death ennobles, and clothes the poor absurd body in unknown formal dress. From now on it is free, even if it had no desire to be. From now on, it is no longer a slave, even if it has shaken off its servitude in waves of tears. Like a king whose major claim to fame is his title of being a king, and who may be laughable as a man, but as a king is superior – in his turn a dead man may be deformed, but is superior as he has been freed by death.

Exhausted, I close the outside shutters, excluding the world, and for a second I possess freedom. Tomorrow, I shall go back to being a slave; but, now, alone, not needing anybody, only afraid lest some voice or some presence comes and disturbs me, I have my small freedom, my moments of grandeur.

Comfortably installed in my chair, I forget the life which oppresses me. It causes me no pain except the pain of having wounded me.

❦

In the pagan era, the perfect man was the perfection of man as he is; for Christians, the perfect man was the perfection of man as he is not; for the Buddhist, the perfect man is the perfection of not existing as a man.

Nature is the difference between the soul and God.

All that a man explains or expresses comprises a note in the margin of a totally erased text. To a greater or lesser extent, given the meaning of the note, we can deduce what should have been the sense of the text; but a doubt is always present and the possible senses multiple.

❦

Since the middle of the eighteenth century, a horrific illness has gradually descended on our civilization. Seventeen centuries of Christian aspiration constantly thwarted, seventeen centuries of pagan aspirations perpetually postponed. Catholicism failing as Christianity, the Renaissance failing as paganism, the Reformation, finally, failing to be a universal phenomenon. The cataclysm of all our dreams, the shame, the shame of all that we had achieved, the abject condition of living a life unworthy to be shared with others, and that non-life of others which we cannot decently even share . . .

All that descended into our souls and poisoned them. The aversion to action, only vile in a vile society, invaded our minds. The higher activity of the soul is perishing; only inferior activity with its greater vitality survives intact; the former having become totally inert, the latter assumes the regency of the world.

Thus, an art and a literature were born, composed of the secondary components of thought – romanticism; and so was born a social life compounded of the secondary components of activity – modern democracy.

Souls destined for leadership had no other alternative but to abstain. Souls destined for creation, inside a society where creative forces were doomed to failure, did not in fact discover any plastic universe capable of being modelled as they wished except in the social world of their dreams and in the sterile introspection of their souls.

We apply the word 'romantic' not only to the great ones who failed, but also to the lesser ones who revealed themselves. In fact, they only have one thing in common: their blatant sentimentality; but for some, sentimentality underlines the impossibility of their using their intelligence actively; for others, it underlines the absence of intelligence itself. A Chateaubriand, a Hugo, a Vigny and a Michelet are the products of the same era. But Chateaubriand is a great soul which has shrunk; Hugo is a mediocre one billowing in the wind of his time; Vigny had genius but was obliged to flee; Michelet is a woman who has seen herself forced into becoming a man of genius. As for the father of them all, Jean-Jacques Rousseau, in him we find both tendencies reunited. In his case, intelligence was that of a creator, sensitivity that of a slave. He affirms both with equal force. But then social conscience raises its head to poison his theories which his intelligence has striven to arrange with clarity. His intellect only served to bewail the horror of coexisting with such a conscience.

J.-J. Rousseau is modern man, but more complete than any modern man. Out of those very flaccid weaknesses condemning him to failure, he knew – for his misfortune and ours – how to find sufficient strength to triumph. What he spawned triumphed, but on the victorious banner, when it entered a city, the word 'rout' was clearly legible. What he left behind, too feeble to triumph, were the sceptres and the crowns, the majesty of commanding and the glory of victory for internal usage.

The world in which we were born suffers, at one and the same time, from renunciation and violence – the renunciation of higher beings and the violence of inferior ones, which is their victory.

No higher quality can affirm itself in modern times, either in action or in thought, either in the political sphere or in the speculative one.

The decline of aristocratic patronage has created an atmosphere of brutality and indifference towards the arts, where no lover of form can find refuge. The contact of the soul with life hurts more and more each time. Efforts are more and more painful as their exterior conditions are more and more hateful.

The decline of classical ideals has rendered everybody a potential artist and, consequently, a bad one. When the criterion of art was a solid base, scrupulous adherence to the rules, few could attempt to be artists, and the majority of those who did were good ones. But when art turned into being the expression of one's feelings, every Tom, Dick and Harry could become an artist since all of them had feelings.

❧

More than once, as I gently strolled through the streets in the afternoon, I have been hit with a terrifying, abrupt violence by the extremely bizarre presence of the way things are organized. It is not so much natural things which create that weighty impression, as, on the contrary, street crossings, street signs, people dressed from top to toe speaking to each other, trades, newspapers, the intelligence of things. Or rather, to be more accurate, it is the very existence of those streets, of those shop signs, of those occupations, man and society – of all that is effortlessly in harmony with the other, following its path and discovering new ones.

I think straight away of mankind, and see that it is as unconscious as a cat or dog; if it speaks, it is with an unconsciousness of a different order, completely inferior to that practised by ants and bees in their social organization. And then, as far as and better than via the existence of organisms, as far as and better than via the existence of rigid physical laws, I see revealed to me in the clearest of lights the intelligence which creates and permeates the world.

At that moment I am struck, every time I have that impression, by the phrase of some scholastic or other: *Deus est anima brutorum*, 'God is the soul of animals.' The author of that wonderful remark wished to explain the sureness of the instinct which guides inferior beasts, in which there is no sign of intelligence, or nothing more than a hint of it. But we are all inferior animals – to speak and to think are nothing more than new instincts, less sure than the others as they are recent. And the scholastic's phrase, so accurate in its elegance, continues by saying: 'God is the soul of everything.'

I have never understood that anyone who has once considered the vast clockwork of the universe could possibly deny the existence of the clockmaker in whom even Voltaire did not refuse to believe. I do understand that. If one takes into consideration certain facts which apparently diverge from a pre-established order (but first one has to know what that order is if one is to know if the facts diverge from it), one can attribute to that supreme intelligence a certain element of imperfection. I understand that without accepting it. I also understand that, if one takes into account the evil which exists in the world, one cannot postulate infinite goodness as an attitude of that creative intelligence. I understand that too without accepting it either. But to deny the existence of that intelligence, that is, the existence of God, seems to me to be one of the lunacies which so often afflicts a part of men's brains, men who for the rest could easily be superior – just like people who make errors of calculation, or, also (to bring into play the intelligence of sensibility), are sensitive neither to music, nor painting, nor poetry.

As I said above, I do not accept either the argument of the

imperfect watchmaker, or that of the evil one. I do not accept the argument of the imperfect watchmaker as those details of order and organization in the world, which appear to us to be lapses and absurdity, cannot be judged as such if we do not possess knowledge of the overall scheme. We see with clarity a plan in everything; we see certain things which seem to lack reason, but we should take into account that, if reason exists for the creation of all things, then it exists in those absurdities as it does in all the rest. We see the reason but not the plan; how then can we affirm, consequently, that certain things do not conform to a plan about which we are totally ignorant? Just as a poet in a subtle rhythmic way may slip in an arhythmical verse for rhythmic reasons, that is to say, in order to achieve precisely the aim he seems to shun, and those critics who yet again are over-attached to a rectilineal purism rather than to rhythm itself will not fail to find fault with that verse – so the Creator may slip in something which our narrow-minded reason considers to be arhythmical in the majestic flow of his metaphysical verse.

As I said, I do not accept the hypothesis of the evil-minded clockmaker. I agree that it is a more difficult argument to refute, but only on the surface. We can safely say that we do not really know what evil is, so we can scarcely affirm whether something is good or bad. However, what is certain is that any pain (even if it is for our own good) is a bad thing in itself; and that is sufficient for evil to exist. A raging toothache suffices for us not to believe in the Goodness of the Creator. But the essential weakness of the argument seems to reside in our total ignorance of the divine plan, and our equally total ignorance of what might possibly be, for an intelligent person, intellectual infinity. The existence of evil is one thing, the reason for its existence another. And yet the distinction is sufficiently subtle as to appear a sophism, but it is true beyond all doubt – the existence of evil cannot be doubted, but the evil of the existence of evil may be refuted. I allow that the problem remains because our imperfection remains.

❧

What a painfully crass error is that distinction, established by revolutionaries, between the bourgeoisie and the people, or the nobility and the people, or between rulers and ruled. The distinction does exist between those who are apt and those who are inapt; the rest is literature, and bad literature. The beggar, if he has adapted, can be king tomorrow, no doubt; by becoming king he has forfeited the virtue of being a beggar. He has crossed the border and has lost his nationality.

This comforts me in this narrow office, whose badly washed windows give on to a gloomy street. It comforts me for I have for brothers the creators of the world's conscience – from the excitable playwright William Shakespeare, to the school-master John Milton, to the vagabond Dante Alighieri . . . and even, if one may cite him, including Jesus Christ who was so little in life that history doubts his existence. The others come from a different race – the government minister Johann Wolfgang Goethe, the senator Victor Hugo, the leader Lenin, the leader Mussolini.

We, in the shadows, between the dockers and the hair-dressers, constitute humanity.

On one side there are kings with their prestige, emperors with their glory, geniuses with their auras, saints with their halos, the village mayors with their power, the prostitutes, the prophets and the rich . . . We are on the other side . . . , the excitable playwright William Shakespeare, the barber with his funny stories, the schoolmaster John Milton, the little shop-keeper, the vagabond Dante Alighieri, those whom death forgets or consecrates and whom life has forgotten without consecrating them.

❧

Context is the heart of the matter. Everything has its own expression, and that expression comes from the outside.

Everything is the intersection of three lines, and those three lines form a thing: a quantity of matter, the way we analyse it and its context. This table, which I write at, is a block of wood, a table and a piece of furniture among the others in the room.

My impression of this table, if I wished to translate it, would have to be made up of the various concepts: that it is made out of wood, that I name such an object a table, attributing to it certain uses and purposes, and that in it are reflected and included, by transforming it, the objects which, by their juxtaposition, bestow on it an outside soul, just as do the objects placed on it. Even the colour it has acquired, today somewhat faded, and including the stains and scratches – all that, please note, came from the outside, and it is that, more than its essence as a piece of wood, which provides it with a soul. And the most intimate part of that soul, which is to be a table, was provided as well by that outside thing which is personality.

So, I believe that it is neither a human nor a literary error to attribute a soul to objects we call inanimate. To be a thing is to be the object of an attribution. Nevertheless, it would be false to say that a tree has a soul, that a river 'runs', that an event is sad, or that the sea is calm (its blue coming from the sky it does not possess), is smiling (smiling because of the sunlight which is exterior to it). But it is equally erroneous to attribute beauty to anything at all. It is equally false to attribute to anything colour, shape and perhaps even existence. This sea is salt water. This sunset is the moment when the sunlight begins to fade, on such a latitude and longitude. This child playing in front of me is an intellectual mass of cells – or even better, a watch mechanism of sub-atomic particles, a bizarre electric conglomeration of millions of miniaturized solar systems.

All arrives from the outside and in turn the human soul is nothing more perhaps than this ray of sunlight which shines on and distinguishes, from the ground where it lies, this heap of manure which is our body.

It is conceivable that one might find a philosophy among all these considerations, provided one had the strength to draw conclusions from them. I no longer have; I can see springing to mind vague ideas with certain logical possibilities, and all turns hazy in a vision of a ray of sunlight which gilds a heap of manure like a pile of damp straw obscurely flattened, lying on the blackened earth next to a clumsily constructed wall.

I am like that. When I want to think, I see. Whenever I want to plumb the depths of my soul, I halt, after a short period of abstraction, on top of the massive spiral staircase, gazing through the open window on the top floor at the sun whose farewell stains with wild dyes the confused pile of roofs.

❦

Metaphysics have always seemed to me to be a prolongation of latent madness. If we could know the truth, we would see it; the rest is nothing but schemas and curlicues. If we think about it, the incomprehensibility of the universe is quite enough; to want to understand it is to be less than a man, since to be a man is to know that it is not understandable.

They offer faith to one like a beautifully wrapped, alien present. They would like us to accept it, without our opening it. They offer us science, like a knife on a plate, to cut the pages of a blank book. They offer us doubt, like dust at the bottom of a box, but why do they offer the box if it contains nothing but dust?

From lack of knowledge, I write; and I employ fine words, alien to truth, according to the needs of my emotions. If the emotion is fatally clear, I speak, naturally, of the gods, and so I frame it inside a consciousness of a multiple world. If the emotion is thought, I speak, naturally, about Fate and so I nail it to the wall.

Sometimes, the very rhythm of the phrase will preconize gods and not God; other times, the two syllables of gods* impose themselves, and verbally I change worlds; other times, the need for an internal rhyme imposes itself, a staggering of the rhythm, an emotional somersault, and polytheism or monotheism follow by necessity and each one in turn has my preference. Gods are a function of style.

❦

---

* *Deuses* in Portuguese has two syllables.

173

Man has very often been defined, and nearly always in opposition to animals. Which is why one frequently finds, in the definitions of man, expressions such as: 'man is an animal ...' followed by an adjective, or 'man is an animal which ...' and we are told what. 'Man is a sick animal,' Rousseau says, and it is partly true. 'Man is a rational animal,' according to the Church, and it is partly true. 'Man is a tool-using animal,' according to Carlyle, and it is partly true. But all those definitions, and others like them, are always incomplete and marginal. And the reason is extremely simple: it is not easy to distinguish man from the animals, there is no sure criterion to distinguish one from the other. Human life passes in the same intimate lack of consciousness as animal life. The identical, deeply rooted laws which govern from the outside animal instinct, govern equally from the exterior man's intelligence, which appears to be nothing but embryonic instinct, as unconscious as any other instinct, and less perfect since still incomplete.

'Absurdity is the mother of invention,' we read in the *Greek Anthology*. And, in truth, all comes from absurdity. Apart from mathematics, which are only concerned with dead numbers and empty formulae, and for that reason can be perfectly logical, science is nothing more than a child's game at dusk, as if one wanted to grasp the shadows of birds and to freeze the shadows of grass in the wind.

And it is both odd and strange to see that, if it is not easy to find the words which really define man in distinction from animals, on the other hand, it is easy to find a way to distinguish the superior man from the common creature.

I have never forgotten that remark made by Haeckel, the biologist, which I read in the infancy of my intelligence, when one loves reading popular books which attack religion. The remark is more or less as follows: 'A superior man is far more distant [citing, I believe, a Kant or a Goethe] from a common man than a common man is from a monkey.' I have never forgotten that remark, because it is true. Between me, who am very small fry in the order of thinkers, and a peasant from Loures there is, no doubt, a greater distance than between him and not even a monkey but rather a cat or a dog. Not one of us, from the cat and including me, controls the life imposed on him, or the destiny he has been given; all of us are drifting away from something or other, shadows of gestures accomplished by somebody else, incarnate effects, consequences doted with the faculty of feeling. But, between the peasant and me, there is a qualitative difference, owing to the presence in me of abstract thought and disinterested emotion; whereas, between him and the cat, there is nothing more than a difference of degree as far as the mind is concerned.

Superior men differ from ordinary men and from their animal brothers in virtue of the simple capacity for irony. Irony is the prime index that the conscience has become conscious of itself. And irony has two stages: the one exemplified by Socrates when he says, 'I only know that I know nothing,' and the other exemplified by Sanchez* when he says, 'I do not even know if I know nothing.' The first stage reaches the point where we doubt ourselves dogmatically, and every superior man attains that level. The second arrives at the point when we doubt both ourselves and our doubt, and very few have attained that during that brief, but already too long, span of time which we, humanity, have seen alternating the day and the night on the variegated surface of the earth.

To know oneself is to err, and the oracle which said 'Know thyself' proposed a labour greater than those of Hercules and an enigma more obscure than that of the Sphinx. To ignore oneself consciously, that is the road to take. To ignore oneself consciously is to employ irony actively. I know nothing greater nor more specific of the truly great man than the patient analysis of the unconsciousness of our consciousnesses, the metaphysics of autonomous shadows, the poetry of the dusk of disillusion.

But something always annoys us, always deadens our analysis; always the truth, though false, is further away than the next corner. And it is that which exhausts me more than life, when it exhausts me, and more than our knowledge and reflection which never cease to exhaust us.

---

* A sixteenth-century Portuguese philosopher.

I get up out of my chair in which, distractedly leaning on the table, I amused myself by recounting to myself these disparate impressions. I get up, making my body erect inside itself, and I go over to the window which opens out over the roofs and from which I can see the city tottering off to sleep in a sluggish onset of silence. The moon, full and white with whiteness, sadly elucidates the camouflaged differences between the houses. And the clarity of the moonlight seems to illuminate, with its icy whiteness, all the mystery of the universe. It seems to hide nothing, and yet there is nothing but shadows welded from false light, deceptive intervals, absurd contours, incoherences of what is visible. There is no breeze, and the mystery appears all the greater. I am nauseated by abstract thought. I have never succeeded in writing one page which said something about myself or about anything at all. A wispy cloud floats over the moon, like a fugitive. I know nothing, like these roofs. I have failed, like the entire universe.

❦

The entire day, in its desolation of damp, insubstantial clouds, has been filled by the news of a revolution. This type of news, whether real or false, always inundates me with a special malaise, a mixture of disdain and physical nausea. It pains my intelligence that someone can imagine himself to be capable of changing anything at all through agitation. Violence, whatever it may be, has always been for me a haggard facet of human stupidity. In addition, all revolutionaries are as idiotic as are, to a lesser extent since less disturbing, reformers.

Whether a revolutionary or a reformer, the error is identical. Impotent to dominate and reform his own attitude towards life, which is vital, or his own self, which is nearly vital, mankind seeks a solution in striving to change others and the outside world. Every revolutionary, every reformer is an escaped convict. To fight is to be unable to fight oneself. To reform is to be incapable of self-improvement.

The man of accurate sensibility and correct reasoning, if he cares about evil and injustice in the world, first of all and quite naturally attempts to ameliorate what is nearest to him: that is to say – himself. That task will keep him occupied during his entire life.

For us, everything depends on our conception of the world; to modify that is for us to modify the world, since it will never be anything else than what it is for us. This personal justice, thanks to which we write a fine, flowing page, this pure reform via which we cause to relive our moribund sensibility – these things are the truth, our truth, the unique truth. The rest of the world is landscape, frames framing our sensations, book-bindings of what we think. And that is so, whether it is a question of a landscape coloured by things and people – plains, houses, posters and costumes – or whether it is a colourless landscape with monotonous beings, rising to the surface for a second, buoyed up by hoary words and exhausted gestures, only to sink back immediately down into the silt of the fundamental idiocy of human expression.

Revolution? Change? All that I truly desire in the entire intimacy of my soul is that these neutrally coloured clouds, which coat the sky with a soapy grey undercoat, vanish; what I long to see is the blue bursting out from in between them, clear certain truth as it is nothing and desires nothing.

PRONUNCIAMENTO OF DIFFERENCE

Matters of state or urban considerations have no power over us. It is of no interest that ministers and civil servants dilapidate the nation's resources. All that happens outside somewhere, like mud on a rainy day. We have nothing to do with all that, and none of that has anything to do with us.

Likewise, we are not interested in major upheavals, such as wars or national crises. As long as they do not cross our thresh-hold, we care little at which door they knock. That, which apparently is based on a gigantic disdain for others, in reality is based on our own rather sceptical opinion of ourselves.

We are neither do-gooders nor over-beautiful – not because we are the opposite, but because we are neither one nor the other. Goodness is the delicate facet of vulgar beings. It only interests us in so far as it is a phenomenon occurring in beings different from us, with other forms of thought. We observe, neither approving nor bothering to disapprove. Our function is to be nothing.

We would have been anarchists if we had been born in those classes which call themselves underprivileged, or in any other from which one can rise or fall. But, in truth, in general we are creatures born in the interstices of social class and division – practically always in that decadent gap between the aristocracy and the upper middle class, that social stratum belonging to geniuses and madmen with whom one can sympathize.

Action disorientates us, partly owing to physical deficiency, but rather owing to moral anorexia. To act seems immoral to us. All thought appears degraded the minute it is put into words, so converting it into something which belongs to another, and which renders it comprehensible to those capable of understanding it.

Our sympathy for occultism and arcane acts is very great. And yet, we are not occultists. What is lacking to turn us into them is the innate will to become one and, in addition, the patience to educate our will, so converting it into the perfect tool for warlocks and hypnotists. But we have sympathy for occultism, principally because in general it expresses itself in such a way that the majority who read it, and those who believe they understand it, in fact understand nothing at all about it. That mysterious attitude is superbly superior. And, further, it is an abundant source of terror and mystery: astral larvae, bizarre creatures with different bodies evoked by ritual magic in temples, fleshless presences of matter operating on our plane, prowling around our paralysed senses in the physical silence of interior noise – all that caresses us like a revolting, viscous hand in the darkness of despair.

But we have no sympathy for occultists when they turn into proselytizers and lovers of humanity, that denudes them of their mystery. The unique reason for an occultist to operate on the astral plane is in the name of a superior aesthetic and not with the pathetic aim of doing good to his neighbour.

Almost without knowing it, we are caught up in an anecdotal empathy for black magic, for the forbidden forms of transcendental science, for the Lords of Power, who sold themselves into Damnation and degraded Reincarnation. Our vision, that of feeble and uncertain creatures, gets lost with a feminine jealousy in the theory of inverted degrees, in perverted rites, in the sinister curve of a descending hierarchy.

Against our will, Satan has a power of seduction over us, like that of the male over the female. The serpent of Materialistic Intelligence is coiled up inside our hearts, as he is round the cadences symbolizing the god of communication: Mercury, Lord of Comprehension.

There are some who are not pederasts but would like to have the courage to be. All lack of appetite for action inevitably feminizes. We have missed our true vocation of being house-wives and chatelaines. Left on the sidelines because of a sexual dysfunction in our present incarnations. Even though we do not totally believe in it, it smacks of an acerbic irony to pretend that we do not believe in it.

All that occurs not out of wickedness, but out of weakness. Alone with ourselves, we love evil, not because of evil in itself, but because it is stronger and more intense than good, and because all that is strong and intense attracts our sensibility which should have been that of womanhood. *Pecca fortiter* cannot apply to us since we lack the strength, even the strength of the intellect which is all we possess. To imagine colossal sins – is the utmost that can be signified to us by that acute injunction. But there are times when even that is denied us: our own interior life possesses a reality which at times wounds us owing to the unique fact it constitutes some reality or other. That laws exist to control the association of ideas, or all the other activities of the mind, is precisely what insults our native lack of discipline.

❦

If I scrutinize the life men lead, I find nothing in it which distinguishes it from that of animals. Both of them are tossed unconsciously right into the middle of things and of the world; both of them find occasional amusement; both of them daily accomplish the identical organic trajectory; both of them think no further than their thoughts, nor live further than their lives. A cat curls up in the sun and sleeps there. A man curls up in life and sleeps there. Neither one of them escapes the fatality of being what he is. Not one of them attempts to rid himself of the burden of living. The greater men love glory, but they love it not as a specific immortality but as an abstract one in which perhaps they do not even participate.

These elucubrations, frequent in my case, provoke a sudden admiration for that type of individual which instinctively I abominate. I refer to mystics and ascetics – to the hermits of all Tibets; to the Simeon Stylites of all columns. Those ones, albeit absurdly, try to escape from animal law; those ones, albeit through madness, try to deny the law of life, to coil up in the sun awaiting death without ever thinking about it. They search, albeit perched on the top of a column; they have desires, albeit from the depths of a dark cell; they lust for what they ignore, including an imposed martyrdom and the wounds inflicted on them.

All of us, living as animals with varying degrees of complexity, traverse the stage like silent walk-ons, content with the solemn vanity of the trajectory. Dogs and men, cats and heroes, fleas and geniuses, we play at existing, never thinking about it (for the best of us only think about thinking), under the mighty tranquillity of the stars. The others – the mystics of the fatal hour and of sacrifice – feel at least in their bodies and their daily lives the magical presence of mystery. They are free as they deny the visible sun; they are replete as they have emptied themselves of the world's vacuum.

I am almost a mystic, like them, when speaking about them, but I would be unable to go further than these words, written at the whim of an odd attraction. I shall remain for ever a man from Douradores Street – just like the whole of humanity. I shall always be – either in verse or in prose – an office clerk. I shall remain, in the mystical of the non-mystical, limited and cowed, slave to my sensations and to the moment I experience them. I shall always be, under the vast blue canopy of a silent sky, the acolyte in some incomprehensible ritual, clothed in life in order to celebrate it and accomplishing, without knowing why, certain gestures and errands, bowings and scrapings, until the feast is over (or my role in it) and I can go off and eat the party food in the big huts which are, they tell me, down there at the end of the garden.

❧

Ever since, as far as I was able, I came to reflect and observe, I have noticed that men recognize that truth is nothing, or are never in agreement about anything in any domain which is of capital importance in life or useful for living it. The most exact science is that of mathematics, which exists cloistered in its own rules and laws; certainly it is of help, in its applications, for the elucidation of other sciences, but it merely elucidates what they have already discovered; it does not help in the discovery. In the other sciences, nothing is sure and accepted except that which holds no interest whatsoever in regard to the supreme aims of life. Physics understands very well the coefficient of dilation of iron, but it does not know the true mechanism at work in the construction of the world. And the higher we climb towards what we could wish to know, the lower we sink down into what we know already. Metaphysics – which might be our supreme guide since it is this and this alone which is focused on the supreme aim of truth and life – does not even constitute a scientific theory, but a mere pile of bricks which make up, in the hands of this One or that One, shapeless, formless houses bound together without any mortar.

Furthermore, I notice that there is no other distinction between human and animal life but the fashion with which both of them make mistakes or errors. Animals know not what they do, they are born, grow, live and die without thought, without reflection, without any real future. But how many men live any differently from animals? All of us sleep and the one difference exists in our dreams, in respect to the intensity and quality they attain. Sometimes death comes and rouses us, but we have no reply to it either – except that of faith, for to believe is already to have it; that of hope, for to desire is to possess; or that of charity, for to give is to receive.

It rains, on this cold and sad wintry afternoon, as if it had been falling with the same monotony ever since the first page of the world. It rains and my feelings, as if the rain flattened them, multiply their stubborn gaze on the soil of the city, where runs a stream which nourishes nothing, washes nothing, makes nothing happy. It rains and abruptly I experience the immense oppressive burden of being an animal who does not know what he is, who dreams his thoughts and emotions, curled up, as if in a warren, in a special region of being, satisfied with a little warmth as if it were eternal truth.

❦

In every mind which is not abnormal there exists a belief in God. In every mind which is not abnormal, there exists no belief in a well-defined god. He is some entity or other, which exists and is impossible, regulating all things; whose personality, if he has one, cannot be defined; whose aims, if they exist, cannot be understood. By calling him God, we say everything, since the word God has no precise sense and so we can affirm him without saying anything. The attributes of infinity, eternal life, omnipotence, total justness and goodness, which we pin on him, fall off by themselves like all unnecessary adjectives when the noun suffices. And he, to whom, being indefinable, we cannot give attributes, is for that reason the absolute noun.

The same certitude and the same vagueness surround the problem of the soul's survival. We all know we will die; we all feel we will never die. It is not exactly a desire or a hope which provides us with that obscure intuition that death is a misunderstanding; it is a ratiocination made by our guts, which refuse . . .

The world belongs to those who feel nothing. The essential condition of being a practical man is the absence of sensibility. The principal quality in the practice of life is that which leads to action, that is to say willpower. Now, the things which put a break on action are sensibility and analytical thought, which itself is nothing more, after all, than thought doted with sensibility. All action is, by its nature, the projection of the personality on to the world outside, and as, for the most part, the exterior world is made up of human beings, it may be deduced that this projection of the personality succeeds essentially by blocking others' paths, by perturbing, wounding and crushing others, in function of our behaviour.

In order to act, it is vital then that we do not easily imagine others' personalities with their joys and their sufferings. If one sympathizes, one stops dead. The man of action sees the outside world as being formed exclusively of inert matter – either inert in itself like a stone he walks on or kicks out of his way; or inert like a human being who, not knowing how to resist him, might just as well be either a man or a stone, since he treats him the same way: either he kicks him aside, or he walks over him.

The ultimate example of the practical man, as it unites the extreme concentration of action with its extreme importance, is that of the strategist. The whole of life is a war, and hence the battle is the synthesis of life. Now, the strategist is a man who plays with human lives like a chess player with his pieces. What would become of the strategist if he thought that his every move brought night to a thousand homes and pain to three thousand hearts? What would become of the world if we were human? If mankind synthesized truth, there would be no civilization. Art serves as a bolt-hole for the sensibility which has persisted in forgetting action. Art is the Cinderella who stayed at home because it had to do so.

[. . .]

Today my employer, Vasquès, concluded a business deal which ruined a sick man and his family. While he was negotiating, he had entirely forgotten the other's existence except as an adversary on the commercial level. Once the deal was concluded, his feelings returned. Of course, only after-wards for if they had come back before, the deal would never have been struck. 'I'm sorry for that wretch,' he said to me. 'He's going to end up in the street.' Then, lighting a cigar, he added, 'Whatever happens, if he ever needs a favour from me' – meaning charity – 'I'll never forget I owe him for a good deal worth quite a packet.'

My employer Vasquès is no crook: he is a man of action. The one who lost his shirt can really count on his future charity, as my employer Vasquès is a generous man.

All men of action resemble my employer, Vasquès – presidents of industrial or commercial enterprises, politicians, military men, religious or social ideologues, great poets and painters, pretty women or spoilt children, who do exactly as they please. He who has no feelings gives orders. The one who wins only thinks about what is necessary to win. The remainder – that is to say humanity in general, the defined and amorphous, sensitive, imaginative and fragile – is only the backdrop against which are silhouetted the principal actors until the moment the whole Punch and Judy Show vanishes; it is simply the banal, flat chess-board where the chess pieces stand until they are taken by the Great Player who, using the stacked deck of his double personality, derives his amusement by always playing against himself.

ON THE ART OF DREAMING WELL

Put everything off. Never do today what can equally be neglected on the morrow.

There is no need to do anything, either today or tomorrow.

Never think about what you are going to do, don't do it.

Live your life. Do not let yourself be lived by it.

In truth as in falsehood, in pleasure and in boredom be your own self. You can only achieve this by dreaming, since your real-life, your human life is that which, far from belonging to you, belongs to others. So, you shall substitute dreams for life and only care about dreaming perfectly. In all your acts of real-life, including those from birth to death, you have not really acted: you were acted on; you did not live: you were merely alive.

Become a grotesque sphinx in the eyes of others. Lock yourself up, but without slamming the door, in your ivory tower. And your ivory tower will be your very self.

And if anybody were to tell you that all this is false and absurd, do not believe a word. But do not believe either what I say to you, because nobody should believe in anything.

(CHAPTER ON INDIFFERENCE OR SOMETHING LIKE THAT)

Every soul worthy of itself longs to live life to the Extreme. To be satisfied with what you have been given is to act like a slave. To ask for more is to behave like a child. To win a bit more is to be mad, as every conquest is . . .

To live life to the Extreme signifies living it to its limit, but there are three ways of going about it and it is every lofty soul's duty to choose the most suitable one. One can live life to the Extreme by possessing it to the utmost, via a Ulyssean periplus through every sensation one experiences, each and every form of exteriorated energy. However, very few are those, at every period of history, who can shut eyes weighed down by an exhaustion which is the sum of all exhaustions, those who have possessed everything in every possible way.

So, rare are those who can demand and obtain that life delivers itself up to them body and soul, and who know, by loving it without restraint, how not to be jealous of it. To be such ones, nevertheless, should be beyond all doubt the desire of every strong lofty soul. But whenever such a soul sees that such a desire cannot be realized, that he is lacking in strength to dominate all the facets of Everything, two other choices are open to him. One is complete renunciation, total rigorous abstention and rejection, in the realm of feelings, of that which it cannot possess in its entirety, in the realm of energetic activity. It is better, infinitely better, not to act rather than to act in vain. Fragmentarily, insufficiently, as does that idiotic, superfluous, overwhelming majority of the human race.

The other option is that of perfect balance, the quest for the limit in Absolute Proportion, because of which the burning desire for the Extreme passes from wilful emotion to Intelligence: the greatest ambition no longer consists of living a full life, nor of experimenting a full life, but of organizing a full life, accomplishing it in intelligent Harmony and Co-ordination.

The yearning to understand, which so often replaces in noble spirits the yearning to act, belongs to the sphere of sensibility. To substitute Intelligence for energy, to break the link between will and emotion, by stripping them of any interest in every act of naturalistic life, that is what, once obtained, is worth far more than life itself, so difficult to possess in its entirety and so sad to possess partially. The Argonauts said that it is necessary to navigate, but not to live. We, the Argonauts, with our sick sensibility, say that it is necessary to feel, but not to live.

❧

As I sometimes look over the abundant production or, at the worst, the finished writings of a certain length, of so many creatures I know or have heard about, I experience a certain vague envy, a disdainful admiration, an incoherent mixture of mixed feelings.

To complete anything entirely, whether good or bad – and, if it is never entirely good, often it is not entirely bad – yes, to achieve a completed thing inspires me, perhaps, more with envy than with any other emotion. It is like a child, it is imperfect, without doubt, like all human beings, but it is ours as children are.

And I, whose critical faculties only permit me to see the

defects, the omissions, I, who do not dare to write more than fragments, short passages, extracts of the non-existent, I myself, in the little I write, am also full of imperfections.

Consequently, the completed work, even if it is bad, nevertheless is a work, is worth more; or else, there is the absence of words, the total silence of the soul which knows itself to be incapable of action.

I sometimes wonder if everything in life is not the degeneration of something else. That being might only be an approximation – some vespers or other or some near miss.

Just as Christianity was never more than the prophetic degeneration of a humiliated neo-Platonism . . . the Romanization of a false Hellenism, as Roman as in our lives, is the multiple deviation of every important proposition, whether congruent or opposed, out of which has arisen the *summum* of negation in which we affirm ourselves.

We live as bibliophilia of the xeroglot.

[. . .]

❧

Since everything, perhaps, is not false, then let nothing, My Love, heal us of the quasi-spasmodic pleasure of lying.

The ultimate refinement! The acme of perversion! The absurd lie combines all the charm of the perverse with the final and greater charm of the innocent. Deliberately innocent perversion – can one go further in ultimate refinement? Perversion which does not aspire to produce pleasure for us, which has not the madness of making us suffer, which falls to earth between pleasure and pain, useless and absurd, like a badly made toy with which an adult would like to amuse himself!

And when lying starts to procure us pleasure, then let us tell the truth to give it the lie. And when it causes us anxiety, then let us cease lying as suffering does not have any meaning for us, nor does it perversely please us.

Have you no idea, Delicious One, of the pleasure in buying unnecessary things? Do you recognize the flavour of those paths which, in our distraction, we might take by mistake? Is there any human act which is so beautiful as those acts of counterfeiting which lie to their own nature and which disavow their own aims?

There is something sublime in wasting a life which might have had a utility, in never completing a work which would necessarily have been sublime, by abandoning halfway the assured path to success!

Ah, My Love, what a glory is that of lost works which will never be rediscovered, of treatises which today only retain their titles, of libraries reduced to ashes, of statues smashed to pieces!

How they are sanctified, in the kingdom of the Absurd, those artists who have burnt a splendid work, or who, capable of producing a masterpiece, have only produced a mediocre one on purpose, or those major poets of silence who, knowing that they could create an absolutely perfect work, have opted for the daring solution of never producing anything at all. (If it had been less than perfect, it would have been unacceptable.)

How much more beautiful the Mona Lisa would be if she were invisible! And if someone happened to steal and burn her, what an artist he would be, greater by far than even the one who praised her!

Why is art what is beautiful? Because it is useless. Why is life what is ugly? Because it is a tissue of aims, plans and intentions. All its roads are conceived to go from one place to another. What would I not give for a road leading to a place from which nobody ever arrives, towards a place towards which nobody ever goes.

How I would love to devote my life to the construction of a road which began slap in the middle of a field and went on to lose itself in the middle of another one; a road which, if prolonged, would be useless, but which would always be sublime, a half of a road.

The beauty of ruins? The fact they are of no use. The beauty of the past? That of recalling it, since to recall it is to make it present – that which it is not and never can be: absurdity, Love of Mine, absurdity.

And I who talk like this – why do I write such a book? Because I know it to be imperfect. Total silence would be perfection; once written, it unperfections itself; for that reason, I write it.

And, above all, because I defend what is useless, absurd – I write this book to lie to myself, to betray my own theory.

And the ultimate glory of all this, My Love, is to imagine that none of this is perhaps true, and I myself do not believe it to be so.

❧

Art consists in making others feel what we feel, in guarding them from themselves, by offering our own personality as a specific liberation. The sensation I feel, in the real matter with which I feel, is totally incommunicable; and the deeper I feel it, the more incommunicable it becomes. So, in order that I might transmit to an other what I feel, I am obliged to translate my feelings into his language, that is to recount things as if they were what I felt, so that, when he needs them, he feels exactly what I felt. And as that other, for reasons of aesthetics, is not such and such a person, but the whole world, what finally I am obliged to do is to convert my feeling into a typical human feeling, despite the fact that by doing so I pervert the true nature of what I feel.

Whatever is abstract is difficult to understand, since it is difficult to hold the reader's attention. I shall give a simple example which makes concrete the abstractions I formulated previously. Let us suppose that, for some reason or other (the tiredness of doing accounts or the boredom of having nothing to do), there descends on me a vague distaste for life, an anguish about myself which troubles and perturbs me. If I attempt to translate that feeling into sentences which describe it clearly, the better I describe it, the more I make it my very own, and, consequently, the less I transmit it to others. And, if it is not capable of being communicated to others, it is more decent and facile to feel it without describing it.

However, let us imagine that I want to communicate it to

189

other people, that is, to create a work of art from it, since art consists in the communication to others of our personal similarity to them; without that, there is no communication, nor any necessity to attempt it. So then I look for, among the range of human emotions, the banal one which represents the tone, the type, the form of emotion I experience at the time, for inhuman and entirely personal reasons because I am an accountant's clerk, or an inhabitant of Lisbon who is bored. And I realize that the type of banal emotion which produces, in banal souls, the identical emotion to mine, is the nostalgia for a lost childhood.

I have in my hand the key to open the door of my subect; I write about and deplore my lost childhood; I emotionally linger over details of people and furniture in that old provincial house; I evoke the joy of not having rights or obligations, of being free from knowing how to think or feel – and that evocation, if it is well done, in visionary prose, will arouse in my reader the exact emotion I experienced, and which has nothing to do with my childhood.

Did I lie? No, I understood. For lying, apart from the spontaneous infantile lie, born of the desire to dream while still awake – is simply the notion of the true existence of others, and of the necessity to harmonize our existence with it. Lying is quite simply the soul's ideal language, since just as we employ words, which are absurdly articulated sounds, in order to translate into a real language the shifts of our most subtle and intimate emotions and of our thoughts which of necessity cannot be put into words, so we employ lies and fictions in order to understand one another, which, if we used truth, distinct and incommunicable, we would never be able to do.

Art lies because it is social. And there are only two major forms of art: the first one which is orientated towards the depths of our soul; the other which is orientated towards our expectant soul. The former is poetry, the novel is the latter. The former starts to lie in its very structure; the latter starts to lie in its very aim. The one pretends to give us truth by means of lines varying in conformity to the rules, which give the lie to the essence of language; the other pretends to give us the truth by means of a reality which we all know never existed.

To feign is to love. I never see a pretty smile or a pensive look without immediately asking myself (and it is of little or no importance who is doing the smiling or the looking) who it is in the bottom of the soul of the person whose face is smiling or looking at me: is it a politician who wants to buy us; or the prostitute who wants us to buy her? But the corrupt politician is more or less enamoured of the act of buying us; and the prostitute is more or less enamaoured of the act of our buying her. We have no escape, no matter how much we may wish to, from universal brotherhood. We all love each other, and lying is the kiss we exchange.

❧

I have always felt disgusted when I read in Amiel's diary the allusions he makes to his published works. His statue immediately is broken. How much greater he would have been if he had not made these references!

Amiel's diary has always caused me pain – for reasons of my own.

When I came to the passage where he says that the fruit of the mind descended on him like 'the consciousness of the consciousness', I saw a direct reference to my soul.

❧

Many might think that this diary, written entirely for my benefit, is exaggeratedly artificial. But it is in my nature to be artificial. And then, how could I amuse myself if I did not edit these notes of my cerebral life? In addition, I do not even write them down carefully, nor do I group them together like an obsessional goldsmith. I naturally think in this refined language of mine.

I am a man for whom the exterior world is an internal reality. I feel this, not metaphysically, but with the normal feelings we use to apprehend reality.

My yesterday's frivolity is today an incessant nostalgia
eroding my life.

[...]

❧

The majority of mankind suffers from the lack of knowing
how to describe what it sees and thinks. It is said that there is
nothing more difficult than to describe a spiral in words: they
say that one should sketch in the air, with the hand, the
movement regularly coiled as it rises, with which that abstract
shape of millstones or certain staircases usually manifests
itself. Yet, if one always remembers that to describe is to
renew, we would have no difficulty in defining a spiral: it is a
circle which rises without ever being complete. The majority
of mankind, believe me, would never attempt such a description, since they imagine that to define is to say what
others want us to say, and not what should be said. Even better:
a spiral is a virtual circle which reproduces itself as it rises
without completion. But no, that is still an abstract definition.
If I took refuge in the concrete, and everything was clear: a
spiral is a serpent whose sinuosity coils vertically around
nothing at all.

The whole of literature is an attempt to make life real. As
everybody knows, even if we act in ignorance, life is totally
unreal in its direct reality; fields, cities, ideas are totally fictive
things, born of our complex realization of ourselves. All our
impressions are not capable of being communicated, unless
we make literature of them. Children are great writers as they
speak as they feel and not how they ought to feel, according to
others. One day, I heard a child say, trying to explain it was on
the verge of tears, not 'I long to cry', as an adult would say, that
is like an idiot, but instead 'I long for tears'; and that phrase,
which is pure writing, so much so that it would seem affected
if employed by a famous poet (if one could be found to write it),
makes a direct allusion to the burning presence of tears
swelling forth from under the eyelids, conscious of that bitter
liquid. 'I long for tears!' That young child perfectly described
his spiral.

To speak! To know how to speak! To know how to exist using the written voice and the intellectual image! Life is worth nothing more; the rest are men and women, imagined loves and false vanities, digestive subterfuges and those of oblivion, people who race around like insects when a stone is lifted, under the vast abstract rock of the unfeeling blue sky.

❀

Art frees us, in an illusory fashion, from that sordid thing which is life. As long as we feel the woes and affronts of Hamlet, Prince of Denmark, we do not feel our own – vile because they are ours, and vile because they are vile.

Love, dreams, drugs and opiates are elemental types of art, or rather, of producing a similar effect. But love, dreams and drugs have their own proper disillusionment. Love either bores or disillusions. One wakes from sleep, and when one slept one did live. Drugs' price is the ruin of the self-same organism they helped to stimulate. But there is no disillusion in art as illusion is permitted from the outset. There is no awakening from art as we do not sleep it, although we dream it. There is no tribute or fine to be paid in art because we took pleasure in it.

The enjoyment it provides, as in one way it does not belong to us, we do not need to pay for or to feel remorse about it.

By art we should understand all that is a source of pleasure without it belonging to us – the trace of a passer-by, the smile proffered to someone else, the sunset, the poem, the objective universe.

To possess is to lose. To feel without possessing is to keep, since it is to extract the essence from something.

THE AESTHETICS OF DISENCHANTMENT

Since we are unable to extract beauty from life, we attempt at least to extract it from our incapacity to extract beauty from life. We turn our rout into a victory, something achieved and positive, with columns, pomp and spiritual consentment.

If life gave us nothing more than an anchorite's cell, we would strive to decorate it, if only with the shadows of our dreams, mixing life and colour, sculpting our oblivion under the tranquil exteriority of the walls.

Like all dreamers, I have always felt that it was my duty to be creative. Since I have never known how to make an effort or realize a plan, creating has always coincided in me with dreaming, wanting or longing; and with making gestures with the dream of the gesture I would have liked to be able to have made.

❦

Literature – that marriage of art to thought, that concretization unsullied by reality – seems to me to be the goal towards which every human effort should be directed, if it were truly human and not an overflow from the animal world. I believe that to say something is to preserve virtue and to dispel terror. Fields are greener in their descriptions than in their greenness. Flowers, if described in sentences which define them in the realm of imagination, will have colours of a longevity disallowed them by cellular life.

To be moved is to be alive, to be sad is to survive. There is nothing real in life which exists unless it has been well described. Second-rate critics love to emphasize that such and such a poem, opulently rhythmical, ultimately says nothing except the weather was good; but it is hard to say the weather was good, and the good weather itself vanishes. So, we have to preserve the good weather in a florid, prolix remembrance, and so constellate from new flowers or new stars the fields and skies of the vacuous and ephemeral exteriority.

Everything that we are and always shall be for those who follow on after us in the diversity of time, will be in conformity with the intense idea we had of it, to the extent that, with all the imaginative powers lodged in our bodies, we will truly have been it ourselves. I do not believe that history is anything else in its vast, turgid panorama, but a flow of interpretations, a confused concordance of absent-minded witnesses. The writer of novels is all of us, and we narrate as much as we see, since seeing is as complex as everything else.

At this moment, I have so many fundamental thoughts, so many truly metaphysical things to say that suddenly I feel exhausted and decide to stop waiting, to stop thinking; I shall allow the *furia* of saying things to bring me sleep, and I shall gently caress with closed eyes, as if they were a cat, all those things I might have said.